Illustration for " Buondelmonte "

Piccarda

Fond Adventures

TALES OF THE YOUTH OF THE WORLD

By
Maurice Hewlett

Harper & Brothers Publishers
New York and London
1905

Contents

The Heart's Key

The Heart's Key

(To the Tune of "A la fontana del vergier")

IT is a tale of love and lovers which they tell, saying that in the hill-country of Toulouse is to be found the walled city of Ventadorn with its castle and long church. Sir Simon was lord of it, a vavasour of good Count Raimon's in the days before his fall. The city towered over two valleys, and the castle over it; there this old vavasour lived, and kept great state once upon a time, with men-at-arms for his walls, and minstrels, chamberlains, pages, and esquires to make cheer within doors. But the days had worsened: his wife was dead, his son Sir Bernart was in the service of King John of England—Landless they called that king, who tricked his father, and was tricked himself; now all that remained to Simon of Ventadorn were his two handsome daughters, Lady Saill and Lady Tibors.

If I were to relate all that the troubadours found to sing of these ladies, I should weary myself and make no way with you; for it is quite true that those women stand highest in esteem of whom

3

history has least to report. So our hopes jump,
and our minds after them. Tell a man that a
woman is fair—fair Helen, fair Cleopatra, lovely
Azalais — and he will make her so in his own
image. But enlarge upon her parts, tell over her
perfections on the fingers, he will say of one at
least, "H'm, not to my taste." This is certain.
Of Lady Saill, then, and of Lady Tibors, I content
myself with this much, that Saill was the elder
and more superb, a golden lady with long yellow
hair like Helen's of Troy, and of fierce face, like
the Siren's when she has drowned a man. Tibors
was brown-haired and rather pale—a sleek, laughing girl. Saill, when she laughed at all, laughed
cruelly, with dreadful mirth. There were no more
lovely ladies in all the County of Toulouse, and
none more various. Men who sang of them—
and all men sang of them—called Saill the Proud
Lady, and Tibors, because of her kindness, the
Laughing Lover. Enough of this and of them:
it will be easily seen from so much whither the
striving went. A man will always sniff at what
lies to hand; if above him, just out of reach, he
sees a prize made rarer by the distance. To Tibors'
one or two, Saill, they say, had fifty lovers; but
the deeds of three are all that can be handled just
now—these, and the deeds of an obscure fourth
lover, who watched the others reap what they sowed,
and afterwards went gleaning, and was content.
The three were Jauffrai of Brieuc, a very noble

4

youth, full of mettle, who made good songs; the Monk of Quesle, a man of the Church, who made better; and the Viscount Ebles, a great man from Roussillon, who made no songs at all unless he were fighting, and then he sang a sharp low song like the whistle of a sword in the air, which indeed was the instrument he played on better than any. As for the fourth lover, he was Guillem of Nantoil, a poor minstrel, with a cropped head, meek eyes, and smooth face, whom nobody thought a lover at all, and who in his service never lifted his looks higher than Lady Saill's knee. He kept his looks thus modestly low, and his thoughts to himself and the Virgin Mary. She, and she only, knew that every night when Saill went to bed Guillem kissed the edge of her bliaut as she left the hall, kissed the lintel of the door where her hand had stayed, and returning when she was gone, kissed the cushion where she had rested her head.

Now, on a day in autumn after the vintage—October was the month, bright and clear the weather—those three great lovers came riding over the brown hills to Ventadorn to pay their vows to Lady Saill; and the time being an hour or so short of noon, the sun high and the wind gentle, they all went into the orchard to sing coblas and talk about love—Tibors and Saill, with Saill's three lovers. And Guillem the minstrel was there on his service, and brought a little table, and set fruit, wine, and snow upon it.

Saill sat in an ivory chair, with Tibors, her sister, a little behind her on her left hand. Tibors was in a red gown, with a jewel on her forehead; but Saill's gown was white, of a thin silk, which fitted her so closely as to be a man's despair, to show how glorious she was and how remote. Her hair was plaited up with pearls and touched the ground behind her. Round her waist was a very broad girdle of gold, plates of gold riveted together with hinges, and stuck with sard and emerald, of the sort they call a Heart's Key, the girdle which virgins must wear until they are wedded. She wore it outwardly by day, and at night next her body; it had never left her yet; and the wonder of the country was, when or how it would. Here, too, was a mockery: not that the country admired, but that no one dared turn the key or unlock the shrine, to lay bare Saill's heart and take it in his hands. And just as the country admired, so now these men looked or longed, each after his kind. Jauffrai of Brieuc grew red: he was a young man. The Monk of Quesle grew gray; but Viscount Ebles would not look at all, for simple fear of what he might be driven to. As for Guillem, I have told you already how far he dared look. Yet he knew very well about the Heart's Key, and every day made a prayer to Madame the Virgin of Ventadorn: "Madame, set the key in my hands. I have within me what will still the fire."

Now, I ask you to note that in the orchard sat

6

The Heart's Key

Saill in her ivory chair, with Tibors a little behind
her on her left hand, but not so far that she could
not lean her cheek to her sister's or put her chin
on her white shoulder. On her right hand, also a
little behind her, sat Sir Jauffrai, where he could
win the fragrance of her hair, and secretly touch it
when his need was sore. The Monk of Quesle was
on her left hand, near enough to brush against her
gown, and a little in front of Tibors. Viscount
Ebles fronted her with folded arms across the table,
watching her, or Tibors, or the other two, as he
felt inclined. Guillem, the minstrel, stood at his
service a certain way off, under a pear-tree.

They made music and songs concerning Saill.
Jauffrai touched first his viol to tune it, then sang
a trembling song of dawn and the white light steal-
ing round the hills, of the sort which in that country they call an *Alba*. "Lady," ran the song, "I wish
that with me you might creep from your father's
house at that hour when the martins peer first from
under the eaves. Not more softly lieth sleep upon
your eyelids, lady, than the white dew upon the
grass. There are no shadows at all, but every tree
and every drowsy flower stands bathed in a lake of
light, that cometh none can tell whence, that is
not shamed by the moon, neither welcometh the
sun. Truly, it would seem that the light is no bor-
rowed thing, but lifteth up, as it were, from the
deep bosom and parted lips of the Earth herself.
So it is with you, lady, whose own fire, whose own

light, and ardent heart suffice you. All night I
watch for you, leaning by the walls of Ventadorn,
just as I watch for the white dawn upon the hills
about it; all night I make prayers to assure myself.
And dawn cometh, and you come, and I lift up
heart and hands, crying, '*Oy, Deus! Oy, Deus!
Deh, l'alba tantost veh!*'—'Ah, Lord God! Ah, Lord
God! Lo, now, the Dawn is here!'"

This was the song that Jauffrai sang; through
which breathed such a tender heat, such rapture
held in check, such hope and wistfulness to make
the music shudder, that all the company was silent
when he had done. Tibors, leaning her chin on her
sister's shoulder, whispered in her ear: "Oh, Saill,
that is a good song, which should not go unrewarded."

Saill said nothing; but she let drop her right hand
behind her chair, and Jauffrai, bowing over it, took
and kissed it.

Then said Viscount Ebles, with an oath in his
beard, "By God's death, Lady Saill, but the song I
sing goes sharper than De Brieuc's. When I sing
it all the listeners begin to wail, urging, 'Quick,
lord, the mercy stroke!' I sing not at dawn, in the
half light, but at broad noon, rather, when the sun
can see my doings. And it is not I who drone the
burden, '*Oy, Deus! Oy, Deus!*' but the people to
whom I sing. When I sing my song one man looks
askance at his neighbor, as if to say, 'Is this a god,
then?' My song hath a note of the scythe in wet
grass, and again of the screaming eagle; it savors

8

of the low-chuckling owl when he hunts the parks of a night, and of the hiss of a snake in a stony place, and of the short snapping bark of the winter wolf. So I call my song the Song of *Lop* (which is to say, Of the Wolf); and when I sing it a blue flame playeth about my head, the spears work in vain, the archers throw away their bows, and my horse picketh up his feet among the spoiled bodies of men. This is the Song of *Lop*, which is my song. If it please you not, lovely Saill, I am sorry, for I cannot amend it. Yet some think it good, and these are the men of Toulouse dressing their vines on the hill; and some think it bad, and these are Frenchmen and the men of the English king."

The Viscount shut his mouth like a trap, and his black beard covered it. He looked a great fighter, who should make a lover no less great; and so Tibors thought and so said. For now she leaned her cheek to Saill's, and whispered, "By the faith of a Christian, Saill, that is a brave singer with a song full of matter. Let him have his reward: it is little enough he asks."

Saill considered these words and Viscount Ebles together. She saw the man goodly, and found that the words fitted him. So then she put her foot out under the table, which, when the Viscount felt, his blood started in his neck and colored all his face with crimson. The courtesy made a giant of him; he dared to look at Saill; but Saill blushed and looked down. So now she had dropped both hand and eyes.

Then the Monk of Quesle, a keen-faced man, touched the strings of his rote, and thus sang he: "Neither the hope of dawn nor the satiety of the noon-heat sing I, Lady Saill; but the blue calms, the very steadfast silver stars, the thin new moon over the hill, the dusk, the end of fret, the evening. My song is a *Sirena*, which goes quietly as my constant heart, saying, 'Peace, my soul, peace, my soul, the long day is done!'

"And I sing it to you, lady, claiming the end of strife. Love in the beginning is a fire, like the flame of kindling wood, which leaps and roars in the heart, and devours the very bones of young lovers. Not so, by insurgent rushes, cry of battle, blood and rage, should a gentle lady be won to her lover's arms. No, no, but by long gazing out of quiet eyes, by patient smiling, by a bent knee and obsequious head, and by the little shrug which says, 'Eh, if she will not, she will not: wait a bit!' Also by a whisper in the hedged garden, and a sigh at the going to bed. For, look you, the age-long lover very well knows that the burden and flood of noon will be done. The shadows creep forward, the bees go home; in the farms they milk the kine. The bats come flickering out, the goat-sucker goes purring through the woods; all look east for the new moon. Then at last the lover lifts his eyes and counts the stars. The light fades, the air is brown, the sky faints out in green; black, black stand up spire and tower when the sun is low behind them.

Through the scented garden, among folded flowers and leaves all breathless with sleep, I see you, Saill, come in a white gown. Both your hands are at the Heart's Key, both of mine at yours. Together we hold the burning thing; under my hands I feel your fingers at the lock. The lock is solved, the girdle loosed, I have the treasure! All in the violet night I cry my *Sirena:* 'Peace, my soul, peace, my soul, the long day is done!'"

Saill breathed fast and deep; but Tibors, with a cheek that pressed her sister's and an arm that embraced her neck, whispered close, "My Saill, that is a pure sweet singer, very constant in love, to whom his reward should be surely given, if the others have theirs. Stoop thy royal head, my dear, that he may touch what I touch. I engage that such velvet is not made at Quesle."

Saill bent her head to the singing Monk of Quesle, and he kissed her on the cheek. So now she had dropped both hand and eyes and head. None the less young Guillem, at his service under the pear-tree, held on with his prayer to the Virgin of Ventadorn, "Madame the Virgin, star of Toulouse, the key, the key, the key!"

When dinner-time was over the three lords took their leave and rode together out of Ventadorn to their own towns. The Monk of Quesle could not contain himself, but turned in his saddle and with uplifted hand began to exult.

"Ha, now, lords," cries he, "am I or not blessed above all men? What! Have I sprung the citadel or not? Have I closed at grapple with the inviolate? Have I lowered the flag or not? You know very well that I have. Did she not stoop her indomitable head? Did I pasture where no man living has laid his lips? Is it done? Oh, is it not done, by the Light of the Earth?"

Viscount Ebles swore with a full oath, "By Saint Gregory, it is not done, thou·half-man. What is such open trifling worth? Catlap, by my Saviour. Why, even as she bowed her head she looked wisely at me; and long before thou couldst touch her my foot had touched hers, and so had touched throughout thy song."

The Monk of Quesle bit his own hand. If ever there was an angry clerk in the country of *Oc* it was he. But Jauffrai threw up his young head like a howling dog and laughed at the sky.

"Judge now between you, O solemn fools," he called out sharply — for he was in pain — "what store to set upon these touchings and lookings of yours. For even when the goat-foot of Ebles bruised her slipper by mischance her hand was snug in mine, and while he sang of his sword-stroke I kissed it; and when the Monk began to sigh of the evening breeze, and when he had done, I kissed again. You prating fools, who is blessed if not I?" Again he laughed bitterly, as a man should not laugh at the deeds of ladies.

Ebles broke out in blasphemy. "Now may God
die twice," said he, "if I deal not death quickly."
He turned his horse towards Ventadorn, which lay
above him shining on the hill, but before he could
pull into a gallop the Monk of Quesle reached after
his bridle, caught and held it.

"Listen, Viscount," he says, "before you do what
becomes you in this ill business. Are we not all
made fools together? Is your case worse than mine,
or mine than Jauffrai's? Not a whit, believe me;
but fool, fool, and fool again, we sit here. Well,
then, shall not the little wisdom of one of us, added
to that of the others, make a wise head at last,—
wiser, at least, than one? We three will act together. Are you willing?"

Cried young Jauffrai de Brieuc with a yapping
laugh, "By my soul, I accord! How long can we
drag the woman? What kennel can we get black
or thick enough for her who mocks good lovers?"

Said the Monk, "Oh, a many." And then the
Viscount, "My lords, I am with you deep in this
matter. Let us set the wits of three offended men
to. work." Riding together over the hills among
the trampled vineyards they concerted a plan. Saill
of Ventadorn saw nothing of them till the winter-
time, but cared little for that.

That winter, about Candlemas, the snow lay very
heavy on all the country, and could not be thawed
because of an iron frost. The sheep died in the

13

fields, fish in the rivers, birds on the trees, and before morning were found frozen hard. A most bitter wind blew night and day, enough to search out and wither the very vitals of a man. But war was awake also. Old Simon of Montfort, kept warm by the Pope, took the field, such as it was; and the good Count Raimon of Toulouse, with him his nephew, the Viscount of Beziers, must needs fight for life, whether snow awaited him or green grass. The mesne lords of the country were summoned by the horn; *sirventes* were the only songs you heard; Sir Simon of Ventadorn made ready for Toulouse against that other Simon; all his knights, squires, and men-at-arms must go with him, and Lady Saill have no lovers, save Guillem the minstrel, who dared look no higher than her knee. Saill sat twisting and untwisting her white fingers by the window; Guillem prayed to the Virgin for the Heart's Key; only Tibors kept snug and warm. She did her loving quietly, saying little; she went laughing low all day long. In the Castle of Ventadorn there were only those two, with Guillem and a few old warders and the women of the household.

Now, on a night of creeping frost, and of mist which froze as it touched, clinging to the bare trees —to Ventadorn, at midnight, came Ebles, De Brieuc, and the Monk of Quesle, in armor, visored, with men, swords, and torches. They broke down the ward of the gate, and came raving into the castle garth. "Ha, death! Ha, Montfort!" they shouted, naming the two old dog-wolves, enemies of Toulouse: "havoc on Ventadorn! Montfort! Fire, sword, and death!" They battered at the gate with their spears.

Guillem sat up scared in his bed, and listened. "This is a bad affair," he said to himself. "Ventadorn is surprised. How shall I save my lady?" He dressed himself in haste and ran down the corridor to her chamber. He opened the door, he crept in; by the light of the lamp he saw Saill, wholly asleep, her cheek on her hand, and all her gold hair streaming over the pillow to the floor.

"Wake, wake, wake, my Lady Saill!" he whispered. "Death is upon us." Then she sat up in bed with fierce, reasonable eyes, and he saw the Heart's Key burning all about her fair body.

"Ventadorn is surprised, lady," he said, blinking before so much glory. "We must come out, if we are not to die."

She said, "Quick, a shift. Thou hast dared too much. Go thou to the door till I come."

Clothed in her linen shift, she came out to him, and they went to awaken Tibors. But Tibors was very sleepy, and would have nothing more to say to them than, "Let them come, but let me sleep. Leave me in peace, Saill." So they let her lie, and crept away down a little stair.

Guillem knew what door to try, a single turret-door which gave on to a swing-bridge, and that on to the privy garden. But the forayers, who knew

it as well as ever he did, waited for him and his
arriving there; and so soon as he opened an inch
or two a foot was in, which prized it wider. The
torches flared in the black fog, a host bayed at the
door; there came a rush, with "Follow, we are in!"
That door which shut the invaders in shut Saill and
Guillem out.

Saill, the delicate lady, shivered and drew her
hair about her neck. In a lit-up circle all round
hustled the gaping soldiers, their pikes, their torches,
the clouds of their freezing breath. "Follow me,
the pair of you, or you win cold quarters in the
fosse," said a man in steel, who wore his visor down.
The shamed couple were led away to the great court-
yard, where, in happier times, Sir Simon of Ventadorn held tourney, and Saill sat in a gallery as Queen
of Love. There, in the trampled snow, frozen into
sharp ridge and furrow, Saill's cut feet left a trail of
red for all to see next day.

"Into the middle with you." There, shivering,
side by side they stood.

Above them soon shone a light in the windows
of the parvise, and showed it full of armed knights.
One set open the windows. Saill saw Ebles, De
Brieuc, and the Monk of Quesle, midmost of their
party, wagging their heads, grinning at each other
and at her.

"Light there, ho!" cried the Monk, in a new,
fierce voice. They beat up the torches into flame.

"Ha, now, proud lady," roared Viscount Ebles

like thunder; "you have heard my song sung, the Song of *Lop*—what do you think of it?"

She said between her teeth, "Shame on you to shame a lady so."

But he answered, "What, then, of a lady that mocks three lovers at once?"

Then the Monk laughed, saying, "Ah, Lady Saill, Lady Saill, now you have found out that my old *Sirena* was more peaceful than my new. What will you do to be let in?"

She asked, "What must I do?"

Jauffrai lifted up his sharp voice, "You shall do to him you have there as you did to us, before we let you in. Give him the hand to kiss which falsely you gave to me."

Saill held out her hand, and Guillem knelt to kiss it.

"Now," said she, "my lords, let me in."

"By the Five Wounds," swore Ebles, "not so. Set you first your foot below his, Saill. What I touched let him touch now."

She put her torn foot out, and Guillem, kneeling still, kissed it many times.

"Is it enough now?" said Saill.

The Monk of Quesle held up his torch that he might see her the better.

"Not enough, my Saill, not enough! Stoop your false head, and turn your false cheek to the lad there. Let him taste what I found bitter!"

She did as she was told; but Guillem, blind with

tears, put up his face at random, and instead of her cheek kissed the side of her frozen mouth. And when he found how cold to death she was, his words burst from him unadvisedly, and he cried to the three lords:

"Ah, sirs, have pity upon so fair a thing! For all the years of my service I have loved this lady, and never yet have dared to touch more than the hem of her gown. If she can stoop so low as this, surely she is punished enough. By Heaven, my lords, you will answer Heaven for it at the Last Day! Let her in!"

They all cried together, "The brave lover! Give him the Heart's Key, Saill. Let him open the door with that, and then we open."

Saill said fiercely, "That shall never be. I will die rather." And Guillem, too, cried out, "I had rather she died here and froze to the ground than that she should suffer, or I do, such indignity as that!"

"Out with you then!" cried the three. "Give it where you will, sell or barter it, but here you shall never trade." Then they shut the windows, and put out all the lights; and soldiers took Saill and Guillem by the shoulders and drove them before to the city gates, and shut them outside. They heard the wind howling round the watch-towers, saw the great icicles stick out like giant's fingers pointing scorn, and before them, dimly, the far-ranging hills all in a shroud of white. Saill struck herself upon the bosom, praying, "Mother of God, send death quickly, Amen!" But Guillem whipped off his jacket, and put it over her shoulders.

"Lady, more dear to me than life," says he, "take my doublet and put it on thee, lest the frost bite in, and thy dreadful prayer be heard. For my part, I will make no such a prayer." She did his bidding, and he fastened the coat across her chest, since her fingers were like stones. He gave her also his shoes and stockings, telling her that they were very necessary for her, seeing they had two valleys to cross. When all was done as he would, Guillem, bare to the shirt, urged her ardently. "Oh, come," he cried; "oh, come, thou loveliest companion in all the world! Come with me now across the bitter fields, on a good pilgrimage."

She looked at him in her fell old way, amazed to see so much spirit in a youth who had served her on his knee, and never looked higher than hers; but remembering how she stood, beggared of all else, and looking down to see what plight she was in, she hid her face in her hands: "O Virgin, Lady of Seven Dolours, what am I to withstand any man born?" she moaned to herself; then gave her hand to Guillem, saying very meekly, "Yes, I will follow thee, good Guillem."

So they set off through the smothered vineyards and fields of olive trees, where the snow was untrampled yet, save by the criss-cross of the anxious birds. They reached the valley, crossed the river

on hard ice, and so gained the flank of the farther
hills, and began to climb, with few words said. Now
and then Saill would sob under her breath, or flag
a little, and then, for certain, Guillem would bear her
up with his arm. She would stop to pant, and he
embrace her so while she recovered herself; she would
lay her head on his shoulder, and Guillem whisper
in her ear, "Cry unto your courage, Proud Lady;
keep a good heart. Shelter is not very far."

"Where is this shelter, Guillem?" she asked him
once.

"It is at Nantoil, lady," he said, "where I was
born."

At the top of the hills they struck the great road
to Marseille, and then at the four ways under a
cross, found a dead man in the snow, frozen to the
degrees of the cross. "God help the fled soul of
him," says Guillem, "as He hath helped me to what
his poor shell hath no need of." He took his doublet, breeches, and sword, and his cloak for Saill, and
so helped her along the better. But now she leaned
on him wholly, and his arm never left her, because
of the wounds in her feet. So with many struggles,
but yet with a heart that could not fail him (so full
it was), to give a brave word or helping arm to her
whose spirit seemed dead, he brought her to the
river-girt city of Nantoil, to his mother's house.

There he encompassed her with every sweet ob-
servance the heart of young lover could devise; and
there, while he humbled himself in her service, she

won back all her old spirit, and a cruel beauty like
the flame of a forest fire. But the more spirit was
in her, the less he dared to woo her. It was not'
that she held him off too much, but that he dared
her too little. You know whether he had a faint
heart or not; yet I will tell you this. Take a bold
way with a lady: if you love her, show little of it.
If she scorn you, it may be bettered; if she pity
you, never in this world. Now, Saill had scorned
enough lovers, but never yet had she been moved
to pity one. But when Guillem dared not kiss her
cheek at the Good-night, nor again the side of her
mouth as in that hour of bitterness he had found
means to do, he lost what he had achieved in the
discovery of what he could not now achieve; she
thought of him again as a foot-boy. And as for the
lad's mother, Madam Bruna, up in arms for her
son, when she rated her, Saill said, "Dear Madam,
I am here safe-caught. He has but to take me, I
suppose. Arms he has, and a mouth, I know, but
I cannot open them for him." To herself she
thought, "I am in a cage with these bird-catchers.
Heaven pity the poor!" In these days, as the winter wore, Guillem longed, and Saill fasted, and
Madam Bruna looked for a stick.

Before long she found one, good soul! The war
shifted from one valley to another like a heavy cloud.
Simon of Montfort laid siege to Nantoil and held a
close leaguer. Guillem went to keep the walls, Madam
Bruna changed her manner, and Saill felt the whip.

Hunger came in, as bitter ally of the cold and Count Simon. Food in Nantoil ran up to famine price. Servants had mouths, but masters no bread; Madam Bruna packed hers out - of - doors. "Get you into the kitchen, my girl," she said to Saill. "I cannot keep you idle when, as God knows, I am hard shifted to keep you at all." So Saill went into the kitchen, and Guillem saw nothing of her; for she was ashamed that he should see her in a kitchen plight, and prevailed upon his mother to give her out as ill in bed. "Have it as you will," said the harassed woman, "lies are cheaper than bread." The lie was told, and Guillem made miserable, but there was worse to come.

That day was soon at hand when food there was none, nor money to buy it. Saill was shivering in the kitchen over the dying ashes of a fire long spent, when Madam Bruna came in, gray with hunger and the waspish rage of hunger. "Get you out, girl," she said, hatred shaking in her voice, "get you out into the city this night and win us bread. Are we to starve, I and my son, and the fault be yours? Is this how you make amends? Out with you."

"How shall I get you any money, dear Madam?" asked the Proud Lady, proud no longer, but trembling at the look of affairs.

Madam Bruna looked her up and down. "Hey," she laughed savagely, "are you so nice? Sell you now your Heart's Key, fool, and my son and I shall be fed."

The Heart's Key

Said Saill, bowing her head down very low, "Madam, for your son I will do it." She went away by herself, and took the Heart's Key, and broke off a square link of it. This she sold to a Jew for a price, and, after the proper time, came back with the money to Madam Bruna. The famished wretch snapped at it, but said nothing of question or comment. She made herself and Guillem a good supper.

Saill had what scraps she could find over, but was so hungry that they were nothing to her. She came at last to lick the dishes in the kitchen and to drink the liquor in which she had washed them. At supper Guillem had said, "Mother, here is better food than ever I tasted this many days. The best of it, as is fitting, should have been given to Lady Saill, who hath always fared deliciously."

"Trust me, my son, and so she has," said his mother, and Guillem believed her. But, following his habit, before he went out to the walls he crept to her door and scratched at it, whispering, "Lady, is all well?" Saill whispered back, as she always did, "I am well, Guillem." But not for all the world would she open to him, lest he should see her as she was, or get news of the Heart's Key.

But starvation had the longer wind. When the great girdle was all gone, link by link, she knew that she had no more to give but life itself. That night Simon Montfort's men made a breach

in the wall through which, like a murderous flood,
they streamed into Nantoil. The kennels ran
smoking red—fire, rapine, lust, and rage stalked
naked through the streets. In Madam Bruna's
house was nothing to eat.

"Girl," she said to Saill, "go out and sell. This
is the night of all others for you."

"Alack, mother," said Saill, "I have nothing to
sell. All is gone."

"Pish," said the other; "beg then; get what
you can. Steal, sin, snatch! Give my son food."
She drove her from the house.

Saill stood cowering in the street, pondering
how to-night she could die. Then there came to
her mind the thought of Guillem fighting for her
life, who had saved her once and loved her always.
"He has neither art nor part in this. No, no," she
said to herself, "that is not the way to reward good
lovers." So she went slippering down the street
like a beggar girl, as indeed she was, among gaping
houses and dead men's bodies, and pale rags which
had once been women, half sodden now in the
gutters.

"That is where I shall lie when they have done
with me," she thought; and just then heard a
horse's hoofs ring like steel on steel, and saw one
come riding on a white charger, and knew she
must adventure him. He was a knight in a golden
cloak, who reined up under a pious lamp, and
looked all ways to find his own. Shivering, Saill

gathered her rags about her neck, and went to lay hold of his stirrup.

"How now, my girl?" said Sir Jauffrai de Brieuc— for it was he. She looked up and spoke to him, sickened at the sound of her own voice, asking him alms, for the love of Mary. He, when he understood her, scoffed aloud. "Off with you, wagtail, unhand me, go your ways. Montfort is in, and you are out. I have nothing for you. I am a lover of ladies, I!"

He spurred his horse till he plunged in the kennel, and sent the mud spattering about. And so he rode his way, looking to the upper windows for ladies.

After that, and after much more deadly skirting of peril (wherein that little which she had left stood to be rifled at ease), she saw the Viscount Ebles stand in the Cathedral Square, very noble, in red armor, with a gold crest to his helm and white cloak over his shoulder. He was a Knight of the Temple, you must know. To him she went, creeping on the tips of her toes, and faltered her petition. But he turned, cursing and railing, and bade her be off, or he would send half a dozen of his men on her heels. "Look you, Mischief," says he, "I have forsworn women since one most injuriously used me. Judge you, little misery, how this was, and learn if it is not too late." So he told her the whole story of herself with those three lords in the orchard. Saill hid her face in her

arm, and, leaning against the church wall, cried
bitterly, as if her heart was broken, as all her
spirit was. The Viscount resumed his meditations.

Now Guillem, at the entry of Montfort's men,
ran quaking by the lanes and alleys of Nantoil
to his mother's house, to save, if he might, all he
loved in it. "Quick, mother, we must look to
ourselves," he told her. "Simon Montfort is in—
we shall be dead or worse. Tell me, where is Lady
Saill? There is no time to lose!"

"Ah, misery and plague be on her," cried the
old woman, despising whom she had used despite-
fully; "where would she be but abroad?"

Guillem turned white. "What is this? Where
is she, then? On such a night!" Madam Bruna
showed herself at last.

"Ah, tell me now, Guillem, where else should
she be? She is out and about selling the Heart's
Key, and so hath been this month of dark days.
How should the house have stood or you been fed
but for that?"

Guillem rebuked his mother. "Peace, woman,
you make me ashamed," he said. "You should be
thankful for the bread she gave you, and honor
her who puts you above honor. Heaven send you
mercy; I must find her."

He turned and hunted among the dead and
dying in the streets. Friend or foe, dying or
killing, he asked them all—"Tell me of my Lady
Saill, for the love of Jesus." He asked Jauffrai de

26

Brieuc, he asked Ebles; neither knew him; but Jauffrai drove him into the kennel, and Ebles kicked him away. So at last, at a corner of the great square, he saw the desolate figure of a woman, who leaned, crying, by the church wall, blown upon by the night wind, the screaming of the sacked city, and all the reproaches of the night. His heart gave a leap, his feet followed: he came to her holding out his arms, kneeling, crying out: "O my heart! O Proud Lady! O Saill, whom I love so dearly, how is it with thee?" She turned and gave a sob, and fell into the shelter he opened.

A party of soldiers came panting by, hunting the houses, like a pack of hounds, for women and liquor. Guillem drew her deep into an archway, and crouched with her there till they had passed. Then from entry to entry they crept, a furtive, fearful way, to the gate. Saill was as wax in his hands, following when he bid her, clinging to him while they waited, and when they ran never loosing his hand; but she was voiceless, neither defending herself nor accusing, neither praying his forgiveness nor justifying his faith. He, who was her hope, must now become her judge as well. So they crawled out of the fire and smoke of sacked Nantoil.

Early in the morning they took the road together in peace: a battered soldier and his drab— who should hurt them? The sun rose over the hill, the light smiled upon their soiled faces, they went along the valley hand-in-hand. But Saill never spoke, for she dared not woo her judge; and Guillem never spoke, for he dared not risk his treasure.

The primroses were out in the banks, in the meadows cowslips nodded their heads, jonquils and lady-smocks. The spring was in, earth quick with it. They came to a little wood which crowned a grassy field, and there they rested on the young moss by a fountain, while they ate what bread they had. Overhead, a pair of wood-doves by a new nest sang to each other. Nantoil was burning that day, but in the wood in the valley the doves sang clear and long. Saill put off her slippers and cooled her feet in the water; she let down the golden race of her hair and threw her head back to shake it free. As Guillem saw that proud fine face fronting, unashamed, the sky, his love leaped hotly in him, rebuking him for his doubt. He prayed his old prayer, "Hey, Madame the Virgin of Ventadorn, give me the Heart's Key!"

Prayer touched him, moved him to courage. His arm was about Saill, his hand pressed her heart. She turned with a face all aflame; but he saw fear in her eyes. That she should fear what he might do whipped him like a rod; then he, too, knew a fear at which his lips went dry.

"Alas, alas!" he whispered, "O Saill, the Heart's Key is gone!"

She blushed a deeper red; but her eyes grew dewy with something softer than alarm.

The Heart's Key

"But not the heart, dear Guillem," she said, "not the heart, O my love!"

He saw how lovely she was, all a burning color, nor did he take away his hand. "Now," said he, "tell me all the truth." So she told him everything from the beginning of their days at Nantoil, and so he learned the holiness and generous pride of her whose pride had once been niggard. Guillem thanked God. "Now kiss me," he said then, "for proud as you are, I am prouder still. You have turned the Heart's Key for me, dear love; now give me thy red heart to keep."

The Monk of Quesle, with a singing company, passed down the road on the way to a Court of Love. In the midst was a lady in a litter. The Monk was dressed in a bright green silken tunic covered with white leopards; on his head was a cap of scarlet; his white horse was trapped in the same hue. He sang to the curtains of the litter and to a fine hand which held them a little way open. Guillem and the Proud Lady let him sing. For them the wood-birds had a more tuneful note.

Brazenhead the Great

Heaven is my witness, I have no taste for prefaces. A story is a story, or verbiage. Yet it is to be remembered by a writer that the public has its feelings no less than he; and if it have met with certain personages before, likes to be reminded of the occasion. Now the actors in the following few pages have all had a hearing, for they are the tellers of some "New Canterbury Tales," to which the public was pleased to listen not so long ago, little thinking that those speakers (as they jogged along the foot-pathways through Hants and Surrey and Kent) had hopes and passions and troubles of their own over and above those which they pretended. They had though: theirs was no peaceful pilgrimage. It began with —— and ended in ——; but let the reader judge for himself.

Brazenhead the Great

PILGRIMAGE to Canterbury and Saint Thomas
of Canterbury, which is in some a piety, in
some a courteous act, for some salvation, for some a
frolic, in others may very well be the covering of
statecraft, of policy, of deep design. So it was with
Captain Salomon Brazenhead in the month of May
and year of our Lord God fourteen hundred and
fifty. With him, "late of Burgundy, formerly of
Milan"—a lean man of six .feet two inches, of in-
ordinate thirst, of two scars on his face, a notched
forefinger, a majestic nose, of a long sword, two
daggers, and a stolen horse, of experience in divers
kinds of villany, yet of simple tastes — with this
free routier, I allow, pilgrimage was certainly a
cloak of dissembling, while none the less a congenial
and (as he would have been the first to admit)
wholesome exercise. If he had served too long in
Italy not to love conspiracy, he had not been to
Compostella and Jerusalem for nothing. Indeed,
he had skirted in his time too close to the rocks of

33

Death not to respect those who (for honorable reasons) had cast themselves upon them. Therefore
he was by no means without devotion in seeking the
Head of Thomas and the Golden Shrine, for all that
he had business, and high business, on the road.
For firstly, in this reign of King Henry the Sixth, he
was a Duke of York's man, a White Rose man.
Secondly, he was one of those who had sworn to
have Jack Nape's head on a charger.[1] Lastly, he
was bosom friend of another Jack, whom he hoped
to meet in Kent; I mean Jack Mend-all, Jack
Cade, Jack Mortimer—call him as you will—that
promising young man, who promised himself a
kingdom and Englishmen a charter, who actually
fought a battle on Blackheath, held London Bridge
against the Mayor, Aldermen, and Citizens, and
hanged Lord Say upon one of his own trees. From
this practical statesman our Captain had received
a roving commission to be his *Vox Clamantis:* he
was to trumpet revolution along the Pilgrims' Way.
This road was the most travelled in the realm; it
led all men into Kent—Captain Cade's country;
it could be safely used: with cockle-shells and
staves enough it could screen an army. Pilgrim
only by the way, therefore, was Captain Salomon
Brazenhead, sometime of Milan, late of Burgundy,
now Deputy-Constable of all England under Letters
Patent of the Captain of Kent.

[1] Jack Nape was Delapole, Duke of Suffolk, the best-hated
man of his day, and no worse served than he deserved.

34

Brazenhead the Great

I have spoken of his leanness, of his inches, of his thirst. It must be added of him that he was plentifully forested with hair, which drooped like ivy from the pent of his brows, leaped fiercely up from his lip to meet the falling tide; gave him a forked beard; crept upward from his chest to the light at his throat; had invaded his very ears, and made his nostrils good cover for dormice in the winter. I might sing of this, or of his eloquent eyes: I prefer a pæan on his nose. Captain Brazenhead had a nose—but an heroic nose, a trumpet, an ensign built on imperial lines; broad-rooted, full of gristle, ridged with sharp bone, abounding in callus, tapering exquisitely to a point, very flexible and quick. With this weapon of offence or defiance he could sneer you from manhood's portly presence to a line of shame, with it comb his mustachios. When he was deferential it kissed his lip; combative, it cocked his hat. It was a nose one could pat with some pretence; scratched, it was set on fire, you could see it smouldering in the dusk. Into the vexed debate, whether great noses are invariable with great men, I shall not enter. Captain Brazenhead was great, and he had a great nose; let this instance go to swell the argument. This fine, tall, hairy man rode directly to Winchester from Southampton, his port of debarkation, entered the city by the West Gate, and stabled his horse at the George, which was then the principal inn. This done, he sent the hostler for a gallon of beer, and in

35

his absence inspected with great care all the animals
tethered in the yard. It was his intention to make
sure of a good one for the morrow, seeing that his
own—if a spavined makeshift levied from an East-
leigh smithy can so be called—did not please him
at all. He chose a handsome, round-barrelled
roan, rising not more than seven, and did not
trouble to change the furniture further than to
add his pack to those already on the saddle. He
was then quite ready to drink his liquor turn and
turn about with the hostler and two Gray Friars
whom he found in a sunny corner—for the Captain was a large-hearted man. He captivated
whatever company he happened to be in; this was
his weakness, and he knew it. So now, with
scarcely a word said, he persuaded those two
friars that they had not seen what they had watched
with some interest a few minutes before: he convinced the hostler that the horse he now saw and
admired was the very horse he had despised when
it came stiffly into the yard. Admirable man! he
set his steel bonnet at a rake over one eye, chewed
a straw, and cocked his sword point to the angle
of a wren's tail. These things nicely adjusted, his
mind at ease, full of the adventurous sense of strange
airs and hidden surprises waiting for him behind
strange walls, he walked abroad into Chepe, intending to pay his devotions to the Shrine of Saint
Swithin, that (by these means) a good ending
might follow so good a beginning; for, as he had

said more than once, honor is due to a dead gentleman from living gentlemen. "If I go," he
would protest, "into such an one's good town and
bend not my knee in his audience-chamber, I
shame my nobility by flouting his. So it is precisely when I visit a Cathedral city, whereover is
set enshrined some ancient deceased man of God.
That worthy wears a crown in Heaven which it
becomes me to acknowledge whiles I am yet upon
the earth. And so I do, by cock!"

With these and other like reflections he passed
by the Pilgrims' Gate, where the meaner sort of
worshippers—pitiful, broken knaves, ambush men,
sheep-stealers, old battered soldiers, witches, torn
wives and drabs—stand at the shining bars, their
hands thrust in towards the Golden Feretory, and
whine their petitions to the good saint's dust; and
entered by the west door, with much ceremony of
bowing and dropping to the knee, and a very
courtly sharing of his finger-load of holy water
with a burgess's wife, who was quite as handsome
as one of her condition had need to be. Within
the church he paused to look about him, but not to
admire the shrine, the fine painting, the gold work
and lamp work with which it abounded. He knew
churches well enough: business was business, that
of Master Mortimer crying business, that of Captain
Brazenhead fisherman's business. Rather, he cast a
shrewd eye at the haunters of the nave, passing over
the women, the apprentices, all the friars. He saw

37

three or four likely blades playing with a dice-box in a corner, and gained one of them by a lucky throw. He picked up a Breton pedler at his prayers, also a shipman from Goole, who had been twice hanged for piracy and twice cut down alive —"Three's the number for you, lucky Tom," he told him by way of encouragement. In the Chapel of the Sepulchre he found an old friend, Stephen Blackbush, of Aldermary-Church, now in hiding for coin-clipping, claimed him, insisted on having him, and got his way. All this was very well indeed, yet the Captain sighed for more. "I have here so much mass," he told himself, "so much brawn; now Mortimer needs brain. This rascaille would as lieve be under the bed as in it any day, and not one of it worth a pinch of salt to the pudding we have in the pot. Give me a stripling of wit, kind Heaven, to outbalance all this dead meat." Scanning the company as he turned over these reflections and framed these prayers, he came plump upon the very thing—came, saw, conquered, as you are to learn.

This was a slim, tall, gracefully made youth, very pretty, who in a pale oval face had a pair of hot, small, greenish eyes, a long nose, a little mouth like a rose-bud, and a sharp chin dimpled; who wore his brown hair smooth and cropped short, and had the shape and tender look of the God's self of love, as you or I might have seen the boy. This young man, whose name was Percival Perceforest, was a scholar in his way, well versed in the books of Ovid, the *De Remedio* and other like works; knowing a great part of the *Romaunt de la Rose* by rote, and also the Songs of Horace. These he was accustomed to cite colloquially, as a priest his psalter. He would speak of the *Vitas hinnuleo*, the *Integer vitae*, or the *Solvitur*, where the clerk would have his *In Exitu Israel* or *Notus in Judaea*. Not that he had not these also as pat upon the tongue: afterwards it came out that, bred for the Church, he was actually in minor orders. Now, with all these advantages of person and training, it is a very strange thing that he should have been found by Captain Brazenhead leaning against a pillar of the nave, crying upon the cuff of his jacket. Yet it was so. Round about him stood unwholesome, too-ready sympathizers, women of the town, harpies; hard-favored, straddling, bold-browed hussies, whose gain is our loss. A short-faced, plainish man stood there too, respectably dressed, who tried to cope, but failed to cope, with two things at once. To the women he was heard to say, "Begone, shameless baggages, tempt not the afflicted"; which made them laugh and hit each other in their mirth. The weeper he urged with a "God help thee, youth, and expound thy misfortunes to me if thou canst not!" But the name of God caused the young man to blubber the more. Captain Brazenhead took a shorter way. He smartly touched his man on the shoulder, calling him his bawcock, his nip and

frizzle, his eye and his minion; at the women he
flung up his hands with a rush, as one starts a grey-
hound. "Off, detriments!" he cried tremendously;
and they slunk or swaggered away with very in-
jurious but muttered expressions to the effect that
they were not going to do for such an old piece what
they actually were doing as they spoke. "Now,
good Master Burgess," said the Captain to the respectable man (whom he had placed at once), "and
now, young Niobus," to the lad, "we will accom-
modate these water-works, if it suit you. Follow
me." He laid a hacked finger to his nose, and scowl-
ed upon the couple with so much hopeful mystery,
such commanding confidence, such an air of give-
and-take-and-be-damned, that follow him they did;
the merchant as one who says, "Well, well, since
your humor is so," and the other with subdued
sniffs. But the merchant, as having a solid founda-
tion upon this earth, trampled stoutly, with a
smack of the shoes upon the pavement, while
Percival Perceforest went a-tiptoe. It is proper to
add that this latter was dressed in a tight jerkin
of green velvet, rather soiled, frayed at the edges,
wanting a button or two at the bosom; that he
wore scarlet stockings, darned in places and not
darned in other places; that his shoes were down
at heel, the feather in his red cap broken-backed;
that he looked rumpled but innocent, unfortunate
rather than debauched, as if he had slept out for a
night or two—which was precisely the fact.

Brazenhead the Great

The Captain, deep in the delights of mystery, conducted his initiates to the stone ledge which ran along the new chantry of Bishop Wykeham. Here he sat down, and courteously invited the merchant to a place at his right hand. This being declined with a "Sir, I thank you,"—"Two feet forever!" said the Captain heartily, and nodded Percival Perceforest to the place at his left hand. Percival meekly took it. "Pretty lamb!" said this fatherly Captain, and put a hand on his shoulder.

Undoubtedly Captain Brazenhead had a notable manner; endearment and command coincided in his tones; he seemed to be pursuing his own generous way when really he was hunting yours. He succeeded with Percival to the point of marvel.

"Name, my suckling?" he asks, and is answered, "Percival Perceforest, sir."

"Could not be better, indeed. Your age, Percival?"

"Of nineteen years, sir." The Captain smacked his leg.

"I knew it; I was certain of it!" he cried with delight, then sobered in a moment to ask:

"Now have you, Percival, in all your nineteen years of travail in this old round, ever let so much water from your eyes as on this day?"

"No, no, indeed, sir. There has been no such occasion," says Percival, and breaks out sobbing like a drawpipe. The Captain thumped him on the back. "No more o' this. Back to your kennel,

4

tears! Down, ramping waters, waste my cheeks no more! Madness of moons—" Percival thought it right to explain. He looked up with all the proper pride of grief in his hot eyes.

"Sir," he said, "I would have you understand, if you please, that I am the most wretched young man in all England."

"Stuff!" says the merchant testily; "windy talk!"

"By cock, not at all," broke in the Captain, "but sound and biting truth, as I can tell. I know something of wretchedness, let me assure you, Scrivener"—the merchant started—"ah, and of English wretchedness too, since I myself have seen the top of a handsome nobleman lying two yards away from his trunk, and his pious lady pondering which morsel she should first embrace—a pitiful sight, I hope. And in Lombardy, you must know, they sow the fields with men's head-pieces, and thereby breed dragons, as Cadman also did in the tillage and common fields about Thebes. Sir, sir, this lad is in an agony, if I have ever known agony. Now, I will lay a thousand marks to your ink-bottle that I can place a finger on the nut of his grief." The Captain spoke so heatedly that Percival was minded to soothe him.

"It is too deep-rooted, dear sir," he said.

"I prick deep," replied the Captain, and raised a finger. "Now mark me, boy. You, in the first delicious flush of manly love, have been torn from your bosom's queen."

42

, "Oh, sir!" says Percival, gasping.

"And she is of high degree."

"Oh, sir!"

"And she is here in this city of Winton—and you have tramped in her steps—and slept under hedges, and in the skirts of brakes—and seen her —and by her been seen—and yet you cannot get at her—hey?"

"Oh, sir!" cries Percival, showing the whites of his eyes, "oh, sir, what magic do you use?" The Captain held out his hand for the other to kiss.

"My magic is the magic of that glowing old puddle of blood, my heart," says this triumphant man. "What difficulty had I? What does youth cry for? Why, youth again. But you tell me much more than such *a, b, c*. Your jacket" (he fingered the sleeve) "was good Genoa velvet once; and is not green her livery? The sun hath printed the badge in your cap and defies your busy fingers; do you bear arms in your own right?" He snapped his fingers. "You have played with your master's daughter, page-boy." Percival hung his head.

The Captain reassured him. "Oh, you have not gone too far. The velvet tells me another tale, my friend. The pile lies down along this line, and this line, and this line"—he drew his finger down Percival's back. "I think your master's staff has been at work here, therefore it was no case for the hemp-collar. And he sent you packing, I see. The white dust of Hampshire cries from those shoes; and

here, as I live by bread, is some Hampshire hay to
tell me where your bed was made last night." He
pulled a long stalk from Percival's trunks and tasted
it. "Whitchurch hay?" he asked.

Percival replied, "No, sir, Sombourn."

"Ah," says the Captain, "I knew it was grown
on the western side of the shire. My palate is out
of order. Where does your master live, then?"

"At Bemerton, sir, in Wilts."

"I know the place." He considered it, gently
rubbing his nose. "Good pasture lands about Avon.
My Lord Moleyns owns the fee; but yours was not
his badge. Would it be—no? Never old Touchett
—Angry Touchett, as we called him in the old
days."

"Sir Simon Touchett is his name, sir," says
Percival. The Captain snapped his fingers and
looked blandly at the merchant.

"Do I prick deep, Scrivener? Now then, to it
once more. Angry Touchett hath a pretty daughter, hey?"

"He hath four," says Percival. The merchant
sniggered, and the Captain tapped his teeth, then
jumped up with a snort, pulling Percival after him.
"Boy," he cried, venturing his all on the main,
"you love the second daughter of Angry Touchett."

He deserved to win. Percival opened his mouth,
words failing him. The merchant said "Tush!"
and walked away; and Captain Brazenhead clasped
the youth in his arms. You may be quite easy

44

in your mind as to whether or no the whole story
was poured out unreservedly.

True it was, according to his own tale, that
Percival Perceforest, foot-page to Sir Simon Touchett, Knight, had loved his master's second daughter,
Mistress Mawdleyn. Certain familiarities growing
unawares, and growing dearer by use; certain innocent natural testimonies given and received; certain
pledges scrupulously observed, were followed by
certain unmistakable tokens. It was all very innocent and passably foolish—a boy-and-girl, kiss-in-
the-dark, dream o' nights affair; but Angry Touchett
had beaten his daughter and trounced his page.
He had packed the girl off to her aunt, the Prioress
of Ambresbury, and Percival to the devil, whom he
conceived to be his natural father. Poor Percival,
deplorably in earnest over his love-making, had
skulked about the shaws and osier-brakes of Bemer-
ton, trudged to Ambresbury over the downs, and
learned the news there—all as much to the detriment of his spirits as of his trim adornment. The
news being that the Prioress would take her niece
on pilgrimage to Canterbury, Percival, too, felt the
call of Saint Thomas: he followed, taking the hos-
pitalities that offered on the road. He saw the
entry of Mawdleyn into Winchester with the Ambresbury retinue; saw her lodged in the stately
Abbey of Hyde beyond the North Gate. He had
seen and been seen, and this mutual grief had been
too many for him. He had opened the brimming

sluices of his heart; he was tired, sick, longing, foot-sore, heartsore, desperate, young. Tears had done him good, but the Captain did him more.

When he had the whole story out, "Now," said this intrepid man, "you and I, Percival, are in the fair way of a classic friendship, as I see very well. What! we have mingled tears"—this was true; "confidences have passed"—they had, but all one way; "we have looked each into the heart of the other! You shall be Patrocleus to a new Achilles, Harmodius to Aristogiton. Or let me stand for Theseus, Duke of Athens, you shall be that noble-man, whose name is on the tip of my tongue, who was followed by his loving attentions to the gates of Hell Town. Now, just as Achilles was kindled by the sparks beaten from the heart of Patrocleus, whom he tenderly loved, so shall I most reasonably be by you, my Perceforest. If Theseus went to Hell after that other gentleman, I will go to Bemer-ton if needs be. But needs will not. Needs call otherwhere. What do you say to a likely manor in Kent, with the title of Lord of Parliament, cousin and councillor to a great king? You have a kingly name, for was not a Perceforest king of all England? Everybody knows it. You may carve out these rewards and have your little Mawdleyn under your arm all the while. Come. I see a part of the way, but I am plaguily a-thirst with all this tongue-work. Come, boy, let us drink. Leave the rest to me: counsel comes on the flood. But let us

by no means omit our respects to the respectable
Saint Swithin, lord of this place, though dead as a
mutton-bone. Come, my gamebird, bend the knee
with me."

II. Wiles of Captain Brazenhead

They bent the knee together, the man of blood
and the weeper, then rose up and went out of the
great church. As they journeyed, the Captain
was good enough to expound his philosophy of
saints and ladies, whom he classed together as
amiable emollients of our frail age, as so much
ointment, necessary to us in early manhood, better,
however, taken early, and always in moderation.
Nearing the inn he became full of thought, and his
face took on so portentous a cast of brooding melan-
choly that Percival dared not break in upon it.
The Captain, as the result showed, had been thinking partly of beer, for he drank deeply and at once
of this fount of solace, with both hands at the flagon.
Percival sipped his beer delicately, without wetting
more than the red of the lips; his little finger pointed
to the sky as he lifted his jug. This was not lost
upon the Captain, who said to himself, "It is easy
to see that you are higher born than you suppose,
my lambkin; so much the better for Jack." But
when he had again drunk copiously, thrown down
the flagon for dogs to sniff at, and wrung out his
beard, mustachios, and eyebrows, regardless of his
birth he slapped his young friend on the thigh,
saying, "I have it, gamepoult, I have it."

"What have you, sir?" asks Percival. The Captain replied, "There is but one thing to have in the world, since you and I are one. I have your Mawdleyn like bird in net." He shut his two hands together to shape a cage; one of his thumbs was stuck up for the inmate. "She is in there, I tell you," he averred. "Do you see her?"

"Yes, sir," says Percival.

"You are a good lad," replied the Captain; "and I'll tell you this for certain-sure; you too shall be in there, billing on the same perch, in three shakes of a leg, if you follow me. Is this to your liking?" Percival seized his friend's hand.

"Oh, I will follow you to the world's end, dear sir!" he cried with fervor; and the Captain, "You shall follow me no farther than Kent at this present. Now listen, and answer me. This Prioress of Ambresbury, what favor hath she? Is she a big lady, or a little mincing, can-I-venture kind of a lady? Is she of fine presence or mean? In a word, doth she favor your tun or your broomstick?"

"She is a fine woman, sir," replied Percival, "with a most notable shape."

"Aha!" says the Captain, "I feel a Turk. Now then, what sort of a train hath she? Many or few?"

"Sir, she is accompanied, as her due is, by two stirrup-boys, half a score men-at-arms, an esquire of the body, a seneschal, a confessor, and five tirewomen, to say nothing of Sister Guiscarda, who hath no teeth to speak of, or of Sister Petronilla, who loves me a little out of pity." The Captain, musing, made a note of Sister Petronilla.

"Very sufficient indeed for an honorable gentlewoman," he said, "and very pleasing to God, I am sure. Now, if I twisted the neck of one of those stirrup-jacks, and put you into his place and breeches, who is the worse?" Percival glowed in his skin. "No one would be the worse, sir," says he, "save perchance the boy whose neck you should be pleased to wring; and, oh, sir, many, many would be the better!"

"Let be then," said the Captain; "I will arrange it for you." Percival sighed.

"How shall I thank you, my noble benefactor?" he said, earnestly. The Captain put hands on his shoulders.

"You shall thank me by your deeds, my lad. I know a youth of parts when I see him—a pale face that knows the look of letters, a thin hand that can curl about a pen-holder. You are exactly what I need. Don't suppose that you are not to work for your bliss. Not at all. You shall do a pretty work in the world before you are a moon older. Now I am for the Abbey of Hyde. Have you any commands for me? A billet for the round eyes of Mawdleyn Touchett? A love-lock? Ah, you are shorn like a Burgundian, I see."

"Sir," says Percival, "I will write if I may."

"Write, write," his friend urged him. "I am

glad you have the knack of that. Presently you shall be writing for the realm!"

Percival, using his knee for desk, wrote in the inn-yard:

My pretty lamb, these words shall kiss thine eyes, letting thee know that I am near at hand, withal crying to be nearer. And so I shall be anon, as I am assured by the noblest friend ever young man had. Start not, color not, be surprised at nothing thou shalt see or hear to-morrow. O my lovely love, my rose, my dear, kiss this paper where my heart is spilt.—From thy true love,

POOR PERCIVAL.

To my Sweet Mistress Mawdleyn Touchett, by a very trusty hand.

"Read it over to me, boy," said Captain Brazenhead. This Percival did, with some confusion of face.

"By the bones of Saint Jezebel," said his friend, "that is the prettiest letter but three I have ever read of—ah, or caused to be written. Soon enough, that gate, you shall wriggle where that will go. Now help me out with my horse and stuff. I lodge at Hyde this night; and do you lie snug in the Strangers' Hall, my dear, and stay there till I send for you."

III. How Captain Brazenhead was Recruited

The deeds of Captain Brazenhead from this point became swift and ruthless; they demand epic treatment wholly beyond my present means, and would be omitted, with a bare mention of the fact accomplished, were it not for one beautiful flaw in them, very characteristic of the man, which (although he had no notion of it then) entirely spoiled his own real design, to Percival Perceforest's incalculable benefit. Let me, therefore, say that the Captain rode (upon his stolen horse) into the stables of the Abbot of Hyde, and told a lay-brother whom he found there that he was to be a guest for that night. Dismounted, he stalked into the stables to see the animals. There was a fat, cream-colored Galician horse there, with a head-stall of red leather. He risked his all upon that.

"What!" he cried out, "is my gossip the Lady of Ambresbury abroad? Is that possible?"

"Her ladyship is here for one night, indeed, sir," says lay-brother Eupeptus. The Captain faced him, with terrible eyes.

"And does she know, thinkest thou, bare-poll, that her dear Cambases is herded with common sumpter-beasts? By my head I will never believe it. Where are her people? Where are her two stirrup-boys, her half a score men-at-arms, her esquire of the body, her seneschal, her confessor, her five tirewomen, to say nothing of Sister Guis-carda, who has no teeth, or of Sister Petronilla, who loves me a little out of pity? Lord of battles, brother, answer me quick!"

"Sir," replied the trembling brother, "I believe they are in chapel at this hour; but the two lads are out in the meads, I am sure, birds'-nesting. I saw them go down this half-hour or more, and

I'll swear to their present occupation (once they be there) by my lively hopes of Heaven."

Captain Brazenhead, with a great air, strode out of the court-yard; but, instead of going into the Abbey, he turned through a wicket-gate into the Abbot's garden, skirted a yew hedge, found a hole in it, wormed himself through, crossed a kitchen plot, a herbary, a nuttery, climbed a wall by means of a fig tree, and dropped ten feet into the meads. Then he took his way over the growing grass towards the river, which he saw coiling between banks of bright green, like a blue snake enlarging under the sun. The evening was very fair, the sun behind the towers of Wolvesey, the rooks circling about the Nun's Walk. Larks soared and sang, a soft wind played over the meadows. The Captain particularly delighted in the cowslips, which, springing everywhere about his feet, appealed to his tenderest feelings, and caused him to skip like a lamb unweaned, lest he should unhappily tread on any nodding crown of them. "My fresh beauties! My dairy-delights!" cried he, "I would as soon trample my mother's grave as your wagging golden heads?" Prancing thus, full of the soft mood which opening adventure always brings to the truly adventurous, carolling and talking secrets to the flowers, he drew near the smooth-flowing, dimpled waters of Itchen, deep and dark just here. Right and left, up and down river he looked, first at the rising trout, next for bigger

game. He clacked his tongue in his cheek at
what he made out. "I am in luck's way this
happy evening," he told himself, "I have divided
the enemy." This was the case. To his left he
saw a figure in dark clothes—or (to be exact) the
lower half of a figure—busy in a clump of osiers;
to his right another, very delicately pink in the
declining sunlight, sitting on the bank of the river,
naked arms clasping naked knees, chin atop. "This
is my game," said the Captain to himself; "I leave
sedge-warblers to the other innocent. This one is a
bather. He shall have a long swim, by my immortal part."

Captain Brazenhead, on his belly, crept warily
up a drain; and it had assuredly gone ill with the
Prioress's stirrup-boy had his stalking enemy not
happened upon some very early forget-me-nots
growing upon the north bank of his covert. This
is one of those star-directed chances which may
change the fates of Empires. Seeing these flowers,
"Oh, patch of heaven's blue! Oh, eyes of the deep
hiding-place of my God!" breathed the prone, delighted Captain Brazenhead. "Oh, color of sacred
hope, what blissful fortune drew my sight to thine?"
He picked two or three of the starry flowers and
peered over the drain, as he did so, at the unconscious youth, who, with his knees clasped between
his hands, still looked at the water. Said the Captain in his thought, "My lad, these azure blossoms
have saved thy virgin life. Thank the Maker of all

53

flowers!" So said, he sprang suddenly upon him
from behind, as a man will throw himself upon a
great fish in a shallow. The boy, smothered under
fold upon fold of Captain, could neither move nor
cry out: one great knee was over his mouth, another pressed the pit of his stomach, his toes were
pricked by a fierce beard. The Captain at leisure
reached over for his captive's shirt, and tore it into
three long strips over his head. With one of these
he securely bound the prisoner's ankles; turning him
over, he next tied his hands behind his back. Lastly he wound up his mouth with three or four thick-
nesses of calico; then carried him off and laid him
snugly in the drain, which was very nearly dry.
He did not forget to choose a place for him close to
the patch of early forget-me-nots. "There, my
chicken," he said, kindly, "your eyes shall be glad-
dened by the sight of the innocent saviors of your
life. Look upon these little blue beauties, and
thank God night and morning for one of the fairest
sights His world can offer you." So said, he picked
up the discarded clothes and ran as fast as he could
towards the Abbey.

He broke through gates and doors, raced down
passages, crossed the Little Cloister, and jostled a
way for himself between the crowd of servants at
the lower end of the refectory. The monks were
at supper under the direction of the Prior, who sat
at the high table. The Lord Abbot, no doubt, was
entertaining guests in his parlor; was therefore more

remote from approach. It would be necessary for
the Captain to roar ıf he wished (as he did wish) to
be heard in there; and yet his sense of fitness told
him that he should not bewail outrageously so slight
a misfortune as he had been able to procure. "The
noise I shall have to make," he had said to himself,
reasoning as he ran, "if I am to penetrate the walls
of the Abbot's parlor, would be extravagant for the
death of a prelate. Tush! and I am to waste it
upon a thin little boy not even drowned in truth.
But what else can I do to serve my friend Perceforest?"

Even as he said the words, being within the doors
of the refectory, he began a wail which might well
wake the dead. Holding on high the limp testimony
of his news, he poured the whole of his magnificent
natural organ into gusts and volleys of woe towards
the rafters. *Tuba mirum spargens sonum!* "Oh,
too much dole to be borne! Oh, misery of men!
Hapless, hapless Narcissus! Hylas, early cut off!
Out and alas! *mes très chers frères*, look upon these
weeds!" It was as if the Seven Vials had been
loosed, as if the Archangel were sounding the Last
Trump, and all the unhappy dead voicing their despair. "O lasso! Oimè! O troppo, troppo dolore!'
pursued the Captain, intoxicated with his fancy,
and breaking easily into the Italian. The monks
and their guests were all on foot, the servants ran
about, the dogs came out from under the tables and
howled at the howling Captain; the Reverend Prior

whipped his napkin from his neck (lest he should strangle) and swallowed a toast before the time. A picture of tragic woe, the Captain stood before him, exhibiting in one hand a pair of murrey breeches and jerkin of leather, in the other a stout shoe, two worsted stockings, and what remained of a shirt.

"Look at these tokens, Reverend Father," says the Captain, "and shudder with me."

"Who are you?" asks the Prior, blowing out his lips. The Captain was ready for that.

"I am Mallecho, the Sorrowful Sprite, the Dark Herald, Testadirame," he announced in bodeful accents.

"And why under Heaven do you show me your old clothes?" the Prior asked him testily. The Captain with sobs enlarged upon the question. Would to God, he cried out, that they had been his! Alas! they had covered a younger, more blossoming body than his old skin could hold. The nymphs, he went on to say, had the beauteous owner of these weeds; Itchen's blue wave rolled over him, fishes explored his armpits, eels and other serpents wreathed his legs. "This man," said the Reverend Prior, "is undoubtedly mad. Let the Almoner be sent for, the Infirmarer, and the Exorciser—" But at that moment a monk, running in from a door in the panel, knelt before the Prior, a messenger from the Lord Abbot to know what this monstrous commotion could be about.

It was wonderful to see the change in Captain

Brazenhead. The usher of woe no more, there stood
erect as keen a man of affairs as ever you saw in
your life. "Your pardon, my reverend brothers, I
had taken this good father for your Lord Abbot.
Conduct me, brother, to his Grace. Unless I gravely mistake, I have sad news for his most cherished
guest."

"Do you mean——?" the Prior began to ask.

Captain Brazenhead laid a finger to his mouth.

"I do mean——" he began to answer.

"Take him with you, Brother Harmonius," said
the Prior; so the Captain with his tokens was led
away to the Abbot's parlor.

In this very stately apartment of black oak and
silver sconces and a statue of the Blessed Virgin,
he saw all that he wanted. The Lord Abbot was
there, a shaggy-browed, portly man, enthroned.
On his right hand sat the Prioress of Ambresbury,
majestic, ox-eyed, slow-moving, with the remains
of beauty carefully husbanded; next to her a yellow
old nun with a few teeth; next to her again the un-
doubted Mawdleyn Touchett of Percival Perceforest's handling, a fine die-away girl, with a creamy
skin, bountiful shape by no means concealed in a
dress of white cloth, and a pair of brimming brown
eyes which, his experience told him, would go through
a diaphragm quicker than a knife through butter.
Upon her further side was another nun, of mild,
repining countenance, whose head mostly inclined
to one side, and who as she talked drew the breath

inward. This must be Sister Petronilla, who loved Percival a little. Other guests there were, of whom this history has nothing to report. Supper was over: the Abbot dallied with a sop in wine, the Prioress with a silver toothpick; Mawdleyn Touchett, who seemed in a melting mood, rather tumbled and very tired, played with her fingers in her lap. A couple of minstrels half kneeled on the floor, and strummed their strings to deaf ears. Captain Brazenhead was a diversion, a healthy gale in a close garden; the singers stopped of their own accord in the middle of an heroic couplet, telling how

> Sire Simonè de Rochefort
> N'i porta pas banière a tort,

and Captain Brazenhead came lightly to the point.

"By your leave, my Lord Abbot," he said, then turned nobly to the Prioress of Ambresbury. "Madam, I bring this sorrowful testimony of the too early demise of one of your servants. A young boy, Madam, whose privilege and hope it was to serve by your foot, seeking the solace of the water, has found eternal solace in the bosom of Our Lady (whom let us bless forever!). I found these clothes by the water, Madam; the tender body I found not."

The Prioress removed the toothpick, as she said, "I recognize the color of my livery, sir, but do not call to mind the wearer. It may be very true what you tell me."

"It is most woundily true, Madam," says the Captain, with a glimpse at Mawdleyn's brown eyes.

"I do not doubt you, sir," returned the Prioress; "but I suppose I can find boys enough in Winchester. Meantime, I am very much obliged to you for your labors."

"Madam," says the Captain, "my labors, as you are pleased to call what I protest to be delights, are but begun, if (as I assume) your Ladyship needs a new stirrup-boy. I hope I know what is due from a man of my degree to a lady of yours. We chevaliers, Madam, are sworn to the succor of ladies; and I should never dare look again into the face of my friend the Duke of Milan (who dubbed me knight) if I were false to that oath. Madam, I found the husk, let me find a kernel; I found the poor weeds, let me find the sprouting bud."

"I confess that I do not altogether understand your desires," said the Prioress, with some hesitation; "but if the Duke's Grace of Milan—"

"Yes, yes," put in the Abbot, "if the Duke's Grace of Milan—"

"Would to God, dear Madam," cried the Captain, with real feeling, "would to God, my Lord Abbot, I could supply you with the kind of lads that flower in my good friend's court! Hey, the bloom, the glitter, the Cupid's limbs of these dexterous youths! They will tie you a shoe, pommel you a cushion, they will trim you a wimple, swing you to a horse, dance, sing, cap verses, tell tales like young gods at play of an evening. I cannot, in this homely land, perform the impossible, alack! but I can get you a very handy youngster of my own retinue, and warrant him no lick-pot neither—if that will serve your Ladyship's turn."

This was a delicate moment, if you please, for the Captain. Directly he had offered, he knew that he had offered too much and too soon; but there was no withdrawing. The Abbot spoke first, leaning back in his chair; plainly he was weary of the thing: "This appears to be a business for my sister of Ambresbury to consider more with her seneschal than with her host. Yet the gentleman's pains merit some courtesy at our hands. Sir," he said to the Captain, "a cup of wine with you."

"My Lord," said Captain Brazenhead, "there spoke a prelate."

The wine was brought; Captain Brazenhead drank deep. After that he began to talk, and the minstrel's office was at an end. He spoke first of his travels in remote and marvellous parts of the world—of the desert between the Church of Saint Catharine and Jerusalem; of the Dry Tree; and of how roses first came into the world. The City of Calamye and its lamentable law of marriage engaged him next; also the evil custom of the Isle of Lamary, and concerning the palace of the King of the Isles of Java. He told of trees that bear

60

meal, honey, wine, and venom; of the herb Edelfla
which is said to resemble a woman; of the realms
of Tharse; of the Devil's head in the Valley Perilous;
and of pismires and their hills of gold. By a
transition as easy as it was abrupt, he passed to
Natural Science, in which he showed himself learned
without pedantry. He spoke of the nine eyes of
the lamprey, and reasoned boldly for the common
opinion of the ostrich, which conceives that it
digesteth iron. This he said he had himself proved,
though he must be excused from telling them how.
I wish you could have heard him upon the vexed
question of whether hares are indeed hermaphro-
dites; he was so adroit in handling, fertile in parallels,
discreet, subtle, provocative of thought. And he
carried his hearers with him. Not so, however, in
the matter of mandrakes, to whom he denied the
virtue of shrieking when pulled by night. Of this
the Prioress of Ambresbury was positive; equally
constant was the Abbot of Hyde in the assertion
that they have thighs. The Captain laughed off
his obstinacy.

He spoke next of perils, painted in battle-pieces
with a broad brush as he went. He took his hearers
with him to sunny foreign courts, to Venice, to
Rimini, to Florence, back again to his dear Milan.
They beheld him head a sortie at the siege of Rhodes.
When the Barbary corsairs chained him naked to a
galley they sat still, crisping their hands, until he
picked up with his toes the half of a file; then while

his escape was in the framing, while the file (wetted
with spittle) ground through the hot, dense nights,
ah, how they held their breath! He whirled them off
with him into the Low Countries, and bade them wait
while he cut the dykes and flooded a whole country-
side. He burned the Pucelle of Orleans before their
dilating eyes, and owned with natural blushes that
it was himself who (for reasons then found good) so
nearly broke the marriage-treaty between King
Harry's Grace and the daughter of King René of
Anjou. In a word, by these his accounts of wide
experiences, of patient, curious research, of gests
and feats of arms, rapidly delivered, copiously
illustrated and exceedingly untrue, he had his
auditory between his finger and thumb; and not
even a little misadventure with Mawdleyn midway
of his oration could throw him off his balance.
The fact is, the Captain greatly admired this fine
girl, and paid her the tribute of his looks and
speech a little more than he need, or was prudent.
This, while it escaped the Prioress, by no means
escaped the vigilance of the sour old nun who sat
at her left hand, and who deliberately brought up
the girl's blue riding-cloak from the back of her
chair, and pulled the hood over her head so as to
cover her eyes. Thus hooded like a hawk the
poor child remained; yet, while the Captain not
so much as paused in his discourse at the cruel act,
he was careful to see the gentler nun on the other
side wince at it, and (good husbandman!) made that

serve his turn, as you will discover. The end of all was that he won over the Prioress of Ambresbury, who, on rising from the table, begged his company for a further private conversation. By this time she had been led to believe that Captain Brazenhead had nearly lost his life in the effort to save her stirrup-boy's, that he had provided interment at his own charges, and written gentlemanly letters (enclosing a sum of money) to the parents. Such are the effects of the art of suggestion in rapid narrative.

At the going out, which was done with great ceremony of ushers, a chaplain and waiting women, the gentle nun fluttered near Captain Brazenhead, wishful, but not daring, to speak. The Captain encouraged her with a sort of eye that takes you more than half-way.

"Oh, sir," said this palpitating creature, "oh, sir, forgive my sister Guiscarda. She hath our charge greatly on her conscience."

"Dear Madam," replied the Captain soothingly, "say no more. She hath a fine heart, I am sure, and a lofty, great soul."

"She is too severe," said the good nun. "Gentleness may lead where harsh dealing may never, never drive." Captain Brazenhead took her hand and whispered over it:

"You share the qualities of the blessed angels, dear Madam," he said. "Be now an angel indeed, a pious messenger. Hist! Come close. You are

63

a friend of our fair prisoner. You are, I know it;
say no more."

The nun quailed to hear him.

"I love the dear child—"

"You do! And she loves—and she is loved—and
she suffers—we suffer—they suffer—ha!"

"Oh, sir—"

"You have a red heart, Madam. Quick, quick!
Take this writing—'tis for her, a balsam for a
bruised little heart. Hearts go bleeding; stanch
the wound. Deliver it as you can, while I hold the
old lady. I dare no more. Oh, sacred bond between you and me!" He thrust into Sister Petronilla's trembling hand Percival Perceforest's love-
letter. Before she could protest or implore he was
gone, had stepped after the Prioress's people, and
was in the thick of new oratory. Here I cannot ask
you to follow him, but from what you know of his
powers already displayed, you must judge the end
of the adventure. He enlisted Master Perceforest,
in the name of his sister's son, Piers Thrustwood
(you mark the disguise) into the place and breeches
of the youth who lay gagged and naked in a ditch
in Winchester Meads, hard by a clump of early forget-me-nots. By this time corroborative testimony
had been brought home by the second stirrup-boy,
the birds'-nester.

That night Mawdleyn Touchett wrote as follows:

O heart! S(ister) P(etronilla) delivered me your paper
after supper. Now it is, you know where, well kissed.

I would I had you there. They pulled my hood over my
face because your soldier looked at me. I saw your face
the better. I *will not see you to-morrow*, as you bid me;
and yet, O shall I not see you?

Good-night, good-night, good-night!

Your pledged,

MAWDLEYN.

Outside this she dared to write, unable to resist
the look of the words, "To my bosom's lord, P. P.,
give this, M. T. dardant desyr," and coaxed Sister
Petronilla into delivering it to the Captain.

That same night Captain Brazenhead lay on his
back upon the Abbot's good flock; Percival moaned
in his half slumber, and rolled about upon the
beaten floor of the Common Hall; and Sister Petronilla, having Mawdleyn's happy cheek against her
bosom, tried to believe herself justified by faith,
not works.

IV. How PERCIVAL PROSPERED

"The humble supplication of Lancelot Corbet,
Citizen and Scrivener of London, Richard Smith,
mariner, of the county of the town of Kingston-
upon-Hull, of Gundrith, his wife, native of Norro-
way, and of Giles Cruttenden of Mereworth, in the
county of Kent, yeoman," was presented in the
morning early to "the Reverend Mother, their Good
Ladyship, the Prioress of Ambresbury"; and was
to the effect that her orators, devoutly disposed by
motions of their spiritual parts in no wise to be
mistaken, were bounden upon the pilgrimage of
Saint Thomas; but because of the disturbed state

65

of the road, owing to these unhappy times of dis-
cord, and the far purposes of Almighty God (not to
be discerned by men alone), they went in peril of
their lives and substance, "being but poor folk un-
friended of any." Their prayer was that they
might be allowed to join the retinue of the Prioress,
and be friends of her friends, foes of her foes; whereby they could not doubt but that Saint Thomas
would be favorable to them, and the Prioress profit
by the added prayers of very grateful persons.
Also her petitioners, as in duty bound, would ever
pray.

The Prioress was inclined to admit these honest
people to her company; but Captain Brazenhead,
who enjoyed some authority with her, said, "Pass
the mariner and his (apparently) heathen wife, pass
Cruttenden into Kent; but leave me to deal with
Corbet the Scrivener, for I know him of old for a
short-faced, snarling rogue." It was true that
Captain Brazenhead knew him for his acquaintance
of yesterday in the Church of Saint Swithin. When,
therefore, the short-faced man came pacing towards the gates of Hyde, cloaked, strapped, and well
embaled, the Captain met him with a short "Ha,
Scrivener, dismount. None enter here."

"By your leave, sir," says the Scrivener.

"You have no leave of mine," said the Captain in
reply; "therefore, come down or I give you number
three." He touched his pommel.

When the Scrivener, after multitudinous un-

66

strappings, was on firm ground, Captain Brazenhead put on a very wise face, and said: "A word
will be enough in your ear. We carry with us a
person of consequence. You love Y—k." The
Scrivener went as white as the favored rose.

"Who—what—how!"

"Precisely," replied the Captain, "you answer
yourself. Say no more: finger on lip; eyes on the
ground; ears wide—pass in." The Scrivener went
slowly in. Captain Brazenhead, his luck still holding, had spoken wiselier than he knew.

At this point you may see, if you will, Percival
Perceforest demurely habited in the murrey jacket
and breeches, the worsted stockings, greasy cap,
and shoes of the Prioress's stirrup-boy; you may
guess what glint lay behind Mawdleyn Touchett's
dewy eyes, with what clouded white and opening
red she flushed and paled as each moment of a
wondrous day brought up its alarms, to melt them
suddenly in rewards; how the heart of Sister Petronilla (thick in the plot) played postman at her ribs;
how greatly Captain Brazenhead behaved, flourish-
ing the party forward out of Hants, how often his
cap was in his hand to the Prioress of Ambresbury,
how often her ear at his tongue's command. I cannot stay longer in Winton, or I would tell you myself. It shall suffice to say that Percival pleased.
The Prioress liked handsome persons about her;
Percival, whose nerves made him vivid, looked very
handsome in his meekness, eagerness-on-the-leash,

and high colors. They had not gone very far before a chance outburst of his in the French tongue —he sang from a full heart and quite unconsciously —gave his mistress a hint that, if the new lad was deficient in stable knowledge, he had other love.

This happened when they were no further on their way than the two miles of deep descent and gentle rise which bring you to Headborne Worthy and its miraculous Rood, which the curious may still see, beaten, dumb, blind, but portentous, in the sacristy of that weathered shrine—a maimed Titan guarded by heroes. Sister Guiscarda had vowed a candle to this image should she be delivered from the face-ache of the previous day. She was delivered. Captain Brazenhead judged it wise to put a prayer out to usury. Mawdleyn, in this heyday of her heart, must needs praise the kindly Saints. But the Prioress sat her saddle, and Percival, seeing his true love depart, took such joy in her mere carriage of the head, had such exuberant savor of the coming day, the coming days, the coming week, which he should spend in her fragrant company, that as he loitered dreaming by the gate he forgot himself and began to sing:

> Si cum j'oi la Rose aprochée,
> Un poi la trovai engroissée,
> Et vi qu'ele iere plus creüe
> Que ge ne l'avoie veüe. . . .

The Prioress pricked up her ears, but let Percival's voice go wandering on; then she said, "Come hither, Piers." Percival started, blushed, but obeyed.

"Dost thou know what thou singest there?"

"Yes, please you, my lady; I sang the 'Roman de la Rose.'"

"Thou hast that piece?"

"I had all of it by heart upon a time, my lady; but have lost the greater part."

"Begin, if you please," said the Prioress; so Percival began:

Maintes gens dient que en songes . . .

and had got as far as:

Ou vintiesme an de mon aage,

when the pilgrims came out of church, and a chance shot from Mawdleyn's eyes threw him out. He helped his beloved to the saddle, he shored up Sister Guiscarda on hers; but the Prioress did not budge. When the confusion of horses was over, she asked her stirrup-boy aloud, whether he could continue this or any other lay?

"Madam, if it please you," said Percival, "I know the "Romaunt" very well; and I know the tale of the "Twelve Peers and Ganelon," and of "Gallien le Rhetoré" (which is very short), and also that of "Le Jouvencel," a didactic piece. Moreover, I know that story of "The Proud Lady in Amours," which they call Blanchardyn, and also "Isofere the

Hardy," and "The Lays of Marie de France."
There are songs in "The Ladies' Orchard" which I
can sing if you wish for them, and another in the
Italian tongue which begins "In the greenwood I
found a shepherdess," and certain "Triumphs of
Petrarch," and very pleasant sonnets which he
wrote to the dear name and fame of Madame Laura,
his mistress—any of these I can sing, whichever the
company desire—"

"Ah!" cried the Prioress, with a little gasp,
"and the airs of these divine inventions, Percival
—where gat you these?"

"Madam," replied he, blushing a little, ' some
of the airs were devised by me for the lute, some
in plain-song, and some in prick-song for three or
four voices, and some, not yet considered, I hope
to achieve as I go."

"I ask you now," said the Captain, with huge
delight, "is this a prodigy I have procreated or
not?" It came natural to him to suppose himself
the father of such a boy; and, after all, a nephew
is not far removed.

The Prioress was observing the speaker with
gravity. Without taking note of Captain Brazenhead's vaunt, she quietly bade him go on where he
had left off. The obedient lad once more put his
hands behind his back, threw up his chin, and
rippled out his French syllables about love, with
his own love's heart beating a little above his own,
and her brown eyes burning through the top of his

head. She lent him eloquence; he sang clear and
loud:

> Or veil cel songe rimaier
> Por vos cuers plus fere esgaier
> Qu'amors le me prie et commande. . . .

At which last words, if the Prioress had been wary,
she could not have failed to see deep hue call unto
deep. For Mawdleyn grew very red, and Percival
was very red; and Mawdleyn dropped her eyes,
and Percival's travelled as high as her chin, and
stayed there. Two others saw as much as they
should—namely, Captain Brazenhead, who thought
it too good to last, and Master Smith, the mariner,
who studied Percival's nose.

"Very pretty," said the Captain to himself, "but
full of jeopardy." He broke in to address the
Prioress. "Madam," he said, "the sun warns me
that we should proceed. Let us have my nephew's
minstrelsy on the way by all means; but let the
ground-bass be our horses' hoofs. We have a far
road to Alton town."

"This swordsman is right, my lady," said Corbet
the Scrivener. "Let your Ladyship's boy sing as he
walks by your Ladyship's foot."

"I could have sworn by Saint John that there
was but one long nose in a pretty face in all this
world," the Shipman thought to himself. "And
whom have we here?" quoth he. The Prioress
took up the Scrivener.

"My boy shall walk by my foot no further than Alresford," she said with decision. "Young man," she turned to Percival, "you are out of your station, I can see. I will look to your advancement if I love music."

"I thank your Ladyship," says Percival; and Captain Brazenhead glossed that text with "Certainly, I did my friend Jack a good turn when I won this throstle-cock. 'Tis a little marvel of science."

Now, the Prioress would have had the "Romaunt of the Rose" in its entirety, though it should have lasted her (as it would) to her first view of the golden angel on Bell Harry. But this was not to be. By the time Percival had failed at the three-hundred-and-fiftieth line, the company was feverish for something which they might possibly understand. I have spoken somewhat of the Shipman who travelled with them, who came from Kingston-upon-Hull, called himself Richard Smith, and thought he knew Percival's nose. This was a bright-eyed, confident, chin-in-the-air kind of fellow, a golden-bearded, apple-colored man, with a thin wife, very much (and too much) at his devotion, who studied the singing-boy sideways the whole time of his singing, watched his feet, his fine long hands, his sharp little chin, his small mouth, his hot little eyes, his fine long nose. He smacked his forehead and talked to himself, he explored the sky, the downs, the birds in the trees, but all to no purpose; he could not put a name to his memories. When Percival faltered, tried back, caught at a line ahead and could not work up to it, this mariner broke in with a laugh.

"Belay there, shipmate, give over your lead," quoth he; "you cannot bottom it. And I, dear Lord, have been in shoal water this three hours. By Blackbeard and Whitebeard, you know a mort of French words, and all of them different, it seemeth. Now, I would like to know of you, where gat you all those words? For you and I, little master, are not strangers."

As Percival looked startled at him, "By my head and heart, Shipman," said Captain Brazenhead, "you have spoilt a pretty dream I was in. For to hear those fair words took me back to the sack of Orleans, where I lay lapped in plenty, and learned that tongue out of as choice a mouth as your wife hath. I have a mind to set my nephew another task. What, Piers, what, game-bird, have at you in Tuscan then!"

"Nay, sir," said the Prioress, "let Piers alone. He has said enough for his turn."

"Is this young man your nephew, soldier?" asked the Shipman. Captain Brazenhead twisted his mustachios.

"I would like to see the older man who denies it," he said with a glitter in his eye.

The Scrivener, who feared bloodshed more than he feared Captain Brazenhead, intervened with a hasty suggestion, that he supposed the friend of the Duke of Milan might have as many nephews as he chose. "Ah," said the Shipman darkly, "and nieces—like the Pope—you would say!" The Captain half drew his sword, but here the Prioress stayed him with a look. A tale from the Scrivener held them as far as their lodging at Alresford on the Hill.

V. How Percival and the Captain was Bold

In the morning very early Percival Perceforest rose from his bed of straw in the stables, and busied himself with the horses' provand, singing softly as he worked,

> Now, Winter, go away,
> And hide thy white array.
> *Gratiâ Magdalenæ*—

while his bedfellow, the true stirrup - groom, gibed as he lay. Yesterday and yesternight had wrought wonders with the young man. He had a clear color, his eyes shone, courage tingled in his fists. So much was this the state of his case that within a short half-hour of his rising he was pommelling that other groom, that other him again, as if all his future bliss were staked upon it. Battle was cried and delivered in the inn-yard, where Captain Brazenhead, his first flagon on his knee, sunned himself and enjoyed the game. Discretion was no part of that great man's equipment, boldness was all. "Stick in your right, Piers—at him again! Now, now, now, land him on the ear! Ah, foul

74

blow! Swing round, boy—paff! now let drive—"
Such were his vociferous comments on the scuffling
youths. In less time than it has taken me to write
this exordium Percival had a black eye, his colleague
a mouth full of red teeth, many of which he was
forced to discard. The air was thick with eyes
and alarms; Mawdleyn Touchett strained in anguish
from an upper window, provocatively dishevelled;
Sister Petronilla watched through a chink in the
shutter; the Prioress in awful majesty descended
to the yard, and required the truth. The real
stirrup-boy, whose name was Jenkin, said, "This
fellow called me a black liar"; snorting yet, Percival
added, "And that art thou, my man." The truth
being demanded, Captain Brazenhead struck in
with many a courtly bow.

"Dear Reverend Madam," he said, "now we may
well discern the truth of the vulgar saw, *Blood will
out*. I speak not of this knave's blood, which is a
very disgustful topic, not to be entered on so early
in the day; but rather of that secret fount of our
life which we call a man's *Blood:* meaning his strain
—that essence, that quick ichor, that imparted jet,
that spring, that far-descended well, which wanders
from the Navel of the World down the Protuberance
of Time, searching for (but when to find?) the Sea
of Eternity. In truth, Reverend Madam, my nephew is something lowly placed in your service. For,
look now, had he been where Nature, that wise parent,
had designed, he had had a dagger in his girdle to

insinuate under that other's girdle—ah, he had carried a sword! Then there had been no rough and
tumble of fisticuffs, Madam: no, but a slick-out and
a slick-in, and a dead knave to bury. I hope I
make my meaning plain. This lout angered my
nephew as he was loyally (O likeness to Apollo!)
serving Queen Admeta—dear Madam, forgive an
old Latinist, incorrigible dog. My nephew says,
'You lie, knave,' meaning that what he dared say of
your Ladyship was far from the truth—no less.
My nephew ups and smacks him on the chops; head
down, fists in the air, lick-pot comes on to his doom.
One, two—one, two—my nephew lands him in the
teeth: up again! down again! Sola! My nephew,
at the cost of an eye, Madam, vindicates his own
lineage and his dear mistress's nobility; at the cost
of one eye, observe. I hope I explain myself, dear
Reverend Madam." Thus the Captain, while Percival tried to temper his breath, and Jenkin tested
tooth after tooth.

The Prioress looked gravely from one to another
—regardless alike of her niece at the upper window
and her household at the gate—at the engaging
candor of Captain Brazenhead, whose explanatory
hands still showed her their palms, at Percival's
flushed cheeks and heaving chest, at Jenkin's preoccupation with the ruin of his teeth. Mostly she
looked at Captain Brazenhead—not because she
liked him the best; for Percival was handsome and
master of the " Romaunt de la Rose," whereas the

Captain was neither; no, but because he was her chief justification for what she was about to do. The Captain put his lineage very high, assumed lightly certain privileges which she held dear. If this personable, scholarly youth were the Captain's nephew —and who proposed to deny it?—then she was acting Admetus to Apollo indeed. Piers had played a gentleman's part without a gentleman's weapons; he had a soft voice, and knew the " Romaunt de la Rose." She must reward Piers—and she did.

"Piers," she said, "go into the house and have your eye dressed. Sister Petronilla will see to it. You say that you have acted rightly; I am sure I hope so. I will talk to you presently. As for you, Jenkin, I shall leave you to the care of Dan Costard"—Dan Costard was the Prioress's chaplain, a fine disciplinarian—"but I hope that, before you see him, you will clean yourself. Captain Brazenhead, I am very much obliged to you for your timely interposition." The captain bowed. He held the lady in conversation for some half an hour, while Percival was having his eye dressed—not by Sister Petronilla. His own lineage, and by implication Percival's, lent him topics. It was exceedingly distinguished. Assurbanipal, King of Syria, by his illicit union with Blandamira, daughter of the Prince of the Kurds, was the root of his title. Those two valiant knights-errant, Sir Partenopex of Blois and Sir Tyrant the White, figured later on, about the time of King Uther Pendragon (inex-

tinguishable enemy of the Brazenheads); and Duke
Regnier of Genoa, one of the twelve Peers of Charlemagne, was a collateral.   Magnificent as this pedigree was, the Captain frankly admitted the irregu-
larity of the tie which bound the exalted pair from
whom it sprang; but attributed it to the loose state
of manners prevailing in their times, the darkness
all over the moral state, and the inexplicably tardy
approach of the Christian dispensation. "All this,"
said he, "I know as well as your Ladyship, and as
heartily deplore it.   But who are we, to judge the
practices of ancient kings?   My ancestor of Syria,
burdened with many lawful wives (another deplorable custom of his age), was hard pressed, what
with his domestic and politic engagements.   There
may not have been a priest handy in Kurdistan at
the time he fell on loving Madam Blandamira—it
is probable that there was not.   And it would ill
become me or my nephew Thrustwood to impeach
an union of hearts, of whose passionate commin-
gling we ourselves are the late, pale flowers.   With
all this," he concluded, "I vex your Ladyship's good
ears, that your Ladyship may see how ill-suited my
nephew must be in a stable jacket, reduced to double
his two fists into cudgels for lack of a fine sword to
grip.   I make bold to add, Advance my nephew, you
do honor to the imperial seed of Assurbanipal and
the noble (if erring) Blandamira!"   The Prioress,
who appeared to be very much impressed with this
long recital, after thanking Captain Brazenhead,

returned thoughtfully to the house, but not in time to see the balm which Mawdleyn Touchett was applying to the eye of the Syrian imp.

In this simple manner Percival Perceforest was advanced from stirrup-groom to secretary, although he could lend no more testimony than a fine color to his kinsman's account of his ancestry. This, however, he lent liberally, with a modesty so becoming that the Prioress gave him a chain of fine gold for his neck. Alresford furnished forth a suit of brown velvet; he now rode the horse which formerly he had curried, and had the boy in his service with whose teeth he had littered the yard. Thus the Fortunate Gods seemed to favor him, or rather his fistic ability. His place was now by the side of his mistress, between her and Mawdleyn Touchett.

The day was still young when they left the town, and had need to be, for they were to reach Waverley that night, and hoped to pass the heat of noon at Alton. Again, as they went, they began with minstrelsy, which Percival (out of a full heart) could pour in a flood. And now the lad was more daring than he had been. "If it do not displease your Ladyship," he said, "I shall sing you a ballade of my own making, which is in honor of Saint Mary Magdalene—my patroness," he added with a thankful, telltale sigh. Mawdleyn Touchett, knowing that song of old, looked scared: Sister Petronilla turned up her eyes; and Captain Brazenhead thought it prudent to change the conversation.

"The conversion which I wrought by means of
that blissful Saint is very dear in my mind," he began. "The Bashaw Korouc, I remember, met me
in the rocky defiles above Ascalon—" but the
Prioress said, "Sing, Piers, of Saint Mary Magdalene," so Percival thrust up his chin, and sang:

Now, Winter, go away,
And hide thy white array,
  Gratiâ Magdalenæ!
Thy pelt is all too rude
To drape her melting mood—
  Dominæ Laus amœnæ!

Come, April, thou, with showers,
Bring daffodils, wind-flowers,
  Gratiâ Magdalenæ;
Bring in the young lamb's bleat,
Soft rain, and gentle heat,
  Dominæ Laus amœnæ!

Let me go clothed in wet,
Tears be my carcanet,
  Gratiâ Magdalenæ;
Silver my extern part,
Deep red about my heart,
  Dominæ Laus amœnæ!

Lady of sweet unrest,
Should I not love her best,
  Gratiâ Magdalenæ?
Unquiet go I, unkist,
Her starvéd rhapsodist,
  Dominæ Laus amœnæ!

"Thus women sing of women, but not men of
women," said Smith the mariner to his wife. "Here
we have for certain old Brazentop's *mye.*"

"What hast thou to do with that since I am with thee, sweetheart?" asked she.

"More than Saints' love went to the making of that song, young gentleman," was the judgment of Dan Costard, the bony old priest from Ambresbury.

"We needs must love as we are able, sir," Percival replied. "And, for my part, I hope Saint Mary Mawdleyn will heed my crying and give me good comfort in the end."

"Comfort is the man's part in crying matters," says the Shipman; "and comfort I have in my pocket for thee."

"I want none of your comfort, I thank you, master Smith," Percival cried: to which the Shipman retorted that he had been glad enough of it once upon a time. With a tale from Dan Costard, which has been told in another place, the day wore to an end. They came out of Hants into Surrey by the sandy way of Farnham, and rested that night within sound of the tumbling weirs of Wey, in the guest-chambers of the Abbot of Waverley. Percival charmed them to sleep by his sweet singing.

VI. How Percival rose where Capt. Brazenhead fell

Next morning it might have seemed that Percival had reached, and over-reached, his zenith of ascension. For the Prioress, rising too early for Mass and walking abroad to meditate, found him with Mawdleyn Touchett in a singular situation. The girl, in fact, was seated by a fish-pond with her

feet bare and still wet from the water, and Percival
on his hands and knees before her, ardently embracing and kissing those same wet feet. "Oh,
dearest feet!" he was saying, and she, "Ah, foolish
boy! Ah, foolish boy!" but manifestly thinking
nothing of the kind. The Prioress coughed, not
loudly; the cuckoo, which happened then to be
calling over the meadows, obscured the discreet
sound. So Percival pursued his amorous transports
and Mawdleyn suffered the raptures afforded by
such homage undisturbed. "Boy and girl," mused
the Prioress, "together in the spring pastures; flowers all about them, flowers in their faces, flowers
making sweet their breath. Shall not flower lean
to flower? What harm do they do? They have
all life before them; mine is rounding its course.
Let life for me end on a mellow note. This Piers
is a gentle boy—good blood, I feel assured, sings in
him; he hath not a pipe so true for nothing. And
if my niece played the mischief with Perceforest,
Piers Thrustwood shall wash away the stain. Pretty
dears, I will not disturb them; but I will question
Captain Brazenhead a little further."

Questioned, the Captain (who had been picking
rose campions) lifted his shoulders to his ears, lowered his brows, produced indefinitely his mouth to
meet them, spread his palms, then solemnly en-
folded his bosom. He gave the effect of an inverted
arch, and implied deference, noble humility, some
philosophy, and a friendly alliance of benevolent

neutrality. "Madam," he said, "may I not add, Reverend Friend, these pretty plays of my en- amoured nephew and your lovely niece may end (why should I not say it?) as they ought to end. If I applaud my nephew's sagacity, may you not in turn approve this tribute to your niece's beauty?"

"Why," said the Prioress, "there has been such tribute paid before—for instance, by one Perce- forest, my brother's page. Sincere enough, I have no doubt; but tribute is to be valued by the worth of the tributary."

"Have at you there, dearest Madam," returned Captain Brazenhead warmly, "have at you there! If we are considering *worth*, for example!"

"You refer, I suppose, to King Assurbanipal and the fair Blandamira?" said the Prioress.

"I did refer to their Majesties, I confess," replied the Captain. The Prioress had no enthusiasm for this exalted pair. "I fear," she said, "that the title and estates have been alienated long since. Such things would have appealed to my brother Sir Simon's understanding before a fine descent. As for lineage, indeed, the Touchetts do pretty well."

"Touchett! Touchett!" said the Captain, "dear, dear, dear! Oh, Touchett is a good Norman house. Your Rolf Touchett held up the Bastard at Peven- sey, I believe. Very fair! very fair! But the King of Assyria, but the Peer of Charlemagne, Parteno- pex of Blois, Palmerin, Tyrant the White!"

"Captain Brazenhead," said the Prioress, with
dignity and point, "when you exalt your house at
the expense of my own, you compel me to ask
myself why the scion of Partenopex of Blois took
the trouble to abduct a stable boy, and hide him
naked in a ditch on Winchester Meads?"

"Thomas on the Pavement!" said the Captain
to himself. "What a still puddle it is!" Aloud
he said, "Rack and pincers, Madam, could not force
me to tell you what that boy had done, or how far
he deserved what he got?" This was perfectly
true, and the Prioress believed it. "I will not apply
such insistence," she said mildly, "for I agree with
you that it would fail."

"Ah, Madam," said the Captain, taking her hand,
"you and I know the world." This pleased the
Prioress, who did not immediately perceive how
little it met her argument. "Madam," the Captain
went on rapidly, "if my dear blood is perhaps too
dear to my barren loins; if in default of lawful issue
—of issue, I should say (if I speak the whole truth),
if mindful of my ancient race, if with a heart over-
full, outvailing head overtaxed; if philogenous, if
stirpiferous, puffed with pedigree, prolific, wily,
fertile in shifts, if one and all these things I stand
naked to the world, do you wonder, dear and gentle
lady, that I run to cloak myself in You? If by the
hand, a shorn lamb, I lead my pretty nephew; if I
bid him curry your nags, hold your stirrup, batter
soft your cushion, sing to you, tell you age-long

romance, bear your napkin on his arm, your livery
on his King-begotten back—if I do this, why do I
do this? Because I love the boy, Madam, and because—" the Captain bared his head, kneeling, "and
because I love your Ladyship! Yes, Madam," he
went on bitterly, "the bloody, crafty, notched,
maimed old soldier is touched at last! You will not
misunderstand me, I know. I love indeed; but as
Plato, as the Seven Sages, as Ptolemy, as Hermes
the Threefold Mage, as the Abbot Ammonius, as
Simeon Stylites, as the Venerable Bede, might love.
Spiritually, that is inwardly, in the skyey places,
under the shadow of angels' feathers. Is it madness to love so? Then Plato was mad, then Venerable Bede was an ass. Is it wicked to love so?
Then it is wicked to seek your shelter for my nephew's nakedness. Is it hopeless? Then I am
damned. Are you angry? Then I hope I am
damned. Are you content? Then I sing *Gloria
Tibi*, and recall memories of my good mother, at
whose knee I learnt to say, *Amo te devote!*"

The Captain, out of breath, but filled instead
with the soft wind of ecstasy, rapturously kissed
the caught hand of the Prioress. She, confused,
had little to say. Percival and Mawdleyn, who
came upon her while their mouths were still much
too close together, had still less to say. They
parted as by a thunder-shock and stood still, their
heads hanging like tired roses. "Children," said
the Prioress, "where have you been?"

"I walked in the meadows, if it please you, good aunt," says Mawdleyn, "and Piers has dried my feet for me."

"Do you understand this service then, Piers, as well as that of minstrelsy?" asked his mistress.

Percival modestly replied that he had done his best to understand it, and so should always do with every office which might please her good ladyship. They went back through the fields to hear Mass and break their fast. The buttercups were so tall that they brushed Mawdleyn's knees and dusted her with gold—a charming sight, which, as Captain Brazenhead remarked, made Danaë of the girl, and so of Percival an object of contempt to all high-minded men. "Perceforest, my young sprig," he improved the occasion by saying, "the pace is too hot to last. We cannot stay, you and I, at such a course. We must break away, Percival, lest we be broken." Percival was too flushed with adventure to heed him. "My cup is full, sir, shall I not drink? For such a morning as this I would contentedly be drubbed every night by Sir Simon himself. Oh, her feet! Oh, her tender hands! Oh, her heart!" And so on, and so on. All this filled his friend with disquiet.

On their way by Crooksbury to Guildford and the White Down, Captain Brazenhead drew from the stores of his garnered experience that remarkable tragic tale which decorates another page;

but interesting as it, and subsequent comments
upon it, might prove, great press of matter drives
me forward to Reigate. Fear of congestion, in
like manner, compels me to pass over the noble
country through which winds the Pilgrims' Way
—Compton and Littleton Cross, Saint Catherine's
Chapel on the side of a chalk down, Shalford Meadows and Shalford Ferry, Guildford town, and the
long grass road which draws you up to Saint Mar-
tyr's Church and the wooded ridge. You shall
picture our company riding there among the boughs,
and guess what opportunities for pilfer—stolen
looks, stolen touches, half - heard sighs, whispers,
vows: "Dearest feet! Dearest feet!" and "Ah,
foolish boy!"—there may have been; what earnest
talk also held the Captain to the side of his Prioress,
and how Master Smith's wife lived silently upon
the sight of her bluff husband's eyes. Those
galliard eyes were much intrigued by Percival's
long nose, out of whose shape the baffled Shipman read mystery, a long - lost sweetheart masquerading as a lad, Captain Brazenhead for a
terrific rival, himself for a flouted man. There
is meat for a tale here. But I am drawn instead
to Reigate, a red town on a hill, where you might
have found a noble Priory of Austin Canons, with
great welcome for their Sister of Ambresbury; a
large inn called the Christopher, and a little beer-
house named The Holy Fish. Thither, under the
shades of evening, Captain Brazenhead drew young

Percival Perceforest, his nephew by adoption, sadly
against inclination and nature.

"By Cock, my bird of the bough," said this
warrior, expostulant, "thou hast had thy fill of
toying with thy dear. Work of men is now on
hand, battle-work, hack-and-hew, blood and bones,
a tragic dish. Am I to remind you that you are
beholden to me? Never in this life, I hope."

"I shall never forget my duty to you, sir," said
Percival warmly, already ashamed of his back-
sliding.

"Why, that is as well," returned the Captain,
"for I assure you there will be every temptation.
But, in my opinion, you hold the iron and should
strike before it cools. The Prioress, let me advise
you, has discovered (how, I know not) my innocent
little device at Winchester; and although I was
able by my arts to give her a check, she is a singling
hound, of whom God alone can predict (if He will)
how soon she will be nose-in-air again. Therefore,
Percival, I say, Time is. Cut the way of Holy
Thomas, tuck your sweetmeat under your arm, take
the road, ride with me—and ho! for war and dead
men's shoe-leather. How does this strike you?"

It seemed a delightful plan to the speaker, whose
surprise was extreme when Percival drew back.
"What, bawcock, art thou faint?" he cried, gen-
erously putting the best excuse foremost. But
Percival was not faint. He was, on the contrary,
very red; his eyes were misty, his lips dry. He had

to use his tongue to them before he could avow the shameful truth to his benefactor.

"Oh, sir," he faltered, after many a false start. "Oh, sir, do not be angry; but I cannot deceive my mistress much longer."

"Hey," cried the Captain, "why? does she smell smoke, do you think?"

"No, no," Percival assured him; "but my con-science—"

"Lord of battles, boy!" the Captain roared, "don't talk of conscience to me. We have our fortunes to make."

"Let it be then," says Percival; "but I dare not add robbery to my fibs." The Captain stopped in mid-street, and raised his eyebrows as if he saw a snake in the gutter.

"Robbery!" he said in a whisper, "why, what are maidens for if not to be robbed?"

"Sir, sir, the Reverend Prioress would be robbed if I took Mawdleyn away," says Percival. The Captain gaped at him.

"Well?" he said, "why not? Why are we here, knights of the road? Why is she here? Why have I told so many falsehoods, and why hath she be-lieved them, hey?"

"I don't think she hath believed them, sir," says Percival humbly.

The Captain scratched his nose." Tush! I must be sadly out then," he said. "Do you think it was Tyrant the White she stuck at?"

"Sir, I think rather it was Blandamira the Kurdish princess. But Partenopex of Blois seemed to me rather a hard morsel."

"Blois is good enough," said the Captain; "it must have been that rascally Tyrant. To tell you the truth, I had hoped that Blois would edge me in the other, a great favorite of mine—especially with a lady who could listen all day to the "Romaunt of the Rose." And now I remember that she seemed to know something about my little contrivance at Winchester. Well, well, I am vexed about this. But everything conspires to further my counsel to you, Percival. Cut and run, my twittering finch, cut and run."

"Sir," said Percival doggedly, "I will run whithersoever you bid me run; but I shall leave Mawdleyn behind."

"Then you tire of her?" asked the Captain. "I am not surprised. The girl is too ripe for her age. Thin ones pall not so soon." Percival's little eyes kindled.

"Captain," he says hotly, "I love my Mawdleyn better than life or heaven; but I will never tempt her to wickedness."

"You will find that quite unnecessary," said the Captain. Percival despaired, and changed the conversation by asking abruptly, What was the duty about to be put upon him, which he was quite ready to perform?

"Why," says the Captain, "it is this. We are

about to visit an exalted friend of mine, here in this town darkly disguised for the exact purpose of meeting with me. He is a gentleman (at present) of greater hope than fortune, and goes—oh, hush!" he sank his voice to a rushing whisper which could have been heard across the street, "and goes — ah, be mum! by the name of CADE. Master John Cade, Jack Cade, Jack Mend-all; so those who love him call him. But, look you here, his name is Mortimer, seed of the loins of King Edward the Third, twin-apple on the stalk which holds King Edward the Fourth—"

"King Edward the—oh, sir!" says Percival in a tremble, "why, this is treason!"

"Treason it is," replied the Captain, chuckling; "damnable treason, and misprision of treason; work for Tower Hill, block-work, chopping-work, my Ganymede."

"Is it this that you would have me do?" Percival asks; and the Captain, taking his arm, says—"It is! It is!"

They stroll on in silence. Presently Percival asks again, How he can serve Mr. Cade? The Captain became very frank.

"Why," he said, "you must know that my friend Mortimer (call him Cade, if you will), although of extremely noble descent, is in this pass, that he can neither read nor write. Other gentlemen of birth and lineage are no better off. We write our names in blood, ha! And here are our

stiles, ha!" He patted his hip. "Now Jack Mortimer," he went on, "corresponds with the D——e of
B——y, the D——e of Y——k, my L——d of
M——h, the K——g of F——e"—these names he in-
dicated in atrocious whispers—"and hitherto hath
done his best to cope therewithal by help of an old
monk of Bury, a Psalter, and the *Gesta Romanorum*.
The result hath been that Jack's correspondence is in
a devil of a mess. Moreover, the monk is recently
dead of a surfeit. You, my lamb, having the
Latin, the French, the Burgundian, the Italian, on
the tip of your red tongue, you I have designed to
be Jack Mortimer's secretary, from the moment
when I first saw you, slim and tearful like Niobus
the Great, in Winton Minster. You say that you
have deceived the Prioress: me you could not deceive. I saw tongues playing about your ingenuous
front; everything you have done since has but confirmed my opinion. Now, I need not tell a youth of
your parts that I open out a golden road for you
to travel. Jack will go far. He is ready at all
points. His men line the roads; London stirs
for him; Kent calls him King. He will give thee
a manor and a title, for thou shalt be his right hand.
Sir Percival Perceforest, knight; Percival, Baron
Perceforest; my lord Viscount Perceforest; *our
trusty and well-beloved Cousin and councillor Percival, by the Grace of Jack, Earl of——* Where the
devil do you come from, my dear?"

"From Gloucester, sir," says Percival.

"I perceive that you speak the truth, for you call it
Glorster. Then you shall be Earl of Gloucester, when
my good Lord R——d is P——e of W——s." Thus
comfortably, as the Captain mused aloud and poor
Percival found nothing to say, they reached the
shuttered green door which announced by a sign
on a string that it was that of The Holy Fish. There
hung the fish, with a hole in the shoulder where St.
Peter's thumb had held it.

"I must disguise myself, boy," says the Captain.
"Mum's the word now; moonlight work begins.
You carry innocence all over your face, but I have
a plaguily fly-by-night appearance, and must by
all means conceal it."

His method of disguise was admirably simple,
for he merely threw his riding-cloak over his head.
Thus he could neither see nor be seen, neither
deceive nor be deceived. This done, he made
Percival take his hand, saying, "Lead on, noble
colleague." Percival followed his nose into the
doorway of The Holy Fish.

A black-haired, stout, blotch-faced man sat in
dirty shirt and breeches at a tressel-board, eating
bacon from a skewer. A jack of beer was at his
elbow, onions reposed in a basin of vinegar beside
him; all about his feet lay letters, parchments,
sealed writs in a heap.

His companions were a miller in his cups and
a Carmelite. Percival stood modestly in the open
doorway, still holding by the hand the muffled,

93

the motionless Captain Brazenhead. The eater of bacon frowned upon the pair.

"What do you want, knave?" then said Master Cade, for this was he, "and who is your mawmet in a shroud?" Captain Brazenhead threw off his disguise with a flourish. "God help this realm, Jack, if I deceive even thee!" he said with fervor. Master Cade resumed his bacon; the Carmelite had never stopped eating onions; the miller went to sleep.

Between bites the great revolutionary asked of his friend, Who was this sprig of jessamy? The Captain introduced his dearest nephew-by-adoption. "He hath a long nose," said Master Cade, "too long for my taste. We are sworn foes of long noses in Kent, as thou knowest. What are we to do with him, Sol?"

"He was born under Sagittarius the Archer," says the Captain, "and is therefore lucky. Start not at his nose: I tell you he is a penman. I have trained him for thy secretary, Jack!"

Master Cade said Humph! to this; but of Percival he asked, "Where gat Sagittarius, your father, you of the body of your mother?"

"Sir," replied Percival, "I fancy that Captain Brazenhead spoke tropically, by a figure. My father's name is John Perceforest; he is a clothier of Gloucester."

"You said he was an archer, Sol," said Master Cade.

"I spoke exuberantly, as this lad says, and in

the tropics," the Captain admitted. "Leave his father and his nose alone, Jack."

"Stop that cackle," cried Master Cade, who seemed excited, "and let me get on with the boy. Now, boy, I have the truth of thy father at last. Is that nose of thine his or thy mother's?"

"My mother, sir, had a longish nose."

"Losh!" said Master Cade. "Now, who was your mother?"

" My mother is dead, sir."

"I asked you not what she is!" Master Cade was very testy. "Plague! will you prevaricate with me? I asked you who she was."

Percival answered, "She was very well descended, sir, as I have been told. Her name before wedlock was Jane Fiennes."

Master Cade grew livid. "Lord of Might! And with a nose like that!" He paused to breathe; presently asked, "And whence came your Jane Fiennes?"

"She came from Kent, sir," says Percival. Cade threw up his hands and brought them down with a crash on the table. The miller rolled on to the floor and the Carmelite slipped out of the room.

"If I knew not his nose among a hundred! Jane Fiennes's son, Jane Fiennes's son!" Master Cade was much perturbed. "Do you know who you are, young gentleman?" Thus he accosted Percival, who answered, "An honest lad, sir, if it please you."

"Honest!" cries Master Cade, "honest! you are better than that, I hope. King Melchior, I'll tell you what you are. You are nephew of Lord Say, that's what you are! Nephew and apparent heir, that's what you are! And you hope yourself honest! Why, sir, you may be a peer of this realm. No need for honesty then, I hope. Honest, quoth he!" He changed his tune abruptly, and turned to the complacent Captain Brazenhead. "Didst thou lay this trap for me, old gallows?" asked his chief. "I'll not deny it, Jack," said the Captain. "It will serve my turn," says Cade, "or may do. When we have cracked the old thief's skull at Sevenoaks, we'll set up this slip of willow in his place, and have a lord on our side. Do you smell? Are you fly?"

The Captain smelt, and was very fly. "Let me talk to my honored young friend," he said, and drew Percival apart.

"Now, Percival," he began, "it appears that you are in a fair way. Your mother was Lord Say's sister, and none the worse in that her brother is an old cut-throat, ill-beseeming dog. You are heir to the wicked man your uncle. Now I propose to you an honorable game, fitting to your name, degree, expectation, and parts. You shall stand in with the noble Mortimer and me. We raise all Kent, attack Sevenoaks, slay your uncle at leisure. You come into title and estates, marry your little Touchett (if she still content you), and reward us after your own generous motions. Do you see your way

96

clear? I protest," cried the delighted Captain, embracing his young friend warmly, "I protest that is as workman-like a little cabinet of villany as I have ever compassed! What is more, it will be of real service to you."

But Percival did not see his way to the murder of his uncle, and told Captain Brazenhead as much with tears of shame in his eyes. "Dear sir," he said, "I know not what you will think of me—ungrateful, unworthy of your continual favors, I owe you all my earthly happiness; but do not ask me to kill my mother's brother. I will die for you, or at your hands, if you choose; but I cannot dabble in my own blood. Slay me now, Captain Brazenhead, where I kneel"—and kneel he did—"and let Percival die blessing the hand that fells him." The Captain, profoundly touched, raised him up and kissed him. "Your sentiments, my Percival, do you honor," he said, "though I deplore their effect upon my plans. I must consider what will be best to do now, for I'll be hanged if I know offhand."

Master Cade had a way of his own. "If the young gentleman can't help us, Sol," says he, "we had better help ourselves. We should put a winger into him at once, I believe. He must never leave Reigate alive." The Captain shook his head: "No, no, my Trojan," he replied, "that is a short-sighted way to work. You may trust Mr. Perceforest, I am sure." He added in a low voice, "A friendly Lord Say will be better than two dead ones, you fool; let

the boy go." Turning to Percival, he kissed him
again, saying, "Remember your old Brazenhead in
after years; for now I must bid you farewell. If I
have served you, I am glad. I love you, my boy,
and shall pray for you every day. Note this also.
You shall do wisely to force your pilgrims on their
way with all speed. Kent will be on fire within a
week. At Canterbury you shall see either myself or
my ghost. Farewell."

"Farewell, dear sir," said Percival brokenly.
They parted affectionately, like father and son;
Percival went out with tears in his eyes.

VII. Incidit in Scyllam, cupiens vitare Charybdim

The Captain gone, not without comment and discussion, in which Percival's explanation played a
poor part, our young man found himself involved
in a new difficulty. Smith the Shipman located
his long nose. "Gloucester knew that nose of
thine," he declared, "as I do verily believe. But
her name was not Thrustwood—no, nor nothing
like Thrustwood." Percival did not deny that he
had been born in Gloucester. "I would like to see
thee deny it," said the Shipman. "I would swear
to thy long nose and button mouth before the Lord
Mayor of London. And how comest thou," he
asked reproachfully, "how comest thou trampling
after a wicked old tosspot mercenary on pretended
pilgrimage, all in a page's breeches? Fie upon such
unwholesome dealing!" Percival grew very angry,
as well he might; hereupon the Shipman turned his

gall to tenderness. "Child, I loved thee once;
pledges we exchanged, we split a coin. I vowed I'd
never forget thee, upon my soul." "I vow that I
have never seen you before, sir, in all my life!" cried
Percival, hotly, "nor your good mistress either!"
"Jealousy," quoth the Shipman, "jealousy is the
mother of lies. What is my wife to thee or to me,
who cry back old dead days?" But here, happily,
that same lady came out to show what she was to
her lord; "Tease not the boy, honey, tease me!"
Thus she wooed him, and left Percival to his other
anxieties. These were to get his people well on the
road before it was taken by the grim Captain Cade,
and to ponder how he could save at once his mistress's skin, his own skin, and the skin of his exalted
uncle.

By ten of the clock—so successful was he—the
whole train was in the Vale of Darent. They baited
at Otford under the shadow of the Archbishop's
house, whence, if Percival could have known it, he
might have seen the threatened turrets of Knole
high on the wooded hill of Sevenoaks. From that
place a very agreeable tale from the Prioress took
them peacefully to Wrotham, where they stayed out
the heat of the day. If Mawdleyn had to complain
that her lover was cold she did him an injustice.
He was consumed with fear on her account; the
country was ominously quiet, with no pilgrim-booths
in Wrotham town, no folk in the inns, few houses
that had not shutters over the windows. They had

halted at a smithy a few miles out of the town:
"You must limp it on three feet, Master," was the
answer Percival got. "There is not a scrap of iron
short of Maidstone, I do believe." "What have
you done with your iron, Master?" asks Percival.
"Ah," says the farrier, "that is telling." A bad
answer: but worse was to come.

After dinner, going by the well-worn lane that
lies snug under the bosom of the hill, they reached
a little place called Trottesclive, some three miles
from Wrotham. Here were an inn, a village-green,
a spreading sycamore with a sign-post, a stocks, and
a pound. Here also was an armed assembly of
peasants, a priest at their head, marching the opposite way, with ribald songs about Jack Nape and
Harry our King. Now Jack Nape was the name they
chose to give the Duke of Suffolk, and the scythes,
bills, falchions, glaives, and other weapons they flour-
ished, boded no good to Harry their King. There
was much confusion here: the men-at-arms of the
Prioress at once became none, by throwing down
their pikes and falling upon their knees. Half a
dozen rascals roared "Down with the fat minchin!"
half a dozen others snatched up the discarded pikes.
Dan Costard showed his mettle. "We are Saint
Thomas's pilgrims, you rogues," cried he. "Touch
us in jeopardy of Saint Thomas"; and Percival, resenting extremely their reference to the Prioress's
condition in this world, drew his dagger.

The Shipman leapt off his horse and caught the

poor young man round the waist. "Vex not thy pretty hands with a man's tools, my fair chuck," he said coaxingly. "What if thy disguise should undisguise thee?"

"Avoid me, by heaven, you red fool!" cries Percival in a fury. "What have you to do with me?"

"Love, my hidden treasure!" said Master Smith, "Love is my goad. I know what I know." Percival flamed up.

"Get you gone, look after your wife, Master, and don't talk your balderdash to me," he said with his teeth together. The Shipman replied that tempest suited a pretty lass better than a flat calm; so women were not like the sea. Percival stared open-mouthed at him. "What is your meaning?" he said aghast. Master Smith might have told him, had he not been recalled to his wife's side by her shrill complaining. Once more, therefore, that thin woman set Percival free. He turned to the fray; but this had been composed by a colloquy between Dan Costard and the priest, the leader of the rabble.

The peasants, it seemed, were marching to Sevenoaks, to meet (it was obvious to Percival) Captain Brazenhead and Captain Cade. The youth could not see without emotion so many scythes turned to the dismemberment of his uncle, my Lord Say. He felt the call of blood as well as the admonitions of piety. "Strange!" he thought. "Yesterday I did not know that his lordship was my uncle, and to-day I must risk my life to save his. But it is so!"

He therefore accosted the rebel priest in the gentlest manner he could, inquiring whether he was leading his forces against any person of consequence. "There is a worthy man dwelling by Sevenoaks," he added, "my uncle, whose estate, though it should fall to me by the fact, I would not willingly have disturbed." The priest, having looked him up and down, said, "Bless your innocence, young man, we shall never hurt any uncle of yours." Percival could afford to say, "I wish I could believe it." "But," he went on, "I fear the worst from what I know of Master Mortimer, your friend."

"Ha!" says the priest, "so you know something." Says Percival, "Yes, I do." The priest rubbed his chin.

"And did he intend any mischief against your uncle, young gentleman?"

"I do verily think so," says Percival.

"Then," said the other, "either you are not what you appear, or Master Mortimer's net hath a small mesh." The Shipman cut in again.

"If he is what he appears to you," he said strongly, "then I am a nun."

"And if he is not what he appears to you and to me," cried the Scrivener, very much excited, "then I was neither deaf nor blind at Winchester, and do know his name, and can shrewdly guess at that of his uncle."

"My reverend," said Percival, who thought it safer to take no notice of this interruption, "I may not tell you my uncle's name, lest you should do a mischief to those I serve here as faithfully as I can. Alack! I have too many interests to serve, I think. But I will ask you to take a message for me to a hidden nobleman who passes under the name of B——d" (he sank his voice in uttering the word of power), "Captain S——n B——d. Are you acquainted with him?" The priest scratched his head.

"Is it a wondrous hairy man? Has he a forest on his nose, hairs on his lip and chin, and fierce hairs which push upwards on his throat like ivy on a stock? Is it a loud talker, speaking of things which he knows little about, and the loudlier speaking the less he knoweth? Is he a kidnapper and a horse-stealer? And doth he affect the use of tongues?"

"In many things you have rightly drawn the man, but in the accusation of various crimes I hope you are wrong towards him," Percival replied with guilty knowledge painting his ingenuous face. "At least I suppose him to be the hairiest man in this realm. Tell him from Piers, That if he loves yet the youth he loved once, he will do nothing to hasten the inheritance nor his own reward." The priest winked one eye as he said:

"Your message is dark. But shall I not essay it?"

"Hush, O hush!" Percival whispered, finger on lip; "you will undo me."

"Tush, my lord," quoth the priest, "all shall be well." He left Percival in a cold sweat; and having made him a profound reverence, drew off his people, who went with songs and cheering for Jack Mend-all. Percival resumed his escort with a heavy heart, and in due time had all safe under the shadow of the famous Rood of Boxley. He could not fail to observe the added respect with which the Scrivener treated him, and was minded to turn that honest man's skill to his own advantage before it might be too late.

For although he knelt before the sacred and wonder-working Image by the side of his tender Mawdleyn, yet the Image cast its spells in vain. He drew no comfortable assurance out of the rolling eyes and wagging head which made the vulgar admire; but the place held an awe for him apart from all that; and the conviction settled down with a weight of lead in his heart that now or on the morrow he must unbosom himself to the Prioress of Ambresbury. And was that to be the end of his fond adventure? Was he to be hounded out of the Prioress's livery as Sir Simon had hounded him out of his? Sir Simon had whipped him for pilfering; might not her Reverence do as much for fibbing? Percival's was that girlish nature that clings the faster for stripes: he knew that the end was not to be then, for Mawdleyn was just such another as he, and when girl's nature loves girl's nature the bond will never be broke. Was such a

love as his to be strangled by a confessed fib?
Could he abandon his dear, soft, loving maid because
his name was Perceforest and not Thrustwood?
He saw Mawdleyn's long lashes brush her cheek,
saw her folded hands, her lovely meekness; he felt
lifted up. Ah, for her sake he had had thwackings
on his back, for her sake had lain in ditches o' nights,
had begged crusts at farmers' doors, had sung dis-
honest songs to thieves and their drabs in tap-
rooms at midnight. For her sake he had been
Captain Brazenhead's nephew, scion of the race of
Assurbanipal and Tyrant the White, he had hob-
nobbed with treason, been misconceived by Smith
the mariner, loosened one groom's teeth, indirectly
drowned another, gained a black eye, and deceived
a noble lady who was so benevolent as to love him.
"Sweet Madonna!" he cried, "how I have deceived
mankind! Sir Simon Touchett thinks I am a common footboy, whereas I am the heir to a lord; Captain Brazenhead thinks I am a rebel, and Captain
Cade thinks I am not; the Prioress thinks me Piers
Thrustwood; Mawdleyn must think me a liar—
which I am; and Master Smith believes me a Glo'ster
girl, discreditably attached to (and forsaken by)
Captain Brazenhead. Alone in my world, the
Scrivener knows me for Percival Perceforest, the
heir of Lord Say; and I am bound to admit that
him too I should have deceived if I had thought
him worth the while. Is there nobody, then, to
whom I have not fibbed or wished to have fibbed?

Yes: I had forgotten Dan Costard. That good man is under no misconception as to my real person, because he has never troubled his head about me. To him I will impart my secret. If I am to receive the Sacrament at Canterbury, I must confess to-morrow. He shall shrive me." He concluded tearfully in prayer, and so remained until the Prioress rose from her knees and took Mawdleyn to bed. Full of resolutions for the morrow, Percival also went to bed.

But Captain Smith drew the Scrivener apart by the parlor fire and said: "Tell me the name of that young spitfire of the Prioress's."

"His name," said the Scrivener, "on his own confession, mind you, is Perceforest."

The Shipman clapped a hand to his thigh with a noise like a carter's whip.

"Perceforest!" he thundered. "Perceforest of Gloucester! I remember the lass to a hair—long-nosed, thin, snuggling girl—spoke softly and kept her eyes cast down. She had a trick of biting her finger I recall, very captivating to youth. Sometimes it would be the corner of her apron—better, as being less fanciful. Why, man alive, she used to lean against the door-post in Hare Lane by the hour together, and all the evening through, listening to my protestations and tales of the sea—and be at that fingering game all the while! Sakes of me, if I remember that long-nosed wench or not. And her name was Perceforest—now, now, now, was it Moll Perceforest? or Nance? It was Nance. It was never Nance? What did she say her name was, old parchment?"

"I don't know what you are talking about, my good friend," said the Scrivener, "and my name is Corbet, descended from Madam Alys, Countess Dowager of Salisbury." The Captain clawed the Scrivener by the knee.

"Her name was Jenny," he shouted, "Jenny Perceforest, christened Jane! Eh, by the Beacon of our Faith, I'll remind her of that i' the morn! Now," he pondered, "how did old Brazenguts get hold of such a good girl as that? And why did she traipse after him across all those shires in a pair of cloth breeches? Is it pure devotion to Thomas? Is it want of heart in the man? It is, by heaven! For why? He has cut and run. Oh, I'll have it out o' Jenny i' the morn."

"You shall do what you please," replied the Scrivener, tired of all this, but I shall go to bed."

"Put me on to a dexterous way," said Captain Smith earnestly; "give me my sailing orders, and I steer dead into the heart of Jane."

"She, as you call him, will deny you point-blank, as I take it," was the Scrivener's judgment.

"I'll wake her up with a parable," said Captain Smith. "I'll tell her a tale to-morrow will open her eyes."

"You had much better leave that to me," said the Scrivener. "I know more tales of wonder and romance than you know creeks and bays of England."

"Then keep your tales of wonder and romance as I keep the creeks and bays of England," said Captain Smith; "and that is until I want 'em to run to. This is my venture."

"It should also be your wife's venture, if she is the fond woman I think her," the Scrivener observed, with one eye more open than the other.

"My wife," replied Captain Smith, "knows her duty, I believe; and if you come to that, where's the harm of old acquaintance? Why, I knew Jenny Perceforest before my wife knew the Christian Dispensation. My wife was a heathen Norse when I was playing hunt-the-slipper wi' Jane. And if a man that hath travelled the lumpy seas may not have a bit o' fun wi' a long-nosed girl he hath known in—"

The Scrivener had gone to bed.

VII. How Percival got more than he deserved

After the conversation of the preceding night, the Shipman became reproachful in his tone to Percival. He disregarded the young man's protests that he was not his own sister, that she was a mother of five at Moreton-in-Marsh, and nearly twice his age. "If so be, Jenny," he said, "that you are mother of five lawful imps, the greater the shame of your cropped head. To dance attendance upon an Italianate cut-throat, an ambusher, a blood-pudding man, with husband and babes crying at home—fie, Jenny, fie! But you and I, my girl, shall be friends yet. You have not seen the last of Dick Smith." Percival despaired; but in point of fact his persecutor seemed to give himself the lie, for he left the Prioress's party at Charing and hastened on to Canterbury direct, leaving his wife behind him.

They reached Harbledown by early afternoon, and stayed there for a few hours, hard by the lazar-house of Saint Nicholas. It was held improper to enter Canterbury unshriven; there was hard work before Dan Costard before any of them dared so much as look for the gold Michael on Bell Harry's top. The lepers came clattering out, the good brothers who served them took the horses, the Prioress with her company went into the Chapel, to touch the relic and prepare for confession. Percival's hour was come. Captain Brazenhead was murdering his uncle, and he was about to murder his own happiness. What a position for a boy in love!

But it seems that not he alone had a weighty conscience to discharge. Consider these facts in order:

I. The Prioress of Ambresbury confessed that Captain Brazenhead loved her after the precepts of Plato and the Venerable Bede; also that she loved Piers Thrustwood more as a son than the nephew he was plainly desirous of becoming.

II. Master Smith's wife confessed that she had

spied upon her husband on many late occasions, but especially on the previous night. She said that Piers Thrustwood was, in reality, one Jenny Perceforest, who had run away with Captain Brazenhead, and been deserted by him; and believed that her husband was intending to renew an old acquaintance with the young woman. She owned that she was not to be trusted if he did. As she spoke mostly in sobs and the Norwegian language, Dan Costard was occasionally at a loss.

III. Mawdleyn Touchett confessed that she loved Piers Thrustwood, who was not what he seemed.

IV. Sister Petronilla confessed that Captain Brazenhead had made her a letter - bearer to Mawdleyn Touchett. She did not know what the letter contained except by hearsay. She had taken back an answer. When the Prioress told her to apply cold meat to Piers Thrustwood's eye, she gave over her office to Mawdleyn Touchett. She did not know what Mawdleyn Touchett applied, except that it was not cold meat.

V. Percival Perceforest admitted that this was his name, that he was and had been in love with Mawdleyn Touchett both before and after his beating; that he was a deceiver of the Prioress, no nephew of Captain Brazenhead, but nephew (on the other hand) of my Lord Say—

"What!" cried Dan Costard, stopping him at this point, "you are not Piers Thrustwood?"

"No, father," says Percival.

"Then," says the priest, "the Prioress does not love you as a son, rather than the nephew you are plainly desirous of becoming."

"Alack, but I do desire it," Percival owned.

"Never mind that now," replied Dan Costard; "one thing at a time. The lady Prioress loves Piers Thrustwood as a son; but if there is no such person she can have no such love." Her absolution, therefore, is easy."

"Then she loves not me, father," said Percival, sorrowfully, "for I have just told you I am not Piers Thrustwood at all."

"But what do you say about Master Smith's wife," the priest continued, "and her ugly tale about Captain Brazenhead?"

Percival felt this to be a comparatively easy matter. "I say, my reverend, that my name is Perceforest, and own that I have a sister Jenny; but I deny that I am she."

"You are sure?" asked Dan Costard. "Very well, then. Smith's wife can be shriven. Now there is Mistress Mawdleyn, loving Piers Thrustwood, who is not what he seems. What have you to say?"

"Oh, sir, oh, sir," Percival urged, with pleading looks, "Mawdleyn loves me, and I love Mawdleyn. And for that reason I was beaten by Sir Simon, and came creeping back; and for that reason I told fibs, and for that reason I confess them. Further, I say, that if I cannot have her, I must die."

"Well," says Dan Costard, hand on chin, "and why not? It will make everything simple, it seems to me."

"But if I die, I cannot have Mawdleyn, good father."

"Tush!" cried Father Costard, "we are beating the air. Get your Lord Say to plead your cause."

"Alas, dear father, I fear the worst for him," says Percival mournfully.

"Then you can plead your own cause, my boy," replied the priest briskly; "for then you will be his lordship. But I must insist upon your making a clean breast of it to my lady; this you shall promise me before I shrive you."

"Sir," said Percival, "it is in the making. I do but wait to ask Master Corbet, the Scrivener, to inscribe it fair upon a sheepskin."

"Very good," said Dan Costard, and shrived him. Percival spent the rest of his time dictating his lowly confession to the Scrivener, but what with the interruptions of his own remorseful tears and the emendations of that worthy man he had got no further than the words, "The humble cry of the heart of P——," when the summons to the road came from the unconscious intended recipient. Percival was called to do his squire's duty, and worse, he was bid to tell a tale. This he did, as all the world may know if it care, with direct application to his case, showing how misadventure

may be piled on misadventure, and misconception
on misconception in affairs of the heart, until (as
in his tale) a young man named Galeotto may wed
a young man named Eugenio, and Camilla (a
young woman), a young woman, Estella, all for
the sake of love. It is not by any means certain
that this entirely met his own position, as he no
doubt intended that it should; what is beyond
controversy is that it did point out the dangerous
state of his relations with the Shipman, and very
much affected the Shipman's true wife.

So much was this the case that when the tale was
ended, which was after supper in the parlor of the
Prior of Christchurch, Mistress Gundrith had a
fit of coughing and weeping intermixed, and retired,
as she said, to bed. But it is now known that
she did not go thither. The intentions also of
Percival were widely different from his perform-
ances. His resolution had been to charm the
Prioress first by his romancing and to melt her
afterwards by his tears. He charmed her, it is
true, but his tears fell on stony ground. For they
fell upon the bosom of Master Richard Smith,
who, having thrown a handkerchief over his head,
had picked him up in the quadrangle (where the
lad had gone to compose his mind), pelted with
him in the dark down Mercery Lane, and now
held him in the cellar of a little beer-house, com-
forting him with flagons and protesting against all
his rage that they should be married in the morn

and sail with the first tide. It was then, and not till then, that Percival found out what he owed to the great Captain Brazenhead. For he—but I anticipate.

At five o'clock in the morning there came a flying messenger into Canterbury bearing letters for the Prioress of Ambresbury's grace. These were from her brother Sir Simon Touchett and thus conceived:

LOVING SISTER—After my hearty commendations, these let you wite that you must by all means do honor to one Master Perceforest who I believe is with you. At the least I traced him as far as Winton, which I know he left in your company. Fail me not herein as you tender my welfare. And the Blessed Trinity preserve you in His keeping, and give you all your desires. From your brother, Si. Touchett, Kt. Postscriptum. I pray you, Sister, be temperate with my daughter Mawdleyn. And if the said Mr. Perceforest will take her with a fair manor of forty pound for dowry, let it be so o' God's name. I fear I have no more to bestow, for times are hard, and the crops very light this year, owing to the dry weather. I pray God amend it. If the said Mr. Perceforest shows signs of grudge against me for misadventure—and for what I must call shameful mishandling—in the past, tell him, I pray you, that I will meet him hereafter on my old knees. Item, I will give two manors of eighty pound clear with my daughter Mawdleyn. I beseech God to grant you a fair reward for your pilgrimage. Your man Costard will marry my daughter to the said Mr. Perceforest. Item, item, I will give a fair thirty-pound land with the said two manors.

S. T., Kt.

A letter for the "right worshipful and his loving friend Mr. Percival Perceforest" was enclosed; and the Prioress, after reading this also, sent for

Piers Thrustwood. At this moment Mawdleyn's soft cheek was against her own, and Mawdleyn's soft heart discerned to be beating in fine disorder. "Dear Madam, dear aunt," said this melting beauty, "I beseech you be a good aunt to poor Mawdleyn. All he did was for love."

"I think so indeed, child," said the Prioress; "and no offence either, it seems. But I ask in vain, why was the poor young man whipped for what he is now to be coaxed back to with forty-pound lands?"

"He will need no coaxing, dear Madam," Mawdleyn assured her. But it appeared that he would need much coaxing. He could not be found. He was not in his bed, had not been in bed, had not been seen since bedtime. Neither had the Shipman's wife been to bed. "Is it possible," thought the Prioress, "is it humanly possible that my brother knows more than I do? Is it humanly possible that Piers, or Percival, is running after Smith's wife?"

Far from that, Smith's wife was at this moment running after Percival. Percival Perceforest in his shirt, breeches, and one of his stockings was flying for his life through the streets of Canterbury. Close at his heels came Smith's wife, behind her a delighted pack of citizens, crying, "Hold, thief, hold! Take the rogue alive! Rope, rope, rope!" and other like words. How long the chase had held, I say not; I know that it could have held

little longer. Percival's breath was gone, his eyes
were dim, his feet cut, his shirt and breeches barely
acquainted. Bricks, mud, sticks, stones whizzed
by his ears; "Peg him down! Peg him down!"
were ominous sounds of preparation. Percival set
his back against a wall and prepared to die hard.
On came the mob; another minute had been his
last. As if rushing upon what he could not avoid,
Percival gave a sudden glad cry and sprang out
towards his enemies. But as he did so, these
parted from behind—whether by express command
or intuitive sense, can never be truly known.
Percival ran through his late pursuers and fell
panting into the arms of a Cardinal who, properly
attended by his foot-page, was advancing down the
street. The amazed inhabitants saw this Prince
of the Church enfold and kiss a young man who
was believed to have murdered a sailor in Mercery
Lane. It need not be said that His Eminence, who
was inordinately hairy, and fierce in the eye, was
Captain Brazenhead in disguise.

His first care was to get rid of the ragtails who
threatened the peace. "Avoid good people," was
his sublime assurance; "he whom you seek is not
here. He is elsewhere." His air, his hair, his hat,
his cassock and tippet of flame-red, did their work.
The men of Canterbury doffed their bonnets to
His Eminence and suffered him to lead away their
murderer whither he would. Mistress Smith raised
shrill cries, but to no purpose. When she de-

nounced Percival, they referred her to the Cardinal. When she scoffed at His Eminence, they referred her to the devil, and so left her. His Eminence led his young friend into the great church, and producing a bundle from under his arm, said with great apparatus of whispering and tapping of the nose, "Take this token, Percival, of my travail for you." Percival unfolded the head of my Lord Say: deeply shocked, he gazed at it.

"Let me not raise false hopes in you, dear Percival," said Captain Brazenhead. "Your late august kinsman was not beheaded, as this gift would seem to imply, and as his rank surely warranted. In fact, the ground of my quarrel with Captain Cade (Mortimer, as he foolishly calls himself) was this, should my Lord Say be hanged or sworded? I named the sword, but Jack would have the rope. I exposed the infamy of this: Jack strung him up. We quarrelled irrevocably. Jack led his men towards London and certain ruin. May Jack go in peace! I believe he is a fool, and know him to be without the feelings of a gentleman. A ridiculous, yet fortunate, adventure brings me to your rescue. You remember the Prioress's knave whom I laid in a drain on your account? This boy (and I speak to his credit), filled with revengeful feelings, followed me all the way, and at Kemsing denounced me to a justice as his ravisher and the thief of his clothes. Unworthy, you say? Far from that, it is for that reason I have advanced him. I was

forced to disguise myself as you see. But what a
plight I find you in! Where is your jacket? Where
are your shoes? Where are your points? What
have you been about? No scandal, I hope?"

"Scandal!" cried Percival, growing very red, "I
say it was scandalous; but I served him well for it."

"Meaning whom?" asked the Captain; and Percival told him, "The Shipman Smith, who would
have it that I was my sister Jane, and carried me
off with a towel over my head."

"The man is a silly fool, as I always knew," said
Captain Brazenhead; "but it must have been simple
to satisfy him."

"Simple or not," says Percival, "I did it. For I
cut his face open with a grindstone."

"You did very well, bawcock, failing a foot and
a half of Toledo," cried the Captain. "By my faith,
I know not how a gentleman of your birth and
parts could have done better. But we have more
solemn business on hand. You and I will go and
declare ourselves to the Lady Prioress. I fancy
your affair—if you are still in the mind for it—will
go better henceforward."

Percival grew suddenly grave. "Alas, dear sir,"
he said, "but I was carried off from my mistress
before I could confess to her the wicked truth."

"You will find the truth not half so wicked as
you suppose, my lord," said the Captain. "Come,
I will conduct your lordship."

"But, sir, consider the danger to yourself," Percival faltered—but, even so, sensibly changing aspect as the new address warmed him.

"Myself, ha?" the Captain snorted. "I am sufficiently protected by my disguise, I hope. I warrant you there will be no trouble on that score. Moreover, that boy who denounced me so took my fancy for the fact that I have engaged him as my foot-page. Have no fear for me, but come, my dear lord, come."

The magnificent Cardinal Brazenhead, every inch a prelate and a prince, took the arm of Percival, who was far from looking what he actually was; and caused the hall porter of the Priory to announce the Lord Cardinal of Magnopolis and my Lord Say, to wait upon the Prioress of Ambresbury. I should fail to find words proper to express the surprise of the venerable lady. But Captain Brazenhead by no means failed. He was at once the courtier, the Churchman, and the deferential lover (in Plato's vein). The moment he was face to face with the lady, he advanced towards her, took and kissed her hand. His page in attendance held his tasselled hat—crimson on a black silk cushion.

"At last, dear lady," he said, with a happy sigh, "at last my tiresome disguises are over! I can greet your Ladyship without fatigue and without embarrassment."

"Oh, my lord! Oh, sir—!" the Prioress began—but he put up a deprecating hand.

"Titles of ceremony between us!" he said, with

gentle amazement. "Lady, you and I know too much evil of the world to affect the world's cozening caresses. We, if you take my meaning, have suffered, and labored, ah, and loved, too long on earth to feel any solace out of things like these. But—" he went on, waving the shamefaced Percival into the discussion—"but with the young it is otherwise. An eyas falcon, dear Madam, may take pride in her opening plumage, I suppose. Here, Madam, is this noble youth, whom you knew as Piers Thrustwood, and I as my dearest nephew, Mr. Percival Perceforest, now (by the unhappy death of his kinsman) my lord Baron of Say; here, Madam, is he for whose advantage I adventured as a Captain of men's bodies, where men's souls, perchance, are more under my care. His dear kinsman is unhappily slain by rebels; and he (barely escaping with his own young golden life) stands before you —ashamed of the deceit forced upon him, glorying in the stripes wherewith your brother anointed his princely back, and burning (if I may speak of such matters) for the tardy bliss he has dared such hardships to win. My dear lord and nephew"— he turned to Percival—"salute my friend the Prioress of Ambresbury." The young Lord Say knelt down before her.

"Oh, Madam, believe me—" he began to stammer; but the Prioress raised him, and gave him a kiss.

"My sweet lord, my dear Percival," she said,

"you shall believe that we love you very much. Come. My charge awaits you."

She shook him by the hand and led him into her chamber, where Mawdleyn Touchett was picking her hem to pieces.

"Master," said the Cardinal's new page, "if my mistress casts an eye on me she'll have me horsed for bathing at Winton."

The Captain looked him over. "My lad," said he, "the Prioress is my very good friend. Moreover, you must have a rind like a porpoise to stand the May frosts on your naked skin. I shall make something of you yet. Go, boy, purvey me beer from the Rainbow. I do furiously thirst."

It is proper to add that the Prioress, Dan Costard, Percival Lord Say, and Mistress Mawdleyn Touchett paid their homage at the Shrine of Saint Thomas; and that Captain Brazenhead was appointed Steward of the Manors of Westerham, Knockholt, and Froghole, with a reversion of the Office of High Bailiff of the Lordship of Sevenoaks.

History knows no more of Master Richard Smith, Mariner of Kingston-upon-Hull, nor of Gundrith his wife, native of Norway.

Buondelmonte's Saga

Buondelmonte's Saga

A S I do not think the worse of a tale because it
may be true, so it is no detriment to it in my
eyes that it has been pieced together from a hundred scraps—remnants, shavings, bits of brick and
plaster, a sentence torn from a letter, a sharp
saying passed into a proverb, the battered stump
of an old tower, the memory (not gone yet) of
wicked old hatreds or high young loves. One
may assume, I take it, a certain decorum in the
process. The raking and scraping, the groping
and poring over rubbish-heaps and rag-bags,
should be done in decent darkness, where a man,
in the company of his shaded candle, may shed
tears without a shameful face: the work has its
poignancy; the refashioned thing should not lack
it either. What my own may want in this last
particular I am not bound to discuss beforehand.
I confess to the raking and scraping, to the shifting and piecing together, and will own to a wet
eye or so, if you press me. No more. I hope
that I have got the dust away, and that the old

bones are none the worse for my galvanism. They
wore great flesh once.

There were three men living in Florence, before
the days of Dante and his friend Giotto, who,
without much previous liking or disliking, were
drawn together and then torn apart. Buondelmonte de' Buondelmonti was the name of one
of them, a gentleman who had a tower in the city,
not far from the river wall. He came from the
west country, from the Val di Greve, where he
had a hill on the edge of the valley, and a castle
upon it, a strong place with a wall all about, and
houses for his servants and laborers and slaves
inside the wall. Here in the old days his grandfather and great-grandfather had lived and taken
toll from all who journeyed by this high-road to
the sea; a thing which vexed the Florentines.
So they attacked them on all sides, drove them
into a corner, and made a bargain with them that
they should become citizens of Florence, and have
privileges there instead of toll. A house called
Degli Uberti had a chief hand in this. It was
Buondelmonte's grandfather who came in, or rather
had started to come. But the Ema was in flood
when he tried to ford it, and he, a very stout man,
was drowned. People told each other this was
a fate upon him, and advised his son to turn back;
but the younger man said: "Not Fate, but Fat
has done this. For if Ema had been thin my

father would have walked over, or if my father had been thin he would have swum over. I shall go on; and it may be that the Uberti will be sorry one of these days." By which he meant that they, in a sense, had drowned his father. He went into Florence, therefore, and married Cunegonda Giandonati, and begat this Buondelmonte, and Ranieri, and some others, and then died. Our man, now head of the house, was rich, young, a good fighter; a pleasant, handsome man, very splendid in his tastes. His blood could not be bettered, he was chief of all the kindreds who dwelt in his country and had their towers near by his in the street by the river wall. Blood relations were the Giandonati, the Gianfigliazzi, and Importuni; other houses, like the Gualterotti, were allied by friendship or common interest. All of these looked to him to play a great part, and to that end, to marry; but he had women enough at his command, and set no store by marriage. He was a great lover, they say; few women could look at him without looking again, and few twice without a stir in the side. He had a very easy way with them and their belongings: to pinch a girl's cheek, or kiss her on the chin, as if to say, "You are worth so much to me, or so much." They called him the Butterfly for this sipping trick of his.

Of a different stamp altogether was Schiatta degli Uberti—chief of that very house which had brought in Buondelmonte's—a big, strong man, very hairy, with arms too long for his height, which was nothing to boast of. His descent—if you may believe all you hear—was the noblest in the city, and his power great; but not so great that it might not grow greater, as he thought. He said that Catiline, the enemy of Rome, was his ancestor, and that, far from being descended from the Emperor's house, the Emperor was derived from some by-blow of his own. This was the sort of talk he held. He had two great castles in Florence, in that quarter of the city which lies behind and below the Badia of the Marquess Ugo; and all his kinsmen and friends lived near about him and assembled at his board. They filled the long tables of the hall, all told; for he had a great family of his own by his first and second wives— sons, strong and warlike young men, and grave daughters, all hungry for power like their father, and proud, and quickly affronted. These were the names of his kindred: the Amidei, who lived north of him in the same quarter of San Piero Scheraggio; the Fifanti and Infangati, close by; the Lamberti, whose tower was west of the Old Market, and of whom Mosca de' Lamberti, the one-eyed man, was chief. He allowed also the claim of the Capon-sacchi to be relatives of his, because they came from Fiesole, whence the wife of Catiline's son Uberto had been taken. "For," as Schiatta used to say, "if your people, Caponsacchi, were as good as you say they were, they must have been the best in Fiesole;

and I am sure my ancestor Uberto would have been content with nothing short of the best. So you may come in." Caponsacchi had to be content with that; and under some similar tossed favor the Gangalandi could confess him chief and lord: the Gangalandi, a great stock, who bore the arms of the Marquess Ugo, and accounted themselves something!

Then there was a man living below Saint Reparata's church, named Forese Donati, a vexed, rather unhappy man. He had made a good marriage, with Gualdrada, the daughter of Guido Bellincione de' Berti; but for all that his affairs had not prospered, and he was very poor. He brooded over this a good deal; for he said that his family was longer in Florence than any other save his wife's, and that while the Uberti were hiding from justice behind rocks on the hills, the Donati were making the Florentine laws and feeding the Fifanti with scrap-meat from their tables. On his wife's side he was akin to the Counts Guidi of the Upper Arno; but this served him little, since most of them took up the cry of the Uberti and helped them to do what they chose with the government of Florence. They were all Emperor's men, while Forese had chosen for the Pope. He had three sons—Buonaccorso was one of them—lean, needy, sulky men, and two daughters, Capuccia and Piccarda, fine slim girls, the younger exceedingly beautiful. On the day that this Piccarda was ten years old, Gualdrada

said to her husband: "Forese, this is a peach to
keep on the wall, but veiled, lest the wasps get at
it. If you take my advice you will lock up this
girl and feed her on the best. And you will put by
all that you can spare in a good coffer with double
keys, to be her dowry. The likes of this girl are
not born in Florence every day; no, nor every
ten years. She is all honey and wine in a lovely
case. You will be able to pick and choose where
you will for a husband; and it will be a strange
thing if you don't better our fortunes." Forese
said that she could do as she pleased; there was
time enough. "Never too early to begin," said
Gualdrada; "as the ass knows, so he bites car-
rots."

From that day forward there was nothing she
did not do for her Piccarda. She washed her every
day and dressed her hair; she gave her rich and
fine food, with cream and butter, wine and the
best fruits that could be had. She caused her to
take the air at a time when nobody was about, and
to sleep at noon and early in the night. So careful was she in what she was doing that no man in
Florence knew of Piccarda. The elder girl, Capuccia, went openly to mass with her mother; but when
Piccarda went she was dressed like a servant and
covered up in a hood. For confessor she chose a
discreet and reverend priest, canon of Santa Reparata and cousin of her own, and knowing that she
could rely upon his counsel, made him partner in

her designs. Piccarda grew up to be a still girl,
excessively beautiful. She had dark-brown hair
which reached the joints of her knees; her head was
small, her face oval in shape, composed and steadfast in expression. Her eyes were long, narrow,
and gray, the lashes of them black; she had a very
red mouth and a smooth, white throat. For all
this, she looked more like a woman than a maiden.
She was not taller than a fine girl should be, had
very little to say; and whether she could love or not,
was not to be determined, since no breath of that
mystery had ever been suffered near her, nor was
any light talk allowed in her presence. She saw no
men except her father and the priest; even her
brothers were not allowed with her.

Whatever Gualdrada could save, by pinching or
shifting, was put into a coffer and kept under two
locks. One way and another she got a good deal
together. Forese and his sons traded or went
to the wars; their return was welcome to Gualdrada according as they came heavy or light to
house. And she kept her ears wide, and looked
askance all ways for her great alliance. She had
heard about Buondelmonte, and thought he might
do for lack of better. But the next thing she
heard about him put her in a fury.

Forese Donati met Buondelmonte outside the
gate of San Pancrazio as he was going to Peretola
upon some business of sheep. Buondelmonte was

coming in from hawking in the meadows by the
river. He had his falcon on his wrist, and two
greyhounds at his horse's heels. His color was
fresh and strong, and his leather coat fitted him
well. Forese gave him the good-day, and Buondelmonte reined up to talk.

"What sport have you had, Buondelmonte?"
asked Forese.

Buondelmonte said it was good. He had a
heron and a crane, and his goshawk had killed
three mallards in the osiers. He asked Forese
where he was going.

"To Peretola," said Forese, "to fetch in some
sheep which have been on the mountains. I have
to look after household affairs, you notice, while
you take your pastime and kill mallards."

Buondelmonte said, laughing, "that his own
household affairs were easily managed."

"You should marry," said Forese, "and then
they would be easier still. Your wife would stay
at home and see that your servants did their work,
and you would have still more time for your mallards, or for warfare and exercise of arms."

"It does not seem to be the case with you,
Forese," said Buondelmonte. "Your wife, I suppose, watches your servants as well as any woman;
but you go after sheep to Peretola."

Forese said: "There are reasons for that. I
have had some bad affairs lately. My son Buonaccorso got into trouble in the Garfagnana and came

home limping; there has been a murrain among
the cattle; and a convoy of mine from Rome,
coming by the Val di Chiana, was set upon by the
Aretines and stripped as bare as my hand. Moreover, I have my daughter's dowry to see to. That
will be worth having, mind you, when I have done
with it."

"Ah," said Buondelmonte, "I have no such
business on my hands."

"It is a business which every man must take
up sooner or later," said Forese. "Think of it,
Buondelmonte."

"I do think of it," said Buondelmonte; and so
they parted.

Buondelmonte rode into the city, to his house
in the Borgo Apostoli. He talked to his friends
of what Forese had said to him; and they all agreed
that he should marry. For, as they put it to him,
a man is not a man until he has made a man. Alberigo degl' Importuni said: "An alliance rightly
framed might bring great advantage to Florence
and to our party. I like hard knocks as well as
any man, but they are best dealt with in the open,
not at the street corner. There has been too much
secret stabbing of late, all done in the dark. If you
do marry, Buondelmonte, let it be in a good kindred."

"Forese Donati was talking about his girl this
morning," said Buondelmonte. "He seemed to
think that she would have something."

"It will be all there is, then," said Viero Gianfigliazzi, who was there; "and what he will find
for the other, except a veil and a pair of sandals,
I should be sorry to say."

"Has he two daughters?" Buondelmonte asked.
"Yes, there are two," said Viero, "as I happen
to know."

They advised him strongly to marry one of the
Uberti kindred. No reason could be urged against
it. There had not been bad blood between Buondelmonte and that house, or what there may have
been in the past seemed all fair now; but between the Uberti and the Donati it had been very
bad.

"If you go on with the Donati," said Alberigo,
"you will draw anew upon our faction all the
misesteem of the Uberti, and no good can come of
that. Choose one of the Uberti; or if they don't
suit, go to the Fifanti or Amidei, settle how much
you will lay out, and see about it as soon as you
can. You are the head of all our race, and should
provide us with an heir. Sons to fight under your
ensign are no bad ensigns in themselves, let me tell
you. And do not let the pretensions of the Uberti
trouble you. When once we are all together under
the tree it will be an odd thing if none of the apples
fall into our laps."

The others agreed.

Buondelmonte said he would talk with Schiatta
degli Uberti about it. Schiatta had treated him

fairly of late. He would give fifty gold florins for Morgengabe—which is what they call the gift paid by the bridegroom for the honor of the bride on the morning after marriage—to a good girl who brought him 1500 *liras* in lands, goods, and money.

In two or three days' time, his mind made up, Buondelmonte went to the house of the Uberti behind the church of San Stefano. He found Schiatta sitting at board in the high seat, with his kinsmen all about him—Lambertuccio degl' Amidei, Mosca de' Lamberti, Oderigo Fifanti, and others of the race. Schiatta made him welcome, gave him a place next to himself at the high table, and asked him how he did.

"Very well," said Buondelmonte, "but not so well that I could not do better."

"That is the case with most of us," said Schiatta, throwing back his shoulders to open his chest. "But how can I serve you in that?"

"Why, perhaps in this way: my kinsmen tell me that I should take a wife."

"Well," said Schiatta, "that is a good thing to do. But do you ask me to give you mine?"

"It is a wife I seek, not a grandmother," said Buondelmonte. "And I am willing to offer so much, if on behalf of one of your girls you will put down so much. This will show you, I hope, that I have no mind for foolish old grudges on the score of our forefathers' misadventures."

Schiatta said: "This is a serious matter, if you

are serious. I shall not deny that I am very glad
of your friendly offer."

"I take the world as lightly as I dare," said
Buondelmonte; "but I am quite serious in this
affair."

"We'll soon see about that," said Schiatta.

"The sooner the better for me," Buondelmonte
said.

All the eyes of the kindred were fixed upon him;
but he bore their scrutiny pleasantly and well.
Some of them began to talk together in undertones;
and Schiatta sat quiet, tapping his teeth with his
dagger. The young men, sons of Schiatta, and the
bastards, nephews, and cousins, as they had been
taught, looked down at their platters while this was
going forward. The minstrel sat at the end of the
board, his rote upon his knee, waiting the sign.

Presently Schiatta looked straight at Buondelmonte, and asked, "How much are you good for,
my friend?"

Buondelmonte said: "I like your frankness,
Schiatta, and will repay it in kind. My wife will
have her portion in my lands of Montebuono in
Val di Greve and my tenements in Signa. She
will have the use of my house in the Borgo, and
of all the gear both there and at Montebuono. In
addition to this, I will give her fifty gold florins
for her honor as Morgengabe, if you will endow
her with 1500 *liras* in movables."

"That's a very handsome offer," said Schiatta; "and I shall advise one of my kindred to take advantage of it."

Mosca de' Lamberti knocked on the table. "I will offer my daughter Lapia to Buondelmonte, Schiatta," he said, and seemed very keen.

Buondelmonte, who had his reasons, said that his business was with Schiatta himself as far as he understood it. He could not abide Mosca, though he had nothing against the man, except an old quarrel in which each of them had been to blame.

"That is very well," said Schiatta, "but it is not in my power to oblige you. Two of my girls are wedded already, and one is promised, and a fourth is too old, and a fifth too young for you. I suppose you to be in a hurry?"

Buondelmonte said, the sooner the better: that brought Mosca to his feet. "I say again, Schiatta," he said, "that I am ready to meet Buondelmonte at this very hour. And I hope he will read in that a sign that I bear him no grudge."

"What says Buondelmonte to that?" Schiatta asked, and Buondelmonte replied that he could not hope to please Mosca de' Lamberti. Mosca sat down.

"That being so," said Schiatta, with a great laugh, "I recommend you to my kinsman Lambertuccio, who has a fine girl to dispose of."

Buondelmonte knew this man well, as being of a house, the Amidei, than which there were few in Florence better descended or on surer ground. He

liked the man, too, and respected him. Lambertuccio was a composed, smooth man, tall and finely
dressed. He had a large house, kept an open table,
and never went. out under the Gonfalon without a
following of fifty men on horseback. He was first
cousin of Schiatta's, and nephew of Mosca de'
Lamberti's, that is, sister's son.

"What do you think, Lambertuccio, of this fine
offer of Buondelmonte's?" said Schiatta; "will it
suit your Cunizza?"

Lambertuccio said that he thought it might, if
Buondelmonte held to it.

"My offer was made to Schiatta," Buondelmonte
said; " but I shall not be far away from him if I go
with you. Is your daughter to be seen?"

"You shall see her this afternoon," said Lambertuccio, "if you will come to my house. At this
hour she will be sleeping, and will look all the better for it afterwards. But come when you please
between noon and sundown."

Buondelmonte replied that he would certainly
come, but without binding himself; and then he took
his leave and went to walk on the Piazza until it
should be time to go. Here he met Forese Donati
by chance, who asked him if he had been thinking
over what he had said the other day. Oh yes,
said Buondelmonte, he had been turning it over in
his mind. Well, Forese said, he believed it would
be a good thing well done, when it was settled.
Buondelmonte owned it would be very good.

"I believe I could meet you," said Forese, "in a reasonable way."

"I have seen your daughter," Buondelmonte said. "She looks a strong, willing girl, and very religious."

Forese said: "She is all that and more. But I have another girl."

"Ah," said Buondelmonte, "I heard something of it, but I have never seen her."

"How would it be if I were to show her to you?" asked Forese.

"There would be no harm done at any rate. But to-day I cannot. I have business."

"As you please and when you please," said Forese, rather red in the face. "We Donati have no need to press our alliances. But it might be worth your while."

"Very easily indeed," said Buondelmonte. Forese cursed him for a dunghill cock, and went off on his affairs. He felt vexed with himself for having cheapened to little purpose, and determined he had best say nothing to his wife about it; for she took these things to heart, and made a noise in the house, so that the neighbors knew as much about his trouble as he did.

Buondelmonte went to the house of the Amidei, and Lambertuccio told his wife to fetch down Cunizza. So she was brought in. Buondelmonte saw that she was a strapping girl, white as milk, with yellow hair, and brown eyes like a deer's,

which had a trick of staring. Well brought up,
too, she proved; not timid, answering whatever
questions were put to her in a quiet voice, without
tremor and with no trouble either in breath or
blood. She was turned fifteen, and had never been
sick or sorry since she was weaned. Buondelmonte
saw that here was a wife who would do him credit,
and get him an heir as soon as he pleased. He
said a few things to her as they came into his head,
jokes and pleasantries. She looked down at her
feet. Then he gave her a kiss upon her cool chin;
and then she was taken away by her mother.

Lambertuccio asked how the business struck
him. He said, "I am ready to go on with it."

"Very well," said Lambertuccio, "we will have
the deed drawn up, and then do you come here
with your witnesses and you shall plight her with
your ring as soon as you have sealed. Will you
drink a cup?"

"Very willingly." Lambertuccio's wife poured
out the cup, and all three drank of it in turn.

The news came into the Old Market that Buondelmonte was betrothed to Lambertuccio's girl
Cunizza, and that the dowry was such and such.
There was plenty of talk, as there always is about
those things. Forese Donati heard of it, and was
very angry; but he said nothing at home. "Take
troubles as they come," he thought; "my wife will
know soon enough."

Buondelmonte's Saga

Gualdrada got the news at San Piero Maggiore when she went to mass. She was in a terrible stew. Half her husband's lands would not have been too much for Buondelmonte; but when they told her of his splendid proposals and of the dowry that went with Cunizza, she could have torn her hair out. "A white slug," she called Cunizza—"a mule, a cow, a bolster, a load of clay." She told Forese all her trouble. Had he heard of it? Yes, he said, he had understood something about it. It was likely to be a fine match, a great alliance on both sides. Buondelmonte would not come empty to the wedding, nor alone. Half the Borgo were his kindred—Giandonati, Gianfigliazzi, Degli Scali, Gualterotti, Importuni. The Uberti would be more careful how they came down the streets with naked swords after this. It was good to have a hostage of theirs in hand. A wife was, as it were, a hostage. Then there would be children—better and better. Forese would have gone on if she had not stopped him with dangerous eyes. "Children! Yes, indeed. But what of my children? They are to be barren, it seems. And kiss the rosary, and have the crucifix for a bed-fellow! And this to go on under your nose, Forese, and all you do is to talk of great matches, and hostages, and advantage to the Borgo. Where is our advantage? What is to be done for my beautiful girl? Is that hair to be sheared off? Is that soft body to be scrubbed by gray serge? Have I

pinched all these years for the advantage of the
Borgo? Gone hungry to my bed so that the
Gualterotti may go safely to theirs? Oh, you
have given me something to dream about, let me
tell you."

"Wife," said Forese, "I cannot force Buondelmonte to take my girl. That is not a becoming
action for the Donati; and so I told him only the
other day."

Gualdrada narrowed her eyes and peered at her
husband.

"Ah, so you have spoken to him about Piccarda?" she said. "Now I am learning something.
And the other day? On his way to the Amidei?"

"No, no," said Forese. "How you take me
up. You have it wrong. I spoke to him then,
sure enough; but we had talked of it before, maybe
a week ago. And I say again I could not force
Piccarda into his arms."

Gualdrada raised her hands and let them fall
with a clap. Then she turned fiercely upon her
husband.

"This is what comes of your grievous secrecy,"
she said, "that holds my dearest hope in the shut
fist of you, and lets it wither sooner than give it
air. Now, what a fine turn you have done me,
and your own daughter, and our affairs—as if they
needed it! Do you suppose I would have let go
of Buondelmonte if I had seen him once or twice?
But no! You must needs go and come, and sit to

eat, and lie in your bed, with all this fast in your mind, and when it is too late and the chance gone for good, you tell me the whole story as if it was news. Now, I shall say to you, Forese—"

He stopped her here, saying: "You have told me too much. Better hold there."

"Then I am to see you bring your family to ruin, and laugh with you at the good-fortune of the Borgo; and perhaps stand gossip to the child?" said Gualdrada, folding her arms.

Forese said: "You are to see what you please, and laugh as you can. But you are not to rail at me. You may tempt me to do that which will give you pain in one part and me pain in another. I don't advise it."

She knew she could not go any further; so held her tongue. But when Forese had gone out, she walked up and down her hall, thinking of her troubles, past and to come. And for many days, as she sat or walked, or went to church, or did her marketing, she kept the bitter thing astir in her mind. She felt that she had a grudge indeed. The Amidei had outwitted her. Nay, they had robbed her. For if Buondelmonte had been to her first, as he as good as promised Forese, it stood to reason that he would have concluded where he was. And the portion that went with Cunizza! She knew the length of her coffer to a finger's-point, and what was in it. She could have given 200 *liras* more than the Amidei. Yes, she had been cheated of the best match in Florence.

One night, as she thought of it all more grievously than ever, she took the lamp in her hand and went into the chamber where her two girls slept together. She held the lamp over her head and turned back the bedclothes. Capuccia lay on her back, but Piccarda on her face, with her cheek turned sideways on the bolster, and all her hair tumbling about her. Her body was white as alabaster, and her cheek flushed like the heart of a rose. Her long eyelashes brushed it and curved upwards. "Ay," said Gualdrada to herself, "there's a bonny shape for a nunnery, and a flower to hide up among cloister weeds." Piccarda, feeling the cold, turned and opened her eyes. Her mother kissed her on the cheek and shoulder a half-dozen times and covered her up again. Then she blundered out of the chamber as best she could, for the tears blinded her.

After the betrothal, Buondelmonte went once or twice to see Cunizza, but to no very good purpose. He found the girl unresponsive, too well-bred by half. "If this is a foretaste of the rest of our commerce," he said to himself, "it promises to be a dull affair." He liked Lambertuccio very well, and his wife; but Schiatta degli Uberti did not please him. Though he knew his own value quite well, he was himself a modest man, which Schiatta was not. And he grew tired of hearing of his good - fortune, of the fine match he had made for himself, and greatly resented being told that his politics were contemptible. Schiatta talked openly when he was well fed; he did not disguise his intention of ruling the city. He had hopes of being Vicar of the Empire: that would do for a beginning. In those days, he said, it would be as well to find yourself on the right side. "You would not choose, Buondelmonte," he continued, "to see your wife and children trudging the hill road to Bologna just because you had held out against her family." Buondelmonte laughed, and said that all roads did not lead to Bologna. "Some go to Arezzo, Schiatta," he said, "where the Tarlati might take pity on the Emperor's cast-offs. And that would be the time for you to reflect whether you had done wisely to refuse the warnings of your niece's husband, between this and Arezzo, my dear friend." Schiatta frowned and said this was poor jesting; his son Farinata, who was a tall, black-browed young man, openly advised Buondelmonte to talk of other things. Buondelmonte held on for a little, to save his face; but he was much annoyed. Mosca de' Lamberti, who was present—he was a grizzled one-eyed man, who grinned fearfully when he was put out—followed him into the street after dark, saying he would walk with him to Por' Santa Maria. "You are a bold man, Buondelmonte," he said, "to go out alone and unarmed after nightfall, having said the things you have."

"I think better of Schiatta than you do, it appears," said Buondelmonte; "for though I consider him a boaster, arrogant, and quarrelsome, I have never suspected him of being a night-stabber."

"He has many friends," said Mosca, "who would be glad to prove their service."

"It would be a strange way of proving it, to my thinking. Are you one of them? Here is your chance if you wish for it. This is a lonely corner, for instance. Would you prefer me to stand still, or can you hit a running deer?"

"This is very foolish talk," said Mosca. "Yet the entry of the gate here would be an ugly place for a man against two or three."

Buondelmonte measured the ground with his eye. There was moonlight, which was reflected in the river, brimful of winter rains. "I could show you a worse in the Borgo," he said. "We fight very close in there. But, to be sure, we don't send out six against one, as a rule."

Mosca came closer and grinned into his face. "One against one is good fighting for me," he said, "by day or by night, with sword or dagger. And so I proved it with you once before."

Buondelmonte had a thought that Mosca wished to pick up the old quarrel with him; but as he had no more ill-will towards the man than what sprang from hearty dislike, he took no notice. He did say, however, that he was glad Mosca could be so easily satisfied. Mosca stopped short; Buondelmonte stopped also. "Yes, I can be satisfied, Buondelmonte," said he, "if it will satisfy you."

"Oh, I don't fight with a one-eyed man," said Buondelmonte. "You had two when we tried conclusions before; and a thing done is done with for me." Mosca took a sharp breath and seemed about to spring at him; but he went on: "And, moreover, to kill the kinsman of my affianced wife, or to be killed by him, if you will, is stupid preparation for a marriage, to my mind."

Mosca seemed to come to his senses after this, muttered some sort of excuse, that he had over-drunk himself, held out his hand, and would have embraced Buondelmonte. This, however, the young man did not feel inclined to accept. He put his hand on his late enemy's shoulder instead. "Remember, Mosca," said he, "that it takes two to make a marriage, and two for a good quarrel. If Lambertuccio has thought it well to give me his daughter, I may have had some thinking to do before I could take her from him. But if Lambertuccio's kinsman thinks well to quarrel with me, why, I may have some more thinking to do," said Buondelmonte. Mosca blurted out his grievance: "You passed me over. You would have nothing to do with me. You chose to follow the Amidei. The Lamberti are the better blood, God knows. And yet you passed me by. I was angry, and well I might be."

"I have had enough talking. Give you good-night, Mosca," said Buondelmonte, and turned about on his heel and walked slowly up the Borgo, picking his way among the puddles. Mosca made the figs at him with his two fists; but Buondelmonte never looked back. He shrugged his shoulders as he went into his house. "A brisk kindred is preparing for me," he thought, "but they are balanced by a stolid wife. When I feel the want of bustle at home, I shall know where to go for it, by my head!"

The Uberti began to think their new kinsman was rather fond of walking in the clouds. Farinata told his father that the talk about Arezzo and the Tarlati was very unbecoming. He thought Buondelmonte ought to be told. Schiatta laughed. "He will learn soon enough where the corn-bin stands," he said. "He has mettle, and should be ridden with a light hand at first. If you put him on the curb now, he will pull your arms out of you. It was I began the jesting."

"You are the head of the house, sir," said Farinata, "and I am your eldest son. You may say what you please; it is your right. And I may resent what is offensive to your honor. That, I conceive, is my right." Schiatta turned upon him.

"If you, Farinata," said he, "intend to quarrel with my new kinsman, you will have first to quarrel

with me. I myself intend quarrels to be done with.
The Certaldesi have asked for a Podesta. They
shall have you. I will send word that you are
coming; and you shall be off this day three weeks.
By that time Buondelmonte will be of the house.
If you snap your fingers under his nose now, you
will scare him off. So let there be an end of it.
Go and snap your fingers in Certaldo."

Farinata said that he would obey. "Of course
you will obey," said Schiatta; "I should like to see
the son of mine who would disobey."

Buondelmonte went to see his affianced the very
next day, and remained with her for an hour or so.
Next he went to the hall of the Uberti, just to show
that he was not to be put down by Schiatta or in-
timidated by his son Farinata. After that he let
a week or more go by, during which he meditated
on the state of his affairs. Then he went again to
each house in turn. Nothing was said which could
offend him. Farinata was not there, Mosca was
very civil, Schiatta as friendly as he knew how to
be. But at the end of dinner, as he mounted his
horse, he knew that he was glad the thing was over.
"I shall hold off that quarter for a week or so
more," he thought. "I will go hunting in Monti
Catini, or to San Casciano to see Gentucca. One
or both of these pastimes I will afford myself."
He rode up the street called "de' Balestrieri," which
leads along the old wall of Florence past the Badia,

until he came to the Corso, which runs east and
west in a straight line; and there hesitated, wondering what he should do. He was in a quarter which
held few of his friends, and was unarmed; instead
of holding on, therefore, he turned west along the
Corso, and rode at a walking pace, the reins loose,
and his thoughts fixed upon his discontent. Richly
dressed, as his custom was, sitting a fine horse, he
had the appearance of a lord of the earth, but of one
who took his signiory lightly, as if it was a play-
thing. Many a woman followed him with her eyes,
or nudged her workmate, and said: "There rides
a winsome young man. Happy is she who gets
him."

Gualdrada Donati was looking out of an upper
window of her house, and saw him coming. Her
heart gave a leap upwards, and she looked the
other way, as people do when they are considering
something they have seen suddenly. Then she
drew a deep breath and opened the shutters wide,
waiting for him to pass. As he came under her
window she took a flower from her dress and dropped
it before him into the street. Buondelmonte saw it
fall, and checked his horse lest it should trample
it. The next minute he looked up, and saw Gualdrada. A boy in the street picked up the flower and
put it in his hand. Buondelmonte, smiling, took
the flower and touched his lips with it, still looking
up at Gualdrada.

"For me, fair lady?" he asked.

"A greeting from your friends," said Gualdrada.

"Happy augury!" he said, and again kissed the flower.

"Why not?" said Gualdrada. "Do not all wish you well? For one so seldom seen you are much loved."

"If I am seldom seen," said he, "it is no fault of mine. If I am seldom invited, I must needs sit at home."

Gualdrada said, "If I invite one, I like to be sure of my guests."

"Then you may invite whom you will, lady," said he.

She said, "What if I take you at your word?"

"Try me," said Buondelmonte. She replied nothing, but looked at him, and smiled wisely and slowly. She was a handsome, sleepy - looking woman, whom it became to smile in that fashion. Buondelmonte called his page to tie up his horse. He dismounted, and looking up to the window, held out the flower. Gualdrada saw him, and drew in her head. He went up the stair.

Gualdrada poured a cup of wine and touched it with her lips, looking at Buondelmonte as she did it. Then she offered it to him silently; and he took it and turned it round, so that the place her lips had touched his should also touch.

"To what shall I drink, lady?"

She said: "To what I did, O Buondelmonte.

To the fair bride, and the marriage-bed, and the rich dowry."

"That is a toast I cannot refuse you," said he, and drank deep. Then they began to talk familiarly together, sitting side by side in the window-seat. She told him she was a diviner, who by secret arts would find out the uttermost places of his heart. Laughing, he said that she would see herself in there.

"I know better than that," she said. "For instance, I know that you have just now been visiting a lady. Is it not so?"

"It is so."

"Now this lady was kind, and not cold at all; and she gave you three kisses. Am I right?"

He laughed again. "No, you are gone astray. The lady whom I visited was neither kind nor cold; and as for her kisses, she harbored them against the proper time."

"The spells have worked awry," said Gualdrada; "but still I seem to see something. I see her cross her arms and bow her head before you, bidding you by those gestures to take her when you are ready. Again, I see her with scissors in her hand cut a strand of her dark hair for your delight. Now I am right."

"You are very wrong indeed. The lady sat all the time by the window, spinning flax for a bridal garment. And in her hair, which is as yellow as corn, the snood was fast, and so it will remain yet awhile. I see that you know very little of this lady, for all your nigromancy."

"In the crystal ball," said Gualdrada, "I saw her speaking a quick welcome; and words came tumbling from her lips. And I saw her take you by the hand and show you her coffer full to the lid with silver and gold, fine linen and wool. And I heard it said that she would scorn to take money from you for her Morgengabe; for as her honor was above price, so she would freely give it you for the asking."

"It may be so," said Buondelmonte. "She speaks when she is spoken to, and said Yes when I asked her a question, and No when I asked her another."

"She could hardly do less, certainly," said Gualdrada. "But she comes of a good house, and a rich house. The coffer may speak for her."

"The coffer is a good orator," Buondelmonte said, "and never tells lies."

She said, "I warrant it has spoken handsomely to you."

"Lady," he answered her, tired of this fencing, "if the coffer is not full, I can fill it up. But you have much to learn of sorcery and divining if you mean to go on with the arts."

"I know," said Gualdrada, "what I have done and what I might have done. I know one more ardent than this bride of yours, who is as beautiful as the flush of dawn; and what she has in hand for the man of my choosing. And Lambertuccio knows too, and Mosca knows very well."

"There is some magic here at all events," said Buondelmonte.

Gualdrada said, "Yes, indeed," and pressed her lips together.

"What is this, Gualdrada," said he, "that you have done? Who is this flushed bride? Who is the man you are to choose for her? Light a candle; it is hard walking in the dark."

Then Gualdrada got up, saying: "You shall judge. Wait a little." She went to the door of a closet, opened it, and called out, "Come, Piccarda." Out there came in a little while a virgin not fifteen years old, as beautiful as the rose of dawn. Gualdrada took her by the hand and led her before Buondelmonte, who was greatly astonished.

She said: "See this girl of mine, Buondelmonte; look at her well. Is she not a lovely person? Look at these smooth arms. Are the bride's as white and warm? Hath the bride hair of this length and texture? Hath she cheeks to flame as quick?" She touched the girl's cheeks and set them on fire. She held up her chin and bade her look Buondelmonte in the face, saying, "Give him look for look, Piccarda; for you may never see again so fine a young man when you are in the cloister, nor so great a lord, unless he be painted upon the walls." Buondelmonte saw that she had gray eyes, narrow and serious, like deep water;

and remembered that Cunizza's were brown and blank. Piccarda had a gown of white silk upon her, and a belt of gold.

"By the Lord Jesus!" said Buondelmonte, "this is a lovely person indeed, and he is a fortunate man who possesses her."

Gualdrada said: "I have no patience with you, Buondelmonte, for your haste and easy temper. For I had kept this girl for you from the hour in which I saw what her worth was. No man has ever looked at her but you, nor she at any man but her father and you. Her very brothers are strangers to her. And now, for some chance word of a fool, you have sold yourself to a girl of stone and little account; and my Piccarda must go into the cloister of the Gray Women."

"That will be a great wrong done her," said Buondelmonte, "and I am sorry on every account. But the Amidei are a good house, well descended, and their kindred are strong men."

"It seems, indeed, that you think them strong men," said Gualdrada. "And it may be that the Uberti and the Lamberti and Fifanti are too much for the Buondelmonti, though formerly it was otherwise."

"How, lady, too much?" he asked her, reddening a little; for, even-tempered as he was, he did not relish this morsel. But he looked again at Piccarda, and kept looking at her.

"Why," said Gualdrada, "if Schiatta had a mind

he could compel you to wed with his cook-maid, and a dowry of a hundred *soldi*."

"You speak lightly," he said, "and as if you were vexed. But you are wide of the mark. He offered me Mosca's daughter, but I refused him. Let me go now, lest I regret something." He said this without offering to go, or removing his gaze from Piccarda, who (for her part) by no means refused pleasure to her own eyes. Her hand lay still in her mother's, but her looks were free.

Then Gualdrada moved lightly towards him, and said, "You fool, you shall regret something indeed." To her daughter she said, "Girl, take him into the closet and show him the marriage-portion." She put their hands together and stood looking at them, tapping her foot on the flags and shaking with rage and disappointment, as the damsel led Buondelmonte towards the closet. There he saw three chests full of fine stuffs, linen and cloth of gold, fine woollen and silken webs, and long table-cloths with scarlet fringes, bedclothes, and coverlets of silk and gold knot-work, hangings of arras for the chambers and hall; and a chest full of gold, and another of silver.

Amazed, he said when he came back, "All this with a damsel so rich in herself!"

"Rich she is indeed," said Gualdrada, "and you have lost her."

"That," said he, "is not so certain, as it would certainly be a pity."

On a sudden Gualdrada said to him, "Take and
kiss her, Buondelmonte, for she was kept for you."

Buondelmonte took Piccarda in his arms and
kissed her on the mouth; and when he felt how
sweet and buxom she was, he could not let her go,
but kissed her again. And she kissed him back;
and so they remained for a space like fond lovers,
until he turned to Gualdrada, but without releasing
the girl, and said, "I must have her, Gualdrada."

"Well," said Gualdrada, "take her, then, and I
will pay forfeit to the Amidei. Few men would
refuse her, I think."

"I am not one, at least," said he; and after an
hour took leave of Gualdrada and his beloved, and
rode to his house.

Forese Donati said, when he heard of it all:
"There will be no good out of such a bargain as
this. I would rather cut my hand off than consent
to it."

"And I would rather see you with a maimed
stump than your child peaking in a cloister," said
Gualdrada.

"It has a bad look, this shifting and veering,"
Forese went on. "How do we know but he will
serve us the same trick?"

"Ah, never, never," said Gualdrada. "And so
would you say if you had seen them together.
Love leaped playing between them like summer
fires on the hills. They were as two pigeons bill-

ing each other; you could not part them. And was
not he bound to us in the beginning? Did he not
agree to come first to you before ever he saw or
thought of the Amidei? And where does our house
stand in Florence if the Uberti and Buondelmonti
and all their kindreds join hands? Do you wish to
bring in a tyrant? And a tyrant like Schiatta?
Your enemy and mine? Do we owe the Uberti so
much? Out upon such weakness! Is your heart
a sponge, holding water instead of blood?"

"You madden me with your questions," said
Forese. He was not convinced, though obliged to
own that he had spoken to Buondelmonte first. He
was for going to Lambertuccio then and there with
the forfeit; but Gualdrada prevailed upon him to
leave the thing alone for a while, for she believed
Buondelmonte would pay it himself.

The year had turned to the spring; March was
in, but Buondelmonte had not been to the Amidei
house for three weeks, nor more than twice in all
that time to see Schiatta degli Uberti. He had
been in the country, it was known; but Mosca de'
Lamberti said he had seen him in the city with his
friends. He understood that a large table was held
in the Buondelmonti house. Schiatta asked him if
he had been a guest at it; but Mosca only grinned
and grated his teeth together. Schiatta, however,
advised Lambertuccio to go to see Buondelmonte.
"It is time something was settled," he said. "I

hear of movements over the mountains which may spread into our plain one of these fine days. They will wait for the snows, yet it is quite as well to have your musters ready. I certainly think you should see Buondelmonte." So Lambertuccio went.

The two men greeted each other, and Lambertuccio said that he had not seen much of his new kinsman lately. It was time that preparations should be made. The year was getting on. Would Buondelmonte be ready for the wedding by Easter? Or what had he to propose?

Buondelmonte sat quiet for a little; presently he said: "I think frankness is a good thing, Lambertuccio, and I will be frank with you. I should have spoken to you before this if opportunity had served me. But I have been in the country, as you know, and troubled with family matters. Now I must tell you that not only shall I not be prepared to go to church with you by Easter, but after Pentecost I don't think I shall be ready."

"What is the meaning of this, Buondelmonte?" said Lambertuccio, raising his eyebrows.

Buondelmonte said: "I think that I was perhaps hasty in my determination. I don't feel myself inclined to marry just yet. I hope I don't set more store by my youth than other men, but I feel that I cannot yet awhile give up those pleasures which young men have a right to. Maybe I do more honor to Cunizza by not marrying her than I

should by fulfilling my bargain. I hope you understand me."

"I hope I do not," said Lambertuccio. "This
is a very unpleasant story you have been keeping
for me, Buondelmonte. I am not prepared with
my answer just yet. Nor will my cousins Schiatta
degli Uberti and Mosca de' Lamberti be prepared,
if they are the prudent men I think them to be."

"Ah!" said Buondelmonte; "since you have
named them, I will add that when I agreed to take
Cunizza, it was after I had declined an offer of
Mosca's and been declined by Schiatta. There I
think that I was right, and Schiatta right. My
politics and his don't agree, and are never likely
to agree; there will be grief over that sooner or later.
It is wiser to forestall grief than to engross it."

"You seem a poor tradesman to me," said Lambertuccio. "Lucky for you that Farinata degli
Uberti is safely out of the way. I have known a
quarrel picked on much less ground than this, and
by him, for instance, on no ground at all, save that
the color of a man's hair displeased him."

"Ah, if you come to the color of hair," Buondelmonte said, thinking, "I have known a bride left in
the lurch for some such reason. But I hope you
are not supposing that I shall decline a quarrel with
Farinata. I did decline one with Mosca the other
day (though before that he had found me ready
enough) because he is short of an eye; and I should
decline one with you, because you are father of a

lady whom I esteem and respect. But the long
and short of it is, Lambertuccio, that I dislike
Schiatta's politics, and that your cousin Mosca is
to me an abhorrence and occasion of nausea. You
will find me liberal, I hope. I am prepared to pay
the forfeit provided by the bond, and to hand over
my fifty florins in addition."

"That is a reasonable offer, I must allow," said
Lambertuccio, after a while; "but I have to think
of my girl's honor. Will you give me your word
not to marry until she is married?"

"No; that I certainly decline to do," said Buondelmonte, "though it is a very probable course of
affairs."

"Well," said Lambertuccio, "you must give me
time to talk over this with my friends."

"I cannot prevent it; it is your right. But I
hope you will not compel me to take the bond
before the Gonfalonier to have it abated. Since
you speak of friends, it had much better be done
quietly, as between friends."

Lambertuccio thought so too, though he made
no such answer. "Friends," he said, "are those
who act friendly." He did not know what to say,
since he was not sure what he ought to do. He
was a slow, deliberate, rather stately man, not soon
put into a rage, but long there when once there.
If Buondelmonte thought the troublesome business
over because Lambertuccio's tongue was at the end
of its tether, he was greatly mistaken. But the

fact is, he thought very little about it, save to be glad it was done with, the ground cleared. The moment Lambertuccio was gone he put a cloak over his face and made haste to reach the Donati house.

He told Forese his news, which Forese received with many shakes of the head. "It is but just begun, the trouble," he said. "I should like to hear Schiatta and the whole brood upon it as they sit at meat. Remember, it was you that approached them in the first place; for they are not likely to forget it. There will be high talk, I'm thinking. You must be wary of your steps, Buondelmonte, and wear chain-mail. They are a dangerous nest to meddle with."

"I shall take my life in my hands when I go to pay the forfeit," said Buondelmonte; "but a man does that when he walks across the street. You understand that you are not an ingredient of this broth of mine."

"There's not much in that," said Forese. "I shall be bobbing about with the best, the roundest pippin there, so soon as the murder's out."

Buondelmonte told him that nothing would be done until his bond was returned to him, and the affair a little blown over. Lambertuccio had wanted a promise out of him, he said, but he would not bind himself to the Uberti a second time.

Forese put a hand on his arm, saying: 'Never mind what you promise, Buondelmonte; but see to it that you hold off until Cunizza is settled,

She is of full age—sixteen if she's a day; they will marry her in a hurry, to save her face. Wait for that, my good friend, wait for that."

Buondelmonte was in a hurry himself, but said he would talk to Gualdrada about it. So he did; but Piccarda was there too. Gualdrada made very light of the whole story. "My husband is a born croaker," she said. "Have you not yet found him out? If there comes a shower—there is to be a flood. If the sun shines—we must prepare for a drought. You will see: the very first thing the Amidei do will be to marry off that girl to one of the house. There are plenty of them to be had; money was never a want of theirs, nor big-boned young men either. And when that is done, or as good as done, what is to prevent your marrying when you choose? Nothing at all. I consider you free as air. I consider the thing done now, and done with." Buondelmonte looked at Piccarda, who returned his gaze steadily, but as if she was troubled at something. Her eyes searched his in pursuit of his secret thought, then turned away; she sighed ever so lightly.

"Why do you sigh, sweetheart?"

"Because I am in love."

"Will you sigh when I wed you?"

"Ah, no."

"Why not, if now you sigh?"

"Because then I shall know that you are in love also."

He took her on his knee, and caressed her. She spoke no more until he urged her very closely. Then she said: "I want you. I have no rest because of you. Before you came I had long nights and days. But now day and night I think of you. I am wretched, in sore need." Buondelmonte kissed her. Such talk was very pleasant to hear, and made him wild for the girl.

Gualdrada, looking at these two, one caught up on the knees of the other, laughed, as rich people laugh. And when Buondelmonte asked her, "How soon will you give her to me, Gualdrada?" she knew that her wages were in her hand, and said: "You are so near together that I care not greatly to delay you. To-morrow you shall plight her with your ring at San Giovanni. Thereafter do what you will, each of you with the other."

Buondelmonte looked at Piccarda. "If I do what I will with thee, Piccarda?" he said, asking.

"That will be what I will," said Piccarda. So he kissed her again.

On the morning after Buondelmonte had broken his news to Lambertuccio, Oderigo Fifanti happened to be passing San Giovanni about the hour of terce when people were coming out from the mass. He waited to watch them for a little, and saw Gualdrada Donati with two unwedded girls. He had always thought her to have but one daughter, whom he knew quite well by sight;

but this other he had never seen before. She
appeared to him of extraordinary beauty, dangerous to men. He was so much taken with her
that when she had passed with her mother and
sister he went into the church to consider whether,
at his age, with grown-up sons of his own, he might
venture upon a second marriage. It would be that
girl or none, he thought, and turned it over and over
in his mind. In the church he saw a young man
offering candles to the Virgin, whose make and shape
seemed familiar. Puzzling idly over this, but more
concerned with his late encounter, presently the
worshipper turned to go out, and Oderigo saw that
it was Buondelmonte. There was nothing surpris-
ing about this, since San Giovanni was the church
where all the factions of his way of thinking heard
mass when they could; and on the great feasts made
a point of taking the Communion. There had been
a Communion this morning, he saw, and afterwards
remembered. Oderigo greeted Buondelmonte and
received his greeting; but they said nothing.

When he came out, not having fully made up
his mind what to do about the girl of the Donati,
he went down to his own house, and heard the
news about the Amidei marriage. Instantly he
connected it in some way with the visit of Buondelmonte to San Giovanni that morning and his offer
of candles to the Virgin. "He has had a vision or
a warning," he told himself; "that is about the
size of it. He has been expiating a vow, or sealing

a new one; or he was giving thanks for a danger averted. Now what will Lambertuccio do? And our kindreds? I must go down to Schiatta's and find out." And away he went.

He found all the kindreds assembled in the hall, Schiatta in the high seat, and Lambertuccio finishing an oration amid murmurs and muttering from the others.

"The sum of the matter, Schiatta," Lambertuccio was saying, "is that I cannot feel offended. I believe Buondelmonte spoke the truth when he owned that he would rather keep his kindred separate from ours. Either he thinks himself strong enough without the Uberti, or he fears to make the Uberti too strong. We know very well that he is wrong in the first, and as for the second, may doubt if he would count for very much. But a man must have his opinions. Another reason of his seems to be that Mosca here tried to pick up an old settled quarrel again, one night last winter. I will not say whether Mosca did well to blow upon dead embers; but it was not a friendly act to me, and Buondelmonte was reasonable in resenting it. He came to us of his own accord, peace upon his tongue; then says Mosca, there shall be no peace between you and me. Well, he would say, then there can be none betwixt me and your kinsfolk. You cannot have it both ways. He has reason on his side, I say. Now Buondelmonte will pay forfeit on his bond, and may have it back when he

166

chooses for all I shall say against it. My Cunizza will wed with Malviso Giantruffetti here, a good man and of our kindred; so her honor will be saved; all the city will believe that we broke off the match. This is all I have to say, Schiatta, about the affair."

Mosca de' Lamberti jumped up the moment he had done. "By·your leave, Schiatta," said he, "I will answer Lambertuccio in your presence. I say that it is well for Buondelmonte that Farinata is tied to the chair at Certaldo; for if he had been here, there would have been wild work in the street. And, for my part, I am not sure that all of us Uberti will sleep in our beds this night, as I gather Lambertuccio intends to sleep in his. Better had it been for all of us if I had settled accounts with my lord Picker-and-Chooser on that winter night. He had not lived then, perhaps, to toss another of the Uberti aside after a little trial. Shall I tell you now why I had my words with Buondelmonte? You think that I bore him a grudge for a very old affair? You wrong me there; it was just the opposite of that was the case. You should remember the day he came into this hall on his wife-buying errand, asking, I'll trouble you for one of the chief's daughters. 'I come for a wife, not a grandmother,' says my young lord. That of Schiatta's lady, look you. A wife he needs, not a grandmother. I know very well what he needs. Well, then, I made an offer on my own account; and Schiatta upheld it, and was right, since I am

his next in degree. Did that have the look of a
grudge? No, indeed. But what says my lord?
'I cannot hope to satisfy Mosca,' are his words.
Great courtesy to me! Oh, the finest! Who
bears the grudge, do you say? He is pleased to
condescend to Lambertuccio's proposals, however,
and will look at the bride, as he might look at a
horse on sale. Vastly pleasant dealing, signori, as
things have turned out. Now that is why I picked
a quarrel with this Butterfly Squire, who thinks
that all our maidens' lips are at his disposal. And
I am ready for another when and how you please.
Lambertuccio's reasonings and reasonableness are
nothing to me. Buondelmonte sought us out,
offering himself: now he throws us over. Can
we bear that, we who are lords of the city? I say
dishonor is done to our name and blood."

There was a good deal of shouting at this, and
some of the young men leaped to their feet. One
raised a cry of "Death to him!" But Schiatta
stopped all this with his hand. "Let no man stir
till I give him leave," said he. "There must be no
bloodshed nor house-burning yet awhile. This
quarrel is Lambertuccio's, who, if he is satisfied,
may be an easy man to satisfy; I say nothing
about that. But I say that Mosca did wrong to
offend Buondelmonte when he was in a state of
becoming my kinsman, and is chiefly to blame in
this which has followed. Had I been Buondelmonte I know not how I could have acted other-

wise. Now I forbid you, Mosca, to move sword
or tongue against Lambertuccio's enemy without
his sanction. Let this be a warning to you to be
civil, and not to take more upon yourself than
your friends are disposed to award you. Has any
man else anything to say in this foolish affair?"

Oderigo Fifanti got up. "I say, Schiatta, that
Lambertuccio is right in his surmises, and will tell
you why. This morning, happening to be by, I
went into San Giovanni, and saw Buondelmonte
there, offering candles at the altar of the Virgin.
Fine candles, too, seven pounds apiece at the least.
Now this is no great feast-day, as we all know;
therefore he must have gone there with design,
and offered his candles with intention. It is clear
as day to me that he offered either because of
a vow he had made, which no man makes except
necessity drive him, or as thanksgiving for a danger
escaped. In either case, it seems, he is to be
excused, as a man is who thinks himself warned
by God. And after the words of Mosca de' Lamberti it is not hard to see what sort of danger a
quiet man has escaped." All the kinsmen shouted
their laughter at this, and Oderigo sat himself
down. Malviso Giantruffetti also said something,
modestly and becomingly for so young a man;
and then Buondelmonte walked into the hall, alone
and unarmed, and courteously saluted Schiatta,
Lambertuccio, and the company at large. There
was a great hush; but all could see that he bore him-

self like a gentleman, and a noble gentleman. His witnesses came after him, three young men—his brother Ranieri, Alberto Giandonati, and one of the Gualterotti, a mere lad — none of them at his ease in the stronghold of the Uberti.

Schiatta, who sincerely admired him, returned his salutation, and said: "Buondelmonte, I guess your errand and am sorry for it. I would have seen you here more gladly on any other; or if this is the end of it, could wish that you had not come at all.

"I can well believe that," said Buondelmonte; "but when a man is told that he must lose his leg, he does not say: 'We will talk about it next week'; but rather, 'Hack it off then, and have done with it.' So I, being forced into a narrow way, make haste to get out even at the price of things which may be dear to me. You say that you know why I have come. I have given reasons to Lambertuccio, which I hope he understands. No doubt he has told them to you. Now, in the presence of you all, his kindred, I pay the forfeit in which I stand engaged, and will take my bond again. Further satisfaction I offer him for the honor of Monna Cunizza — namely, the fifty florins which I should have laid down for Morgengabe. This seems to be justly her due, since I believe from my soul every good thing of her. So I pay it now in your sight."

"It is greatly done," said Schiatta; "I own that." And so all confessed to one another that it was.

Lambertuccio said: "Noble offer should have noble response. I shall not accept from Buondelmonte more than is my due, nor money for that which he has not had. This Morgengabe will undoubtedly be paid by the satisfied man, and it must not be supposed that it is due from Buondelmonte. That is Malviso's business here, to whom my girl is betrothed."

"That alters the case," said Buondelmonte. "I should be doing Malviso a great offence." So he took back his purse of fifty florins, and shortly after withdrew, he and his witnesses.

The assembly broke up; the kindreds left the hall upon their several affairs; but Oderigo Fifanti stayed behind for a talk with Schiatta about his own affair of the girl of the Donati. Schiatta advised him against it. "This is an idle itch of yours," he said, "tending neither to good husbandry nor good comfort. How will you get a young wife to settle down with your sons, who are themselves old enough to marry her? Remember the grief of Obizzo of Este, whose son fell in love with his stepmother, and perished, and caused her to perish, miserably. Yet you are not to blame Obizzo for maintaining his rights, since he had chosen to make them so, with a strong hand. Again, the Donati are a good house, I'll not deny, though not so good as they have been, and no friends of mine. But mark you this, when the hour comes, the Donati will be on one side of the ramparts and the Uberti on the other. This must infallibly be."

"The same would have been true of the Buondelmonti, in my opinion," said Oderigo.

"Buondelmonte is a young man," replied Schiatta, "and more supple than the Donati. And his is a growing tree, where the other is rotting at the heart. I warn you off this quest of yours, kinsman."

"Well," said Oderigo, "maybe I shall not take your advice."

"Oh, if you confess yourself an old fool, I have nothing more to say," Schiatta answered. To which Oderigo replied with heat that if everybody was a fool who did not hold Schiatta's opinions, Florence held a goodly number of fools.

"I think it does," said Schiatta, "but that is no reason why you should add to the number."

"He is a fool," said Oderigo, "who follows blindly where another leads him. Knowledge of this, and not profundity of wisdom, makes a shepherd master of sheep."

"Go your ways, Oderigo," said Schiatta, "go your ways. Let January wed young May if he can. But let not January quarrel with the nature of things if he freeze May to death, or May fritter him to water with her awakened fires."

"I shall certainly try my fortune," said Oderigo, "and thank you for your friendly warnings."

Buondelmonte's Saga

Buondelmonte, who had a journey to make, laid
out his fifty florins in a gold crown, the finest that
money could buy in Florence or the world. It was
made of two hoops of gold, one above another,
joined together by flowers in red and white enamel;
above was a garland of lilies in the same work, with
a star in the midst, to be over the forehead, and in
the midst of that again an emerald of large size.
He took it to the house of the Donati, and before
he left her that night set it upon Piccarda's head.
"Let this speak to thee of my love while I am away.
I shall come soon, my dear heart," said he, and departed in a torment of love by no means allayed.
Gualdrada embraced her beautiful daughter. "He
is bound to you, my child, hand and foot. Think
not that by giving you have nothing left to give.
A fine skein is in your hand, to be wound as you
please. Though it be of thin silk, it will drag this
man to heaven or hell." Piccarda had nothing to
say; or else she did not choose to speak of Buondelmonte.

Gualdrada heard steps upon the stair, which she
thought were those of Forese coming in. "Stay
you there, Piccarda," she said, "and let your father
see what a lordly husband you have won." So she
sat still where she was, looking like a queen.

Forese came into the chamber with Oderigo Fifanti, who, when he saw Piccarda with the crown
upon her head, stayed by the door as one dazed.
Forese said: "Wife, here is Messer Oderigo come

173

a-wooing, wanting our Capuccia. What have you
to say to that?"

Gualdrada made a little demur; her head was
turned by the happy conduct 'of Piccarda's affair,
and she had never set much store by her elder
daughter. It would have to be considered, she
said; there was much to be said for and against
such a match; and then to Piccarda: "Go into
your closet and put off that ornament you have
on. Your father shall see it another time." Piccarda got up to go; whereupon Oderigo recovered
his senses. "Hold," he said; "you have my story
wrong, Forese. This is the damsel I seek for a
wife."

"Bad Easter to me," says Forese, "I am sorry
for that."

Gualdrada said: "You choose your words strangely, husband. Messer Oderigo, you are too late.
This girl of mine is betrothed; the crown she wears
now is a wedding-gift from her affianced. Not
every damsel hath so rich an offering as that. But
the bridegroom is a young man, of an age with herself or near it, and well found in goods, as you see."

"It is evident," said Oderigo, putting the best
face he could upon it. "There cannot be many of
his sort in Florence. Might a man know his name?"

Forese looked at his wife, doubtful what she
would have him do. Gualdrada made haste to
answer.

"Indeed, there would be every reason why you

should know, and sooner than most," she said. "But this is the true state of the case; the bridegroom has gone to Siena on business of some moment for himself and the state. Lest any shame should fall upon our daughter by failure of his, or accident, or any such thing—which God mercifully avert!—he has charged me to withhold his name and the betrothal itself until he is happily back. But you have surprised us out of one of these, through no fault of your own or of mine."

"Your secret is safe with me," said Oderigo; "but indeed you have found a tender bridegroom, singular in Florence on every account."

"You may be sure that he is," said Gualdrada.

After a few courteous speeches Oderigo, having no further errand with the Donati, departed. He owned himself for a fool; but for all that he was greatly puzzled at the mystery. Meeting by chance with Mosca de' Lamberti as he crossed the New Market, he clean forgot his assurance of secrecy, and told him the whole of the story, except the part he himself had played in it. Mosca said at once: "I met Buondelmonte on the bridge even now, on the Siena road. What if he were your man? What then, my friend?"

At once it jumped into Oderigo's mind that he had seen Buondelmonte that morning in San Giovanni, offering candles to the Virgin, and that in the same church had been Gualdrada Donati and her daughter. The remembrance of this, and the thought of what it involved, flushed him all over; but knowing Mosca for a pickstrife, a mischievous man, he said nothing about it. It might have been an accident, and the offering made for safety on his journey. So also there might have been the Communion there and yet neither Buondelmonte nor Piccarda have communicated. But if there were no accidents at all, and everything had been as it looked, then the Uberti were very much offended. Lambertuccio must then be told, and Schiatta. While he thought of all this, Mosca clapped him on the shoulder. "We are two fools," he said. "There is but one man can make such a gold crown as that. He is Lapo of Lucca. We will soon have the Donati secret in our hands."

Lapo the garland-maker, who lived by the bridge, made no secret of his part in the traffic. It had been Buondelmonte who had bought the crown this very morning. Mosca and Oderigo looked at each other without saying anything. By the Piazza of San Stefano they were about to separate, when Oderigo took Mosca by the arm, and held him fast, saying nothing.

"Let me go, cousin," said Mosca, struggling; "I have business."

Oderigo was no coward, to shrink from a quarrel or many quarrels; but he was a serious man, who considered fighting a serious business; and he saw that such fighting as might now be on hand would be no ordinary scuffle. So he held on to Mosca by

176

his gown. "By Jesus Christ, Mosca," he said, "you shall tell me to whom is your business. For I see that it lies in a different direction from that in which it lay when I first met you."

"Let me go, Oderigo," he said again. "I am not bound to tell you of my affairs."

"But this affair is mine as well as yours; so I mean to have it out of you."

Mosca looked this way and that with his one quick eye—up at Oderigo, who was looking at the men in the river drawing their nets below the weir; down at his feet; about and about. "Well," he said at last, "there is no reason why I should not tell you. I am going to Schiatta's."

"Then you may go," said Oderigo. If he had said "To Lambertuccio's," Oderigo would have forced him to silence; but he cared little what he said to Schiatta, because he knew nothing positive, and Schiatta would see that it amounted to nothing. A man is at liberty to plight himself with a woman when he has broken his plight to another, but not until. Now Oderigo knew very well, but Mosca did not, that Buondelmonte must have been with this girl long before. Therefore he had insulted the Amidei. But whether Lambertuccio would choose to avenge his own injuries or to share his rights with the Uberti, he was not yet sure.

He went to the Amidei house and told Lambertuccio the whole case, not concealing from him his own share in it. Lambertuccio listened without movement or sign, save that his face took a darker tinge, and that this tinge was darkest at his neck. At the end he said:

"If this is true, as fate seems to have it, he must die. No doubt of that."

"If you are for that work," said Oderigo, "I shall stand in with you. For you are not the only man offended."

"As you please," said Lambertuccio. "I need no help from any man. You brought your trouble on yourself. At your time of life, he who goes running after maids unwed deserves what he gets. My case is very different. I shall kill Buondelmonte."

Oderigo said: "He will be in Siena by to-morrow night; it could be done very handsomely there. Any of the Tolomei would do it. Or Farinata could arrange it easily for you from Certaldo."

"It will be done very handsomely here, you will find," said Lambertuccio quietly. "There is plenty of time. But I have just supped, and this is the hour at which I usually sleep. Forgive me, and many thanks."

"You will let me know when you are ready?" said Oderigo.

"Certainly. There is plenty of time."

"Good repose to you, Lambertuccio."

"Many thanks."

Schiatta heard Mosca's story, and put his finger on the weak spot at once. "A man freed is a free man," he said," and not less free for being that moment free. Buondelmonte may have known the Donati girl before, or he may not. He has acted within the letter of his rights. You cannot prove anything against him, and you cannot touch him."

"Your son Farinata would touch him," said Mosca.

"My son Farinata would do nothing of the kind," Schiatta replied. "You know very little about it."

But afterwards, when Lambertuccio came with his new story, Schiatta saw differently. "If this is the state of the case," he said, "the family is grievously offended—no less with the Donati than with Buondelmonte, except in this, that the Donati have always been open enemies. But the other came to us unasked, professing the need of alliance. Black treachery. Our name cannot endure this, Lambertuccio. I must certainly interfere. And it is a good occasion, after all, for what we have in the back of our minds. For if we go sagely to work, I don't know why we should have an enemy left in Florence."

Lambertuccio said: "You are head of the house. Do as you think proper. The quarrel is certainly mine first of all—but do as you think proper."

"I shall call a council of the kindreds," said Schiatta; "that is what I shall do."

They all came together in the hall of the Uberti; Lambertuccio and Oderigo, the Infangati, Mosca de' Lamberti, the Caponsacchi and Gangalandi, and Ruggiero Giantruffetti with his son Malviso, who was to marry Cunizza.

Oderigo Fifanti, when called upon, confirmed his story. He said that he agreed with Lambertuccio that the Amidei were chiefly concerned in the quarrel; but he considered that he came next on account of his private intentions towards the girl. He should stand by Lambertuccio in whatever he should chose to do.

There were cries for Lambertuccio degli Amidei. He rose unwillingly, and said little. "It is distasteful to me to speak of my private affairs, and by your leave I shall not. I have made up my mind what I ought to do; if possible, and Heaven on my side, I shall perform it. I speak as a man, father of a maiden wronged, not as kinsman of any other. If, however, you push your claims upon me, as being of my blood or intimacy or some such, I shall not refuse you. Forgive me; I am little of a speaker at these times."

Mosca de' Lamberti spoke next, not fiercely, but moderately and with show of reason. "There are two things to do," he said, "which equally become us. Firstly, we must stand by our offended kinsman; secondly, we must seek the benefit of the whole name and blood. Now, as to the first, it is plain what we ought to do; but the second, to my thinking, is no less easy. It is, To do the first. I am not the only man to say what I say now, that a thing done is done with. Buondelmonte said those very words to me upon a time. But I tell you now, a thing done is done with. If we act with Lambertuccio in his quarrel, we act justly, paying our debts. If anything follows upon that, it will have been begun by those who have thought themselves injured by what we may have done. We can be ready to meet them, and more than half-way. Therefore, by doing what is in your right you bring that to be done which is within your desire; and it will be done in the course of nature, without any seeking of ours or show of design. Do you wish the Florentines to say to each other, "These Uberti use a private grudge to make a tyranny over us"? That will breed a maggot of discontent and turn the whole city into fermentation. No, no. But if the friends of the Buondelmonti, all the kindreds in the Borgo and San Pancrazio, and all the Donati and their likes, draw sword upon us and seek publicly to requite what we have privately and most justly performed, they put themselves in the wrong, signori; they themselves pick the quarrel. We defend ourselves; we are in the right from the beginning; our advantage flows naturally, like Arno from Falterona. This is my sentence, kinsmen. A thing done is done with. Let them begin a new thing if they choose."

Schiatta said at once: "Upon my soul and conscience, I am in a case I never was in before, to agree with Mosca here. My first counsel would

have been for war on all these houses; but he is
right. Now let us send the lads away and settle
matters between us. Let Malviso, however, remain, since he is a party to the quarrel." This
was done. Lambertuccio and Mosca, Oderigo Fifanti, Leone Gangalandi, Malviso Giantruffetti,
kept their places beside Schiatta. Lambertuccio
would not talk, and Oderigo said nothing new;
Malviso was timid; Schiatta and Mosca settled
everything. Farinata was to be written to at
Certaldo. He was to watch for Buondelmonte
upon the road home from Siena, at Poggibonsi
where the fork begins, and send a messenger with
word of his coming. If the man went over the
hills, by Torre in Val di Pesa, he would gain three
hours on Buondelmonte. The six Uberti would
wait for him in the church of San Stefano, and go
out to the bridge-end and meet him. He would
probably be unarmed, at least without mail, because he would be going to the Donati. Mosca
said that this was certain, because a man does not
give his betrothed a gold crown unless she has something to give him in return. No doubt that he was
mad for her. When they were all agreed, and on
the point of going away, young Malviso, with a
very troubled face, said that he could have no part
in it. Schiatta stared up at the rafters. "What
does this mean?" he said. "Treachery," said
Mosca.

Malviso stammered out his meaning as well as

he could. Here was an unarmed man, lightly accompanied, upon whom were to set six with weapons in their hands, and counsel in their heads, and half the city at their backs.

"Well," said Mosca, "how many more do you want to help you?" Malviso took no notice, but looked at Schiatta.

"I am concerned in this, sir," he said, "since I am to marry the offended lady. But certainly I could not have married her if she had not been offended by Buondelmonte. So it seems that he has by no means offended me, but served me rather."

"What!" cried Mosca, twitching his arms; "by insulting your lady?"

"No, no," said Lambertuccio; "you are too sharp with the lad. It is easy to see what he means. So long as this is my quarrel, it is not his. He has my consent to stand out."

"And mine also," Schiatta said. "I consider his feelings only right and proper, though they are far from being mine."

"Or mine, either," said Mosca, "luckily for us."

They all went their ways.

Buondelmonte settled the affairs of the commune with which he had been intrusted, and his own; then he sent word to his friends that he should be in Florence on the morning of Easter, and started on Good-Friday night. He reached Poggibonsi and slept there.

Next morning, as he came out of Poggibonsi,
Farinata degli Uberti saw him from a good way
off, and said immediately to a young man with
him, "Off you go." The young man departed at
once on foot, more fleetly than any horse could
have fared in such a country, and as long in the
wind. Farinata himself waited to see how Buondelmonte was accompanied, and saw to his great
surprise that he was alone. It came into his heart
for a moment to warn him of his danger, so that
he might at least make a show to fight. Two
grooms would have been something, with his own
long sword. While he was turning it over, thinking it a shame that a fine man should be killed like
a pig in a sty, and, on the other hand, that it was
no business of his, he saw that Buondelmonte had
observed him. It would not do to make off now.
So he stayed.

Buondelmonte greeted him, wishing him a good
Easter. Farinata smiled.

"You too look for a good Easter, I expect,
Buondelmonte," he said.

Yes, Buondelmonte said, he thought it might
prove the best in his life.

Farinata, looking at him, said, "I should hope
that the more heartily if you had not put a hitch
in our affairs."

"I am sorry to confess that I did," said Buondelmonte. "I did not behave well, but I behaved as
well as I could. Look, Farinata, you and I are

nearly of an age, so that I can expect you to understand me when I tell you this. I saw Monna Piccarda by chance, and her extraordinary beauty
troubled me not a little. Also I admit that the
dowry she brought with her was a very fine thing,
much better than Cunizza would have had. But
both of these advantages would have been got over.
I have had my share of them, and still have. Do
you know what inflamed me to such a pitch that
I knew I could not live without Piccarda? It was
this, that when I kissed her for the first time, she
kissed me back. Ah, and earnestly. Do you not
see, my friend, that she gave me her heart there
on her mouth. I have no words ready to exhibit
my thought or understanding, but I was touched
very nearly by that, and on a quick spot. I could
not tell Lambertuccio all this, still less your father
Schiatta; but I may tell you."

"I understand you," said Farinata. Then he
sighed: "It is a pity."

"Yes," Buondelmonte said, "it is a pity; but I
can see a greater pity avoided. For say that I had
been wedded to Cunizza before I had met Piccarda,
it would have made no difference. What is was
bound to be. And, to my thinking, that would
have been more shameful in me than what I have
done."

"Maybe," said Farinata. "Who knows?"

"I have mentioned this to nobody," Buondelmonte said; "and shall rely upon your confidence."

"You have it. Rest assured of that," said Farinata. "But I am keeping you from your way."

"I have a good horse," Buondelmonte said, "which will take me to the Impruneta by nightfall. I shall find my servants and baggage, and sleep there. It will not do to go to see my beloved in a suit of sweat and mire."

Buondelmonte rode on his way. He felt much more at ease since he had unburdened himself to Farinata, and began to sing a song he had learned in Siena. Folgore of San Gimigiano had made it. It was a good song.

Farinata's messenger reached Schiatta very late on the eve of Easter, but Schiatta judged that there was no chance of Buondelmonte's coming in that night. He put men on the lookout, one by the Certosa and another at Porta Romana; and then he went to bed. The kindreds were informed; bidden to assemble, those who were concerned, in the church of San Stefano in time for the first mass.

In the morning twilight young Malviso Giantruffetti's heart misgave him. He had not slept much all night for thinking of the work on hand, and wondering what he ought to do. "He has done me a service, he has done me a service," were the words running in his head; and then he thought: "What harm will there be if I do him a service in my turn? Let him at least make a fight of it." With the earliest light, unable to endure himself

any longer, he put on his clothes and a cloak, and
went out of the house without disturbing any one
in it. The streets were empty; but he knew the
gates would be open by the time he reached them.
He crossed by the Rubaconte bridge for fear of
being seen by Schiatta's outposts, and picked up
the Siena road at a point below the Certosa. Not
knowing where Buondelmonte had lain that night,
he went too far and overshot him; but he found
out his mistake before he got to San Casciano, stole
a horse there, and pelted back the way he had
come. Such good pace did he get out of the horse
that he was again on the Rubaconte before the bell
of the Badia had struck for terce. But he had not
caught Buondelmonte for all that, and now dared
not go to look for him, for he knew he must be in
or near the city. So he held his horse by the rein,
and leaned upon the one bridge, in the angle of one
of the little chapels which used to be there, looking
over to the other. It was a fine morning, with
very clear air and sunlight. At first he saw peasants coming in, by twos and threes, to the mass of
the Resurrection; but by-and-by a horseman at a
foot-pace, and he came from Over-Arno. He looked
immediately to the foot of the bridge and all about
the old Por' Santa Maria, which stood there in those
days, but could see no men there. "If that is Buondelmonte, he will get over yet," he said to himself.
But then he saw that it was not Buondelmonte,
but a much older man. The Badia bell rang, and

the sound was taken up by Santa Reparata and San
Piero Maggiore, by San Frediano Over-Arno and
other towers; and then he saw two men come at a
trot through the gateway and pass over the bridge,
going to Over-Arno. One was in green and bareheaded; the other wore a hood. He heard the green
rider laugh and the other reprove him, the air was
so still. "That is a boy," he said. "That will be
Gualtiero Gualterotti going to meet his cousin. The
other has the air of Ranieri Buondelmonte, but I
can't be sure. So they expect him."

Not long after the riders had gone by he saw
a party of men come slowly round the buttress of
the old gateway. He counted them; there were
four, two in cloaks and two without. If they were
the Uberti, there should be a fifth man: where was
he? He soon saw that they were the Uberti. He
knew Lambertuccio by his height, and Mosca by
his stooping shoulders, and head incessantly on the
move; and Leone Gangalandi by a white eagle's tail-
feather he was fond of wearing. The fourth must
be Oderigo Fifanti, because he seemed to feel the
wind; he kept his cloak high up round his ears. He
saw them turn: then Schiatta degli Uberti joined
them. His head was bare, as usual with him. They
all talked together. He saw Mosca drive away a
cripple who came whining about, with his hands
held out over his crutches. Various people passed
in one direction or the other over the bridge. Presently Leone Gangalandi went through the gate at

a brisk run, and the others waited about. Ten minutes or more passed in this way, Oderigo taking sharp turns up and down the bridge, Mosca leaning over to look at the water, Lambertuccio quite motionless, and Schiatta looking up at the sculptures on the gate. Malviso wondered what was going on. Leone Gangalandi came back with half a dozen men on horseback, who went over the bridge, while he himself stayed with his friends. "I see the game now," said Malviso to himself; "these will go to detach Gualtiero and Ranieri, so that Buondelmonte can be dealt with separately. This is a bad business."

As the day wore, so increased the number of those coming and going over the bridge; but it was still easy to observe the riders. Malviso saw one such come leading a pack-horse, and then two others, also leading horses. They wore green jackets. He guessed that they might be Buondelmonte's servants; but whoever they were, they passed over unmolested and seemed to suspect nothing. When the last of them was through the gate, Oderigo Fifanti took off his cloak, and Lambertuccio followed his example. They folded the two cloaks together and put them into the empty gate-house. There was shadow on the east side of the bridge where they were standing. Malviso saw Oderigo Fifanti cross over and stand in the sun. He hated the cold.

A drove of pigs appeared on the bridge, from

Over-Arno. Their herd ran backwards and for-
wards, beating with his stick to get them together.
Malviso saw that the pigs were all over the bridge,
and was wondering what would happen if Buondelmonte should come up behind them, when the herd
stopped, looked round, then threw up his hand for
a signal, and began beating the pigs to one side. A
white horse, having a rider all in white, came at a
quick trot on to the bridge, followed by a party of
seven or eight at least. "Here is their man," said
Malviso to himself. "Ser Martino drives pigs to
the shambles, and these horsemen drive Buondelmonte. If I could stop him even now, I would do
it." He stood up on the balustrade of the bridge
and waved his hand, shouting, "Back, Buondelmonte, back!" Three or four times he shouted
thus, and at the fourth time Buondelmonte, who
was riding very fast, turned his head. Malviso
went on shouting and signalling; then Buondelmonte called out clearly over the water, "Buona
Pasqua," and lifted his hand. He rode on, his
companions about ten yards behind. Malviso saw
that the waiting men had come out and were standing in the gateway at the end of the bridge, blocking
the passage. Buondelmonte reined up for fear of
being into them; and Lambertuccio walked out
slowly to meet him.

To return to Buondelmonte. He had started be-
times from the Impruneta, and made such good

pace that he met his friends well on this side of
the Certosa. He had on clothes to suit the feast-
day, a long tunic of white velvet, with white hose
and boots of red leather, a white bonnet on his
head, and a short cloak. He had no arms but his
dagger. Very glad he was to see his brother
Ranieri, and still more that Gualtiero Gualterotti
had come, for he loved that boy; but he would not
stop or slow down, though he was all agog for news.
They had to talk as best they could. He said he
should go directly to the house of the Donati. "It
is full six weeks since I have seen my beloved Wonder of the World," he said, "and I am on fire to
learn what new beauties she has grown by now."
They told him that Cunizza was to wed with Malviso
Giantruffetti the next day. "The gentle Cunizza!"
said he. "It is only proper she should have the
start of me. She has a worthy youth for her husband. I have a good deal of friendship for Malviso."
Talking of this, that, and the other, they came into
the Via Romana by the gate, and there the young
men whom Malviso had seen met them, as if coming round by the steep road which leads from San
Miniato al Monte by the Porta San Giorgio. Two
of these were Uberti, one a Gangalandi, one was of
the Greci. Buondelmonte and his friends greeted
them and would have gone on their way; but Tacuino degli Uberti called out that he had a message.
"For me?" asked Buondelmonte. "No," said
Tacuino, "for your brother." So Ranieri stopped,

and was overtaken by two or three of these men,
who held him in talk while the rest of them pushed
forward, and got in between Gualtiero and Buondelmonte, talking and laughing among themselves.
Buondelmonte kept up his pace. Thus they came
to the bridge and into the sun, and crossed it, just
as Malviso had seen them.

The sun was full in Buondelmonte's eyes; but as
he neared the Stone of Mars and the old gateway
he could see that there were people in the road, not
to distinguish them. He reined in his horse and
put his hand up as a warning to the others; and .
just then Lambertuccio came out to meet him,
with a hand to take hold of his bridle; and he saw
who it was. Now he began to suspect something.
"Stay me not now, Lambertuccio," he said, and
turned quickly to see where his friends were. They
seemed to be in some difficulty, he thought. The
horses were all huddled together. He heard Ranieri talking in a rage and the others laughing at
him. Then Schiatta came up behind him as he
sat half turned, and jumped for him, and pulled
him suddenly from his horse to the ground; and
Mosca leapt forward from behind Schiatta and
stuck his knife in deep. He stabbed between the
collar-bone and the neck. Buondelmonte cried out,
"Rescue! Rescue!" and felt himself losing blood
very fast. "One at a time," he said, pleasantly;
but had no more words, for Mosca stabbed him

again, and Lambertuccio came up in his deliberate
way, pulled off Mosca, and put his knee on Buondelmonte's neck and drove at him twice in the heart.
He never spoke again; but Oderigo Fifanti did his
part for all that.

A crowd of onlookers had gathered, but no one
interfered; and as for Ranieri and Gualtiero, they
were prisoners and could do nothing. When the
Uberti saw that their work was done, they wiped
their daggers and walked away. Oderigo went for
his cloak; but Lambertuccio had to be reminded
of his, and went back for it. Going off, Schiatta
held up his hand for a signal, and the six horsemen
parted to allow the Buondelmonti passage room.
No harm had been done to them.

Ranieri spurred directly into the city up the Via
Por' Santa Maria, shouting as he went, "The bells!
the bells! Treason! Buondelmonti!" but young
Gualtiero went and sat beside Buondelmonte and
put his head on his knees, and covered his face with
his cloak, or what was left of it. The moment the
Uberti had left the bridge all the bystanders ran in
various directions, and almost immediately the great
bell of the SS. Apostoli began to toll. Others followed in no long time.

Ranieri, riding full gallop up the Calimala, met
Buonaccorso Donati coming down to see what the
crying was about. He was buckling his sword-
belt as he came. Ranieri told him the news, and

193

Buonaccorso ran back to fetch his father. Ranieri hastened on to find, if possible,, one of the Uberti who should not have been warned. As luck would have it, in the Via Condotta, he did meet with Malviso Giantruffetti returning from the Rubaconte bridge. "Treason! Treason!" he cried, and, "Death to the Uberti!" and rode him down. The fighting began within a few hours; but by that time they had taken Buondelmonte to his house and laid him on a bier.

Gualdrada came with her daughter soon after they had got him home. They let her in through the chains which had been put up at the head of the Borgo. Fires were burning in the Quarter of San Piero Scheraggio and all the bridges were held; but Gualdrada said, "There will be place made for the dead." She chose that Piccarda should sit upon the bier, with Buondelmonte's head on her knees; and Piccarda had nothing to say. She only stared at the window. Even while they were making ready, the Gonfalon was being brought down the Borgo. Men heard the roar of the fight in the north parts. The Donati were driving the Uberti down towards the river.

The Love Chase

The Love Chase

I. NELLO NELLI

IN the Civic Museum of Padua you may see the
portrait of a fair - haired young poet wreathed
with myrtle, a pretty youth indeed. He has a
chubby, blooming face, a long mouth, a pair of
eyes softly brown enough to make any girl's heart
beat; masquerading as I know not what sort of a
shepherd—Daphnis or another—he wears the shepherd's leather chlamys and twirls in his fingers the
shepherd's reed. And yet he perplexes. You
think of Saint Sebastian, and of Dionysus; you see
a sinner turned saint, a crucified Cupid: he looks
luxurious, drowsy with luxury; clever and aware of
it—he looks, in fact, a dreamer by choice who yet
has a root of good conceit in him which might one
day urge him to put his dreaming to the test of
practice. In the picture he can hardly be more
than two or three and twenty, by which time—for
his age was precocious—all his light-hearted piping
had been done, and his soft lips tempered to a more
measured music. When that was painted he had

been in prison and out of it, at death's door and
beyond its shadow for some two years; for that is
the portrait of Nello Nelli the humanist who, with
more philosophy in him than most Venetians, and
more poetry than any, entered this history and the
Gabbia of Mantua at the tender age of eighteen.
Even by then he had been a lover, was a scholar
and a poet, and on the fair way to some dignified
position or another—a professorate, a doctor's
gown, Latin correspondence. Stranger things had
happened in his country and century than that he,
at five-and-twenty, should have gained the red hat.
That he never did, was the result of putting dreams
into practice—a thing unheard of in Cardinals—
and is the subject of this tale.

Venice had him first, but did not keep him long.
His early years, conception, parentage, cradling,
tutelage are no great matter. The *sestiere* of San
Pietro in Castello is famous for easy marriages, and
it is probable that that of Masuccio Agnelli (viva-
cious man!) with Carlotta, the ruddy-haired laun-
dress, was as easy as most. Masuccio was a scribe
in the great monastery of San Gregorio, able enough
for much better things, but too idle to attain them.
He was singularly handsome, and not without
kindness; therefore, when Carlotta told him with
flames in her eyes that he must marry her, he
pinched her cheek, smiled tenderly, and said, half
to himself, "I have never yet been a parent." By
so doing he quenched Carlotta's flames in happy

tears. He hired a room in the *sestiere* where she worked, was in it as often as not, and soon had that new joy to add to his experiences. A golden-haired child was born, with his smile and Carlotta's carnations. Masuccio was enchanted, and gave instructions for the christening. They called it Agnello, because it had been born on Saint Agnes's day, and because she carries a lamb; also because of the patronymic. Agnello Agnelli—Nello Nelli —could anything go more trippingly? "Dear girl," said Masuccio to his wife, "you tripped and I tripped, with this result. Let him trip forever in story to keep our memories green." Masuccio gave a feast and illuminated the *rio* through all its length. They had music, as much as they would; they danced into the small hours; and then he came and kissed his Carlotta and her babe.

But she gave him no more children and died still a young mother. In such wise were the birth and baptism of Nello Nelli, the friend and correspondent of Politian.

Nello, to his widowed father, proved a charming consolation, always good-humored, always engaged in sucking health into his plump body; as a short-smocked urchin, sprawling with fine contempt for display on the quays and canal steps, he was so compact of beauty, grace, and bright-eyed mischief as to be the envy of all women not yet blessed with motherhood. But Masuccio tripped no more—he was too happy in his son. And while he aided him

in his escapades up and down the water, and fished
him out whenever he fell in, he succeeded also in
being his friend. He taught him all he knew, which
was much; grew enthusiastic over the youngster's
aptitudes and his own, and ended in a perfect passion for learning, that he might teach this most
teachable, lovable boy. The pair became fellow-
students, egged each other on, even quarrelled, as
scholars will, over particles and such small trophies
of the chase, and were reconciled with tears, kisses,
and generous concessions. Nello had Latin by the
time he was nine, Greek at twelve, and at fourteen
might have been in Hebrew but for an accident.
At that age he fell in love with a lady ten years
older than himself, and found out that he was a
poet.

Zenobia Belforte was the name of this lady, a
Greek, and wife to a man three times her senior, a
very learned jurist, who was then lecturing in the
cloister of San Pancrazio. Her bright black eyes
and slim fingers, always engaged with this most
promising pupil, spoiled the chances of the Talmud,
while they enriched the vernacular with some very
sugary *canzoni* and *ballate*. Master Nello rhymed
away, and in his own person enacted his rhymes.
At his age you must be thorough—that's the time
for logic. He was in all the categories of this uni-
versal science, and he rhymed them all. Languid
ecstasies, complaints, laments—*Anima mia sono in
tormento! Ah, bella crudel, odi il mio lamento!* the

dutiful rascal played out this music to Zenobia's fingering, and revelled in the most delicious pain. It was make-believe, of course; Nello was not in love with Zenobia—he was in love with *amor*, which rhymes with *cuor*. But Zenobia was in love with Nello, and Masuccio, his father, seeing how the land lay, considered the lad's fortune made. With his entire approbation the enamoured lady, with her professor and her Cupid, left Venice for Padua. "I've made him, and he me. He'll do well. And that's the way of the world," Masuccio told himself. He knew he should never see his son again, and never did.

In Padua, that happy little city, flowering away quietly under the Euganeans, Nello made a mark by his good looks, extreme youth, and learning. He was hailed as a prodigy; for it was a wonderful time, when at any moment a God might burn upon the earth—and fortunate were he who discerned and hailed him first. He gave lectures of his own, commenting, if you please, upon the *Attis* of Catullus. He invented and caused to be enacted in a green garden by the Ponte Corbo, a piece, half masque, half satire, abominably clever, absurd, and audacious, which he called "The Priapeia." He became the height of fashion, and Zenobia went mad with jealousy. But the exercise of his proper talents was her greatest rival: he cared nothing for her the moment he became interesting to himself. From Padua to Este, from Este to Ferrara and else-

where, however, he went at the call of her moods.
Finally she took him to Mantua, in an evil hour
for herself. In that city of water-worn palaces he
totally forgot her under the charm of the great
Politian. It was time—he had been four years in
bondage; but what was better still was that he forgot himself. He was in a fair way to become a
real scholar, for now he loved learning only.

Eighteen as he now was, and in most things astonishingly premature, he was happily wise before
the time in this, that he was no great lover of
women. Women loved him much, but his adventures in their particular affair were seldom of his
own seeking. He was critic as well as minstrel,
and always judged his own cause to the detriment
of his advocacy. Certain traits, tricks, habits, accidents, whatsoever they might be in women,
touched him and drew poetry out of him like a
stream of honey from a comb; he had a strain of
asceticism, or took a pleasure of the senses from the
contemplation of it. Frugality, economy of beauty
he thought exquisite; recluse beauty—the hidden
rose; a beauty unconscious of its own excellence—
Apollo playing cowherd; meek beauty, beauty in
bondage, beauty discreet, beauty wise: these kind
interested him, or he told himself that they would.
No such beauty had been observable in Zenobia, a
hardy-flowering stock; Zenobia became his abhorrence. She vanished, and left him alone with his
dreams, his studies, and his youth. Nor did he

find any wise beauty in Mantua which he might
worthily celebrate; but instead, the opportunity of
putting a dream into practice, a prison, a patron,
a torment, a martyrdom, and a wife. These things
are vitally bound up with him and his conduct in
this tale.

To end my prologue. He had been six months
in Mantua, the willing bondsman of Politian (his
senior by two years) and a perfected Greek style.
With that profound young man he had explored all
known mines of learning, and had sunk a good few
shafts for unopened seams. He was very well inclined, too, to let the world share his adventures.
He commented upon the *Hymns* of Callimachus in
an "Interpretatio Mystica" of such excellent piety
that Cardinal Gonzaga was to show it to Pope
Sixtus, and did not forget it for a day and a half;
his *Scholia* upon Propertius lost nothing by the discretion with which he treated that poet's vexed
loves. He became enamoured of physical science,
did not shun to probe the recesses of our nature.
He bottomed, for instance, the habits of infants in
a treatise—"Why babies, when they hear the
nurse's lullaby, cease their squalling, and soon, indeed, fall asleep; but with men otherwise?" Plato
helped him, or the Platonic system, and some very
elegant Latinity. He passed, by an easy transition,
to consider the difficulties of drunkards. "Cur
nonnulli ebrii gemina vident?" is the title of his
work—a gloss upon the *Problems* of Alexander

Aphrodisius. Intimate thoughts concerning animals and lovers occupied him next. "Why mules are not fertile?" "Why the extremities of lovers are at one time hot, at another cold?" "Why the bearers of loads sing as they go?" "Why insects die in oil?" These excursions delighted Mantua; and Nello, instead of following Politian to Florence, when the poet was summoned by Lorenzo, stayed where he was in the hope of preferment. Cardinal Guido Gonzaga, brother of the Marquess and Regent of the State, was understood to be benevolently inclined.

II. We Taste his Quality

The society of the learned had by no means cut him off that of the gay. In that Italian spring there was no dismal science. Nello took his learning lightly, as became so pretty a scholar, adorned his person to be in tune with his mind, could compliment a lady or flatter a great man, with any courtier in Lombardy. The Marquess of Mantua, Lodovico the Turk, as they called him, was a big-boned soldier in the main, a man of hard knocks and lightning judgments, who chose a minister like a battle-ground, and met arguments like hostile squadrons. He respected the Church and Church-manship, and as for art and letters, he sincerely admired what he made no pretence towards himself—sound book-learning. He had made Master Nello free of his Court, recommended him to his more accomplished brother, the Cardinal, and en-

couraged his sons to be intimate with the youth.
These two, in character very different, were Federigo and Francesco, the latter a mild-mannered
boy, shy, and much under his uncle's thumb, intended for the Church. He did not greatly interest
Nello, but Federigo did—a hot-blooded, handsome,
rebellious fellow, able, idle, and a rake. With him
our poet struck up a Horace - Mæcenas, patron-
client kind of friendship, which ended abruptly,
and in the following manner.

Among the less reputable, but not on that account least reputed inhabitants of Mantua, was a
very handsome young woman, known as La Pernetta. She lived in the Via Sant' Agata, between
the Castello and the Ponte Mulina (where, over the
rushing weirs, the Twelve Apostles preside at their
mills, and diligently grind out the corn of the faithful); and being as prodigal of her lover's bounty as
of her own, she attracted, whenever she chose to
ask for it, a large company. It was upon a hot
July night that Nello found himself in her supper-
room, one of a half-dozen women and as many
young men who were eating and drinking there.
Federigo Gonzaga, flushed as the Wine-God himself, with vine-leaves in his black hair, was there
too. He was, as always, bitter in his cups. There
were others—Amedeo Castiglione and his brother
Baldassare, sedate and master of himself; a beautiful little creature, all roses and gold, called Giulia
Romana; a Lionello d'Este (by a side-wind) with

his broken nose and hare-lip; a shameful old man
who thought it not robbery to beshame his silver
hair; Sirena of Forli, Violante Senese—to name no
more, since their names tell nothing. There had
been songs, hiccoughings, bickerings, loud talk, high
words; now and then already a man had bitten his
lip, or started and felt for his dagger. Throned in
the midst, magnificently disarrayed and magnificently sulky, crowned with roses, and the color of
them, Pernetta sat and gloomed at her company.
She was in a bad humor.

"Drink, drink, my pantheress," Lionello urged
her, grinning horribly through his split lip; "pour
to Lyaeus. See him over there in his ferment.
Sleek yourself for his sake."

"Silence, satyr," said she, "and let me alone.
Baldassare"—she beckoned to the grave young
man—"Baldassare, good friend, go and ask the little Venetian to sing me out of this hubbub."

Baldassare bowed his way from lady to lad.

"Messer Nello Nelli, our lady is sick of love and
all sweet food. You are to comfort her with music,
since flagons are her loathing. Let it be of your best,
I beseech you—but not inflammatory, my dear sir."

"May the fate of Pentheus be mine," said Nello,
blinking his long eyelids—"of Pentheus whom the
Mænads tore, if I provoke that God of theirs."

"You rebuke me well, sir," Baldassare said. "I
speak with a man of soul. When ladies fall to
their knees, poets spread their wings."

Nello said, "I shall certainly do my best for Monna Pernetta." He swung free his lute, and struck a chord or two.

I do not reproduce his song. He had a sweet and gallant voice, whose hardihood and adventurous ease had the power to draw tears. A discretion which was natural to him bade him select a county song, his own wholesomeness secured its honesty: it had been born in the Garfagnana of Tuscany, upon some green and wooded slope of that pious land, and breathed of a love artless, innocent, and tragic at once, that of a girl for a man out of reach, which hurt her and wounded her notes. It was a girl who had sung it in his hearing, some such poor drifting creature as he had before him now; and Pernetta may have been of her country, or may have wished to be of it. Whether it was pity or regret wrought the *catharsis* is not to be known. Her eyes were blind when he had done. What cool breath of what familiar pastures blew upon her from his notes, what memories of peace and young love, wonderful, hopeful, triumphant—who is to say? She was deeply moved, and being vehement in all that she did, rose suddenly, wine-cup in hand, and threw over her chair in her haste. Nello, having ended, sat down again and took the applause of his company sedately; but before long he was aware of La Pernetta clamoring for a clear road.

"Let me pass, herded swine," ,he could hear her

scolding, "let me pass, you who run swilling to the
wine-trough so soon as you dare. Let me pass, I
say. I am going to kneel to the first clean heart
I have met with in Mantua." She was half crying,
half railing, more than half tipsy. Nello considered her with a chill, critical eye, not withholding admiration of her bountiful parts, but putting no
heart into their study. She was like a Roman
Bacchante, with her loose hair, hot, stained face,
and gown slipped off one shoulder. If you must
have enthusiasm in a nymph, he preferred that
shown by Scopas. The conception, he thought,
was none the worse for being circumscribed; it was
not necessary to spill over so much. And yet it
was curious to him to see this sumptuous animal
strive with the God.

Misused, misusing, burning creature, she came
towards him with a hasty lurch; came stumbling
on, was quite near him, a goblet in one hand,
crushed in the other a rose-wreath torn from her
hair. Her color of fire, wild breath, disorder, nearly scorched him. A little nervously, he rose to receive her.

"Hail, poet!" she cried out, swaying in her balance. "Hail, thou that singest of good love! Look
at me well—look. I am the Shame of Mantua, and
I kneel to you!"

Then and there she dropped to her two knees
and began to struggle with her passion of penitence.
Tears came hardly from eyes long dry; to sob was

horrible pain. It was a sudden and dangerous
frenzy she was in. Nello, greatly concerned, would
have lifted her up.

"Ah, Madonna, never kneel to me!" But she
looked at him with a shocked and empty face.

"Madonna!" She gestured her despair—"Do
you call me Madonna—naming the holiest? Call
me Robaccia—call me Corruption, for such am I."

As he stooped, full of gentle disregard of this
sort of fury, to lift her up, his fine manners were
a sting. Her shame was driven sharply inwards
and maddened her. It was a tense moment,
chosen, of all others, by that misshapen devil
Lionello as one in which to crow like a cock. Then
some fool laughed, as fools will, and Pernetta turned,
furious. Even then the storm might have grumbled out, had not Federigo hereupon put his arm
round her from behind and whispered in her ear—
some catchword of her class. That cut her deep;
at that she sprang away from him and found her
feet, mortification adding fuel to the blazing heart.
She swung herself clear of him, and "Dog!" she
cried at him, and hit him full in the forehead with
the metal cup. The edge cut him open; he staggered back and fell with a thump in puddled blood
and wine. There was a moment of absolute quiet
until he was down, and then the roomful swarmed
about him, about the tragic woman, and about poor
Nello, dazed author of all these harms. The uproar
was like nothing so much as a disturbed rookery—

cries, whirling arms, foolish laughter, abandoned sobbing from little Giulia Romana. One, more unmanly than the rest, ran out screaming into the night.

"Morte! Morte!" they heard him shrilling down the street. "Treachery! Treachery! To me!" Nello grew scared, the women were tussling to get at the door. Lionello d'Este, spurred by his familiar fiend, locked and set his back to it until the guard came.

The soldiery clattered into the house; their heels and jingling accoutrements soon quieted down the clamor. Lionello threw open the door with a flourish; way was made to the body in the midst of the wreck of feasting.

"Whose work, gentlemen?" The lieutenant was standing over the red and motionless Federigo—heir to the Mantuan dignity, good lack! Nobody cared to claim the honor of having laid him there. Pernetta was crouched, shaking in a corner; this was a hangman's business. Nello, only, saw her, and pitied her. Besides, she had praised his singing.

"My work, lieutenant," he said. No one else spoke. Pernetta, white to the lips, stared at her champion.

"You are my prisoner," said the lieutenant; "kindly hand me your weapons." Nello gravely handed over his lute, and somebody sniggered. It had fluttering ribbons, and was a pretty instrument; as a weapon a mouse would have laughed at it.

But you can never make an officer of the law look
foolish. The lieutenant took it all as a matter of
course. Nello's hands were strapped behind him,
and all names were taken down.

"To the Gabbia," said the officer, "*avanti!*"

Now the Gabbia is an iron cage eighty feet up
the face of a tower, and is six feet by four by four.

III. He Philosophizes on High

The time is before dawn. Imagine Nello Nelli,
a bloom-faced, golden-haired lad in green velvet
doublet and trunks, green and white hose, and
dainty shoes, crouched in an iron cage in mid-air
—a cage six feet by four by four—but do not imagine him miserable. His undimmed eyes searched
the firmament with interest; expectancy kept his
red lips moist, and gave color to his cheeks; he
held a keen lookout for stars, and the first stirring
of light. "There burns Sirius," he mused, "there
falls, tired, the Wain. We have not the Pleiades
from our eyrie; the Way of Milk is paling already
before the flushed face of Eôs. Courage, courage—
what a blessing it is that my lodging faces the east!
She comes, the nymph Eôs comes—

"all red,
Blushing to be so new from Tithon's bed!

a pretty line, and I think new in conceit." He
gave ease to his numbed right leg by doing violence
to his left; he found, also, that to clasp a knee was
comfortable to the reins; but he was forced to

admit that rectangular bars of iron make a bad mattress. The air, however, was balm after the wine-charged heat of Monna Pernetta's banquet. He had been bathing in its freshness for two or three hours already, and was not chilled by it yet. That was famous, because the sun could not now be far off, and its first rays must strike him at the height he was. A faint breeze came to play about his forehead—a sigh from love-lorn Eôs; the whole city lay slumbrous beneath him, muffled in the slipping shrouds of night. Probably he alone was watching and waiting for the day.

His earliest sure premonition came from overhead. A pigeon began to coo, softly at first, as if tentatively; then, gaining assurance with volume, pouring out a comfortable stream of sound, full of brooding, contented preparation, of monotonous peace. "Good," said Nello, "good! I am on a level with the birds, always friends of mine—and now neighbors. That householder up there has not, perhaps, so various a pipe as mine, but he sings of what he knows, and in that does wiselier than I. Did I do so at Monna Pernetta's Bacchic interlude? I doubted nothing at the moment, but now I doubt—rebuked by this cool air, by the cadences of this peaceful songster, my more reasonable colleague. All Nature is in tune; but I have been an alien to her, fatally out of tune." He shook his head. "I was cooler than the others; I love not over-ripe women—I was more at peace with my soul than poor spilt Pernetta; but I gave her none of my peace, and so she broke Federigo's head, and I pay the bill." He clasped both his knees, he put his chin between them, and gave ineffable repose to his backbone. "There is a surer foothold for me than singing of Nature in a painted lady's bower; love of books, love of learning, love of God, love of stainless things—things unshadowed and unsmirched —love of a sweet-breathed lass. Ah!" he cried, in a sudden flood of ecstasy; "ah, soft, Nello, soft! See that fluttering out yonder, that stretching of a silver cord; see the creeping light, the whisper of our hidden world. Oh, pledge of Heaven, the Dawn, the Dawn!"

Slowly the gray cup of the sky filled and flushed with fire; the belfry of Santa Barbara caught it first. A bird or two cheeped, in the poplars sixty feet below him some watcher rustled the leaves; the wind came on more assured, the light broadened, and paled as it spread. He saw the sheeted lagoon, the long bar of the bridge run out like a spit of sand; he saw the reeds bend, a heron flap heavily by the shore; then reddening cloud-wings caught his eyes, a band of rose and gray, burning at the edge, intensely bright. The chorus of the birds opened full; the birds were at prime: roof beyond roof Mantua lay out in ridges, like a mountain prospect—with the belfries for the great skyey peaks, the gables for cornices, ledges of rock, the chimneys for splintered pikes, the domes like breasted hills—

oh, the wonder and the still delight of this daily miracle, to be seen only from the Gabbia, and only savored by the condemned criminal! Nello lived at fever-rate for an astonishing hour, and would not have changed his cage with the tenant of Saint Peter's throne; the very Courts of Heaven, one may say, would have seemed a doubtful bargain.

The pigeon, meantime, went chanting on, a sweet and homely descant on the glowing theme. Nello rubbed his hands. "O benissimo, benissimo! I am in the happiest case," he told himself. "I survey the open country. I see more sky than His Magnificence the Marquess of Mantua, or His Eminence the Cardinal Guido Gonzaga. My lodging is aërial; certainly there is a draught, but no soul in Mantua has seen what I have seen this day. And, after all, it is satisfactory to remember that I had nothing to do with cutting open Federigo's head. That being so, I fancy that I suffer considerably less than the real sinner. Monna Pernetta is, I hope, lonely in her bed, thinking ruefully of recent excesses, and deriving (it may even be) some glimmer of wisdom from my chivalrous rebuke. For if a distempered woman is not rebuked by a stranger offering to take her offence upon himself there is no merit in vicarious sacrifice. I did well by her, better by myself, I am sure of it. The woman had been moved to better desires by my singing—lifted up, set on her feet; but while she rose, as on wings, Federigo was left behind, still grovelling in the mire where she had once been. His muddy touch shocked her: ah, believe it, there is a cleanliness attainable by us all! She did virtuously to cut him down—she could not have done otherwise—she was armed by Heaven. And I, the cause of her great act, did well to pay the shot; for nobody ever paid so high a compliment to my muse as to shed blood in its honor. At this rate, Nello, a poet may command armies in the field, and a philosopher may yet be king."

Warm fires leaping over a ridded world assured him that he spoke the truth; the sun's good face, which at that moment sent a kindly ray into his cage, gave him the heart of a warrior. He ate his bread—it was capital. He sipped his cup of water—the night had iced it for him. "If I die within the next hour," he said to himself, "I can be very sure that I have lived greatly during its predecessor." He awaited his summons with confidence, and as he watched Mantua crawling (like a nest of ants) to its labors, was in such high good-humor with himself and it that he forgot that one of Mantua's labors was to be his execution, and that there were to be no more labors for him in this world.

He was in the Cage of the Condemned on his own confession of having cut open the head of Don Federigo Gonzaga, heir to the Marquessate of Mantua, with a silver goblet. At half-past ten in the morning the Turnkey came to take him out. "Master Poet," said he, "the time has come." "Sir," replied Nello, "I have been expecting him a long while. I hope he is as ready as I am."

"There is a guard below, sir, to take you immediately to His Eminence."

"Master Turnkey," says Nello, with sparkling eyes, *"moriturus te salutat."*

IV. THE CARDINAL

Cardinal Guido Gonzaga, who, in the absence of the Marquess his brother, was Regent of Mantua, was a prince of this world and a man of it in the first place, a Prince of the Church when it suited him so to be, and forty years old. His proportions were massive and imposing; he was square-shouldered and necked like a bull. His chest was a buttress, his chin manifold, his hands were somewhat gross. He had staring, black eyes, which had the faculty of seeming to be aware of nothing, and consequently of telling you nothing; and yet he was by no means without insight, humor, or a pleasurable sense. He had lived without scandal in a quasi-married state with a lady of the noble house of Pico; he had earned fame as a warrior, and plumed himself upon his statesmanship. Since the death of his companion, without issue, no disorders had been observable in his life and conversation; in fact, he took particular care that the world, admiring him as he trampled its ways, should take due note of his fine discretion. He was no ascetic; his reason, which told him that appetite was not given us for nothing, made the thought absurd. But he was accustomed to say that heartache was as sure a sign of ill-health as the headache, and as easily avoided. He took his pleasures therefore, temperately, and enjoyed them all the more.

It was before this stately personage that young Francesco, his mild-mannered nephew, knelt and blushed as he told the tale of overnight's revel and tragic upshot. It seems that La Pernetta had embarrassed him with her confidence, and assailed him with prayer that the truly guilty might suffer. The Cardinal smiled, partly at the story, partly at the teller of it.

"You report a Magdalen in our midst, my nephew," says he.

"My lord," replied Francesco, "the woman has led a deplorable life by her own confession. She has told me all—she is a beautiful, wild creature. It was she alone who did the deed, provoked by the untimely acts of my poor brother. The poet, on the other hand, had moved her to repentance. She is, as I say, exceedingly—"

"As you saw, nephew, I think you would have said."

Francesco was fluttered. "Your Eminence, as a candidate for holy orders—"

"Never protest, my son," said his uncle, cross-
ing his legs, "and never explain, if you hope to
be a Prince of the Church. Do, rather, and do
strongly. Let the woman be what she is, or what
she appears to you to be, we have the means of
proving her contrition under our hands. I will
examine the poet myself, but believe that I understand the affair very well. Your brother Federigo will be none the worse for his cupping,
and I suspect that the girl has given him no
more than his deserts. But the little philosopher moves my admiration. No doubt the whole
affair was very flattering to his vanity—yet it
was a gallant return to make to a lady who
praised his verses, to be ready to be hanged in
her stead. I like the spirit of him much more
than I do his discourses on the classical authors.
Send him to me, Francesco."

Francesco, having kissed the princely ring, was
about to withdraw, but the Cardinal laid a heavy
hand on his young shoulder. "Mind me now,
Francis," he said, "be discreet. Do not interfere
with wiser heads than your own, nor with the
hopes of your country. We shall not make very
much of Federigo, I believe. Already I know
that he is not docile in this Bavarian marriage we
are getting him. The road he is upon now leads
to Ruffianism; I see him a bravo, a dunghill cock
'flapping his wings among cutthroats. Now, my
boy, with you in your scarlet and Mantua under

your hand, what is to keep you from the Vatican?"
He shrugged as the lad drooped. "At least, be
it not said against you that some slobber-cheeked
baggage of a girl kept you from it. Now go, my
boy, and send the poet to me."

By this means Nello's meteorological observa-
tions were cut short at half-past ten in the morning. He lost no time in presenting himself in the
Cardinal's antechamber. He had already a bowing acquaintance with the great man.

"Master Nello," said the Prince, "your invention surprises me. What part did you propose
yourself to play up there in the Gabbia?"

"The part of a gentleman, my lord, had been
in my thoughts," replied Nello, "but predilections are unmanageable. I found myself study-
ing the weather."

"Did you consider it a gentleman's business to
tell lies for worthless women, sir?"

"Ah," said Nello, waving his hand to one side,
"Your Eminence knows better than I do whether
a man may not sometimes prevaricate. As to
the lady's worth, I know nothing of her, except
that she praised my singing."

"At the cost of my nephew's head, young man."

"That is so, Eminence. Her flattery took a
practical form. But if I may be permitted to
explain, Don Federigo's head happened to be the
next to her hand. In reality she was as guiltless
as he was, and I alone culpable. For undoubted-

ly, if I had not sung she had not repented her way of life; and if she had remained in sin, Don Federigo had remained in health, but in sin also with her. So that I cannot but feel that in chastising Don Federigo she did him a good service, and that in moving her as I did a good service was done to her. For such things as these, though I may deserve the penalty of the Civil Arm, I shall not shrink from a higher tribunal."

The Cardinal was pleased. He tossed his head and laughed.

"Bravo!" he said. "Either you have learned that frankness is acceptable to my family, or (which is better still) that it is acceptable to yourself. I agree with your estimate of the service done to my nephew, and can perhaps do you one in return. What are your plans, Master Nello? Have you ever thought of the Church?"

"Eminence," Nello replied, "I think of Holy Church every day. It is the duty of every man who would be thought wise."

"No doubt," said the Cardinal. "In a Christian State—"

"Eminence," said Nello, quickly, "in every State. I am of the opinion of Plato, that a wise man bows his knee to the divinity of the place in which he may happen to be, not as a token of acquaintance, but lest, by the omission, some god may be offended."

"I had not remarked that passage in the philosopher," said Gonzaga dryly; "but we Churchmen cling mainly to Aristotle. He, we think, is not so apt to commit himself. I do not wish to press you —yet it is a fine career."

"Learning also appears to me a fine career," Nello ventured to say. The Cardinal nodded.

He said, after a pause, "I have a place in my Secretariate empty, which I shall be glad to put at your disposal. It is a very personal affair, requiring tact, amiability, power of invention, some reasoning, and a knowledge of tongues. Arabic will be useful; you should learn that language. I have heard nothing but good of you from Agnolo Poliziano; Vittorino da Feltre speaks well of you. But your best credentials are your own. What do you say, my friend?"

"I say that I will serve you to the utmost of my wit," said Nello, sedately, and kissed the ring. The Cardinal, moved by some paternal humor, patted his bent head, and with a "State sano, figliuolo mio" nodded him away. He went out of the Castle as if on wings. He had been long enough in the world to know the worth of such a friendship as he had made; it justified him in a long visit to the tailor in the Via Broletta.

"Battista," he said to that careworn artist, "I invite you to share my good-fortune. This day I enter the Cardinal-Regent's service, and consider your accounts as good as paid." Battista rounded his dutiful shoulders, and rubbed his hands together.

"Let us not speak of such things, dear sir. What are little accounts between you and me?"

"Trifles," said Nello. "My way is clear before me, stocked with the miraculous. Consider the variations of my fortune. At five this morning I was in the Gabbia, able to remark that you did not attend the first, nor indeed the fourth, mass in Sant' Andrea. At eleven I was in the study of His Eminence. Now, at noon, I am in your shop, ordering a suit which is to do you credit, as surely as you will give credit for it to me. Make me a black cloth doublet and trunks, of the finest web. There shall be slashes on the shoulders and at the hips— slashes in which you will insert black satin, Battista, and liberally, lest it should be said of me that I display all my goods to the market. I will have black silk hose, my friend, and fine lace at the neck and wrists. No color, my genius, no color, save one scarlet garter on the left leg to mark the rank of my patron; and a scarlet cap of the present fashion, with a pheasant's feather therein, pointing ever forward, to indicate my sanguine future. Let all this be done with speed, for I have much to perform before we go to Milan, the Cardinal and his secretary. Let me have also a cloak of black velvet with a lining of honorable purple."

"Benissimo, benissimo, dear sir," murmured Battista. "And a sword? And a hanger? Yes?"

"A fig for your andirons!" cried the youth. "You should know well enough that the weapons I work

with are here." He touched his smooth forehead,
and the rebuked Battista hastened to his tapes.
"You have the person of the young David, dear
sir—"

"Ah," said Nello, "let us accept the augury. I
observed that Goliath was very civil."

He dined at the Castiglione Palace, and later in
the day paid La Pernetta a visit of inquiry. This
he did deliberately, feeling that he could afford
himself the luxury. "It is not given to every
young man in the world to play the part of a saviour," he said to himself. "If I stung the soul of
that deplorable, pretty woman by a light verse, I
did as well as Saint Benedict of Norcia, who made
an oration to a dozen of them, and moved no more
than I did. She has been a baggage, and put
great heart into the business. Who knows what she
may become under my handling?"

He found her pensive and bashful; she had been
weeping, but her disorder became her. She was
soft, lax, repentant, and rapturous at once—a
troubled Magdalen, but a Magdalen *pur sang*. He
took her hand, and asked her how she did; he
thanked her warmly for her advocacy; was very
discreet, gentle, dispassionate; he treated her, indeed, as if she were a lady of condition, flattered
and tormented her at once. After premonitory
signs of approaching storm, quivering lip and heaving breast, she suddenly threw herself with passion
at his feet, and clasped his knees.

"Save me, save me, sir," she sobbed. "I am bad,
but would be better. I am a shame before all the
world—an animal—"

"You are wrong," says Nello; "nobody is shameful who feels himself so. Nobody is below his nature who knows it. How did Nature make us men?
To be free, generous, pious! How do we know that?
In this way: what other creature blushes? What
other creature is capable of shame? None. Pernetta,
by your blushes you are saved."

She looked at him, kneeling there before him,
open-mouthed—in wonder. "Are you sent from
God to be my salvation? Are you an angel—a
messenger from Heaven?"

"Who knows?" said he. "I desire your salvation. You are too handsome to be wicked; it is
horrible waste. I would have you—I would have
all women—remember what they are—poets at
once and their poems, painters and their pictures.
Good Heavens, Pernetta, if my song, which dies
with the shutting of the lips, moved you to wholesome tears, how much the more might that lovely
person of yours, quick so long as your blood throbs,
move your sisters to wholesome living! My friend,
there are two things worth doing in this world—
one is to be at peace, the other to declare it. These
are what poets, philosophers, and gracious women
can best accomplish, but few others. So, then, you
and I are in the fair way. What have I gained by
peace of mind? The Cardinal-Regent's friendship,

your friendship, a fine velvet suit, and an Arabic grammar! What may you gain? Your own respect; mine, if you care to have it. Pursue, Pernetta, pursue. To be breathless, to be torn, to flush, to pant, to crush the breast, these are no ways to peace of mind. Forgetfulness is not peace, but assured memory, rather. Adieu—be your own poet, your own poem. Live your music before the world. We shall meet again."

"Oh, talk to me again," she implored. "Touch me—"

"Never," said Nello; "but I will certainly see you again. Adieu, my sister."

"That is a woman of great appetite," he told himself. "I can imagine her becoming a very glutton for frugality one of these days. I will make use of her when I need her—which is not now. Unless I am greatly mistaken she has done with Coän vests and scented ointments and crowns of blown roses. Will she become a saint or a wife? She might be both, with care, especially if she have children."

The rest of his day was spent in his lodging with a lamp. He began the study of Arabic; but first he wrote to his friend Politian.

IV. THE VOW IN THE WOOD

Messer Nello Nelli, the golden-haired little humanist, having been started in life with a patron, experience, and an Arabic grammar, I must go behind the scene to set up some other figures for my

225

stage. It is a common mistake of the story-teller's
—perhaps a generous fault—to suppose the business of our planet suspended while his hero buckles
on his greaves and sets his lance in rest to go out
and conquer it. He ought to remember that this
poor globe is peopled with such heroes, who are all
bent on the same enterprise at her expense, and that
through their clashing together and frequent slaugh-
ter business is actually carried on. Nello Nelli had
been racing for the goal since his fourteenth birth-
day, and had no notion but that he was sure of his
prize. He had heard by report of Simone della
Prova, the Black Dog of Cittadella and hired soldier of Venice, for all North Italy had heard of his
doings; but how was he to guess him a competitor?
What had he to do with condottieri—he the scholar,
poet, saviour of Magdalens, student of Arabic? But
the three women in the mountain-glen who weave
the thread and keep the shears at hand (as he at
least devoutly believed) had another spool to un-
wind, whose yarn was to cross his own. Long ago,
when Nello, at fourteen or so, was kissing the
hand of mature Donna Zenobia, Simone della
Prova, two years older, was kissing the cold lips
of Emilia Fiordispina, a child of scarcely Nello's
age.

La Colombina, they called her, because of her
quiet allure, her sleekness and gentle ways; pet
names she always had—La Madonnina was one of
them, and La Nina another, to be given her in due

time by her mates at the Court of Milan, when the soft dove-habit was to be in danger of soiling, and the soft dove's ways were to be the only shield she could have. But this is to anticipate her story and Nello Nelli's, to whose coincidence we approach by sure stages. The tale finds her now, a growing slip of a girl, with but little trace of that enigmatic, pondering beauty for which she was afterwards made famous by Luini's pencil, in the arms of Simone della Prova, swearing, in response to his fierce adjurations, a little matter of eternal fidelity. They were alone in a myrtle thicket, the hour the tired close of a long August day. The sun, low in the sky, covered them with a cloud of gold-dust, warmed her white gown, and set his buff on fire. Like a pitiful epitome of the Lovers' Hell (the tragedy in small, jigged by puppets) was the scene —dusky fire, clinging figures, straining and despair, kisses which could not satisfy and hearts which could not believe. So straitly he held her, so fierce were his words, if this were matter of life to him, it might be one of death to her.

"Swear, my Emilia, swear! Swear by the Holy Virgin and her tears; by her most bitter tears over the body of her Son, and by all tears of unhappy women, that you love me forever."

"Ah, yes, I swear it—I have sworn it, my love."

"Swear by the True Cross and Him that hung there all day long; by the Five Wounds, the Sponge, and the Spear; by the Crown of Thorns and the threefold writing over the Holy Head! Swear, my Emilia, swear!"

"Oh, dear Simone, dearest love, dearest soul, I swear, I swear! Ah, but you hurt me, dear love. I am frightened—but I shall die of this love!"

Her words, rather than her faint struggle to free herself, moved him to set her free. He did it, however, and stood looking at her as moodily as if she had denied him everything. This made her tremble, and her eyes to search his timidly as if asking for a spark of belief. Simone's arms were folded over the place where she had been; he was scowling as if he knew for certain that, as they held nothing now but emptiness, so she would never fill them again. He was, I take it, of that exorbitant sort which always feels empty. He was a handsome, swarthy, hulking young man, magnificent to look at, built after the antique Roman fashion—cropped in the head, low and square in the brow, stern and square in the chin, with fixed lips and sullen, deep-set eyes. Of his strength there could be no doubt; it ran through him from within to without, and transfigured him. He was flat in the right place— his calves were flat, and his upper arms; so were his brows and the broad stretch from cheek-bone to ear. He looked cruel, but was not so by nature; he was perfectly ruthless, however, and could only think of one thing at a time.

Of the child before him now there is not much more to say. Her beauty, which was not then re-

markable, lay in her hair, in the shape of her head,
in her eyes—dark gray shot with black. She was
growing fast, was thin, was very pale, even to the
lips; but her mouth had begun to take the curve
of the bow which Luini made immortal, and already
she could make the most of herself. Young as she
was she had her troubles before her; for here was
Simone della Prova, after all her oaths, scowling
at her as if she had done him a wrong.

Woman-like, she began to coax him as soon as
she dared, to woo the evil out of him by deference
and caress. She snuggled near, she slipped one
hand into his, she put another on his shoulder,
then stroked his hair. Simone, very full of his
trouble, did not stay her. He found himself listening to the cooing of her voice much against his
will.

"Dear Simone, what will your poor child do
without you? All Peschiera, all the blue lake, all
the islands for her alone! I shall not be able to
look upon the mountains without tears, nor watch
the boats draw in, nor walk in the meadows—you
will be gone! What will become of Emilia?" She
sighed as she lifted his brown hand and stroked her
cheek against it. Simone quivered, but said nothing. She pursued him and her thought—"Ah, my
Simone, never forget me!"

He looked at her then. "Forget you? O
Christ! She blushed, exulted in him, laughed her
glory.

"I would be happy with that cry in my ears.
Listen to what I shall do when you are gone. Every
morning after mass I shall light a candle before the
Madonna del Lago, and pray to her for you and
me. 'Madonna mia,' I shall say, 'keep me for
Simone, the bravest, the noblest, and the best—'"

"Ah," he groaned, "you will have need to pray.
You will grow old praying."

"Wait, wait. Nobody, not even my mother will
know why I do this devotion—nobody, not even
Father Pandolfo. You do not confess your merits,
but only your sins. And this will be a merit, I
am sure. Will it not be, Simone?"

She waited for his assurance, but did not get it.
Simone was fighting his despair—very real to him
at this hour. Emilia leaned to him, and took his
chin in her little white hand. La Colombina, they
called her later, when she was wiser but not more
wheedling than now. Her voice was very low and
calling; it sounded hurt, it appealed.

"Must it be to-morrow, dear one? Can we not
have to-morrow—the feast of the Assunta? We
could begin my devotion together."

"Pooh," said Simone, his face to the sky, "pooh,
devotions! There will be no time for such things.
I must be in the saddle with the light. You know
that I must go."

"To fight for the Republic!"

Simone squared his jaw, and took some bitter
comfort from the fact that he was to fight against

the party of his beloved—his cruel, about-to-be-faithless beloved. "To fight against your Milan, at least."

"You care against whom you fight? Not on whose account? You hate many, love but one?"

He looked down at her with those storm-wrecked eyes of his. She knew what he was going to say, and thrilled to know it coming. He took her in his arms again.

"I love nobody but you—nobody. Why should I love the Republic? I am no Venetian, *Deo gratias!* It is true that they have always been friends of my house, and my house of them—but what of that? I fight because I have my way to make. Love? It is you I love—you—you." He sealed his words upon her lips. "Dearest Simone, you are my lover indeed," sighed the little Emilia.

The sun was down, it began to grow dusk all at once. Emilia shivered and longed suddenly to be alone. She was tired to death. "They will come to look for me; I must go," she pleaded.

"Listen first—then you shall go." She clung to him, obedient to the call, looking up into his hard face. Her two imploring hands were on his breast. But he put her away, made her stand alone and in front of him. It became rather like a lecture.

"I love you so cruelly that, in truth, my heart seems to me afire. I know not whether I am to live or die in the fighting, but this I know well, that I had sooner die believing you true than live on in

231

the state I see ahead. I have a mind to kill you myself where you stand—that you might die with no other kisses on your lips than mine, and no other name but mine upon your tongue. That would be the only certainty, I do believe. You are a child; you have no strength, as men have, no purpose, no will of your own. You will be easy to bend this way or that way. They will seek to betroth you, to marry you here or there—by Heaven, they will be at you day after day. Now, I tell you, Emilia, that, as I shall be unutterably true, look at no women, think of none but you, so I shall expect of you. Is that too much? If I, a man, can do that, cannot you? A man's nature is different from a woman's—it does more, it asks and needs more. Why, I am setting myself an enormous task in this pledge. If I prove false—but let us not talk of absurdities. If you prove false, Emilia, I shall kill you. Certainly I shall kill you. It would be just. God would demand it. Is it not so?"

"Yes, Simone, it would be just." She looked deplorable, drooping there before him, and felt as though she had been beaten. Such a lover was a glory—but ah! he was terrible in this mood.

"And now we must part, my child, my girl, my dove—" He tried to hold himself sternly, and might have succeeded if he could have kept her at a distance. But at the first break in his voice her own sorrow broke over her like a wave. She was in his arms again, sobbing her fear, her abandonment, imploring him not to leave her, not to love her so, not to frighten her, to love her more. This pure tide of her misery knocked out his guard: two children, they clung and kissed together, tearing the very heart out of passion. "My soul, my white dove. Let no one call thee Colombina but me!" She swore him that also. Was there anything she would not have given him then?

From beyond the trees, up from the darkling sheeted lake came the stroke of a bell. One by one the belfries of Peschiera took up the cry. They started apart. Emilia held her side. "Oh, I must go," she said, brokenly; but "Not yet," said Simone, "come to me." This was more than she could bear—she fell on her knees, hid her face, and wept unfeignedly. She frightened and humbled him; he dared not touch her. At the last deep clangor of the bell she rose, and slipped guiltily through the trees. As for Simone, he cried unto God, not with his voice, and threw himself face to the ground. There the night dews found him, there the stars.

VI. The Lover and the Lass

What the parents of this Colombina were about to allow such desperate heart-probings as I have had to relate can be easily explained. They knew nothing about them, and were too hungry to inquire. Spinello Fiordispina was the lord of a tower and a few leagues about it, including a strip of the shore of Garda. In his dark old stronghold down

there he maintained himself and Monna Lucia, his
wife, his two old sisters, his Colombina, and some
twenty servants, on what he could exact from the
fishermen of the place. That, in fact, was very
little; whence it arose that care for the bodies of
all these people usurped the rights of their more
subtle needs. It was literally a matter of food
sometimes. His family was ancient, the towers
and poor lands about them represented what had
once been a great fief of the Empire; and just in
the same way he himself was a ruin. He had been
a notable warrior in his day, warring in Tuscany,
Umbria, on the March, here and anywhere with old
Sforza-Attendolo, founder of the robber-house of
Milan. When that renegade shepherd, and king of
men, went down in the flood, whither he had swept
his enemy's horse, Spinello found that he was too
old to stomach the new Sforza—or the new Sforza
may have found himself too young. At any rate,
Spinello was squeamish; he knew he was a good
man still, but doubted he was getting past his work.
He was painfully sensitive, sniffed about for offences
where none were, and thought that he could detect
an odor. He withdrew himself, his dignity, and
his spearmen, to Garda, and was chagrined to find
that the affairs of Milan continued to prosper.
This embittered, while it stiffened him. It also
caused him to be exceedingly hungry.

His own affairs certainly did not prosper. His
spearmen ate up every green thing. He had to

disband them, to sell land, to see some slip from him without price asked or offered. At the time I am now reporting his household was, as I have put it—three old ladies, Colombina, twenty servants, himself, and Simone della Prova—rueful, reckoning for the Lord of a tower, a Fiordispina, and a knight of the Empire.

What was this shrunken gentleman doing with a Simone della Prova in his household? It is to be remembered that he was a great, as well as a shrunken gentleman, and the holder still of fine old traditions of warfare. None knew this better than another battered warrior, Malipiero della Prova, lord of Cittadella, that red citadel within turreted walls which may still be seen by the traveller much as it was in an earlier day. Della Prova had always taken the other side—he was too near Venice to do otherwise, just as Fiordispina was too near Milan; but though they had dealt each other hard knocks, they had no less mutual esteem—indeed, they had more. It was in an interval of peace that the old Venetian sent his boy, Simone, to Garda to learn the arts of knighthood from a man who had proved his science to Cittadella's detriment. And while Simone learned those arts, he learned others, as we have seen.

That young Simone, swarthy in blood as in hue, a fighter by inheritance, proved an unconscionable lover. It was an affair of a moment; the child Emilia, whose gravity made her look older than

her little tale of years could warrant—those pondering eyes of hers, that sweet, slow smile, the pallor
and tired grace she had even then—stung him
sharply. Instantly he stormed the enemy, stormed,
fired, and had her at discretion. She had no time
to judge, no leisure to choose, no choice, no voice.
He assumed the position of her lover before she
knew that she loved. She never did really love.
She was gentle, she was timid, greatly flattered by
the homage of this wild, scowling youth; she was a
girl, she was twelve years old, she was lonely—and
what more is there to say? She was a very sweet-
tempered, meek-mannered child, who could never
refuse anything to any one. When Simone came
spurring up to storm her with cries to surrender,
she lowered the flag at once. The donjon was his,
and he sat down as tyrant of the poor little city.
There were sweets for the conquered, of course.
It is sweet to dispense one's bounties, and sweet
to be needed. She had cool, soft hands. Simone
brought her headaches to be cured, fits of the sulks,
fevers to be soothed, horrible suspicions to be explained away. He scolded her, threatened her, was
madly and unreasonably jealous—he thought that
no girl who was loved should kiss her parents'
hands; and as for Father Pandolfo, the old priest,
O horrible! why, she owned that she loved him!
She suffered more than can be said, but she never
dreamed of rebellion; and it's not to be denied that
she had hours when her glorious estate as the be-

loved of so strenuous a youth seemed almost more than she could bear. She responded wonderfully to all his moods; she was penitent, ardent, passionate, thoughtful, virginal as he willed her. Of course he learned to play upon her as upon an instrument, and got the most piercing, whispering, or wailing music from her that ever you heard. For two years he scorched himself and drained her thus; then came the summons to arms: Mantua and Milan at war with Venice; he must join his father in the cause of the Republic. The children were torn apart; Simone scoured away, riding on a storm-cloud of his own brewing. Her last sight of him had been with his sword in his hand, threatening her from his horse, daring her to forget him, daring her to let some other mouth her name; and for weeks afterwards the poor girl sat dry-eyed in the myrtle woods, remembering her hero; or prayed without end before the Madonna del Lago; lit up little candles in secret; crisped her little hands; held her little foolish heart, and wondered sadly why it did not ache; looked about her askance, half in panic, half in awe, at a new world which could be so dispassionate, or at daily customs which could dare go on while Simone was so far and she so forlorn.

She was wretched that she could not be more wretched; her conscience tormented her as cruelly as Simone had ever done. For six months she dragged herself about, white and weak, hollow-

eyed, listless, and morose. Then the fever spent
itself; she heard nothing; Simone was no penman.
She still believed herself wretched, still lighted little candles and prayed to the Madonna—the ritual
itself was her best comforter. The snow came
down, Garda had a rim of ice; the days crept out,
the almonds flowered; there were orchids and
fritillaries in the water-meadows, cyclamen in the
woods. Spring came laughing into Lombardy with
the sound of the shepherd's pipe; and Emilia, turned fourteen, began to peer about for columbines,
her own flower. The year went peacefully round;
no word from Simone, no rumor of him, made all
the difference to the girl. Behold Emilia at fifteen,
a maiden grown—and behold her if you can as
Luini painted her, of womanly parts and wisdom
so early compact, with the considering eyes and
heavy eyelids of a beautiful, much-courted woman,
the mysterious smile of a woman with secrets which
amuse her, but the curves and tender bloom of a
girl to make her the more dangerous. Luini's picture, now at St. Petersburg, calls her La Colombina,
and shows her in a dress of loose brocade, caught
at the bosom by a jewel, but leaving one breast
bare, with a hand holding jasmine in her lap, the
other delicately lifting for contemplation the flower,
her namesake. Her hair is crisped and plaited
closely, to show the shape of her head; it is brought
below and round the ears. It represents Emilia
at twenty; she had lovers then and to spare, and

less matter for pleasant thought than for patience
to be got out of them. It is a more mature Emilia
than we can yet consider, but all the charms so
ripely there were in bud at this earlier age. She
was sleek at fifteen, dainty in movement, dainty in
pose, deliberate in speech, witty when she chose,
demurely sharp in reply without being malicious.
She was very kind, and in her ways showed it; her
hands besought your patience, her head was meekly
disposed; she had quick, affectionate motions; wom-
en always liked her, and without meaning it she
had a fatal charm for men. Much as she was in
flower at twenty, such she was in bud at fifteen,
when, in a straight silk gown of white and red, with
a necklace of pearls and a fillet of silver daisies for
her hair, with a deep-red cloak and hood of the
same for her journey, she kissed her parents and
two old aunts, and rode brightly forth into the
world to begin her adventures. She was for the
Court of Milan, to be maid of honor to the Duchess
Bianca. It was nearly three years since she had
watched Simone ride away to the wars and had
been threatened by the gleaming of his sword. She
had heard nothing of him since, and his name, if
ever mentioned in talk, caused her no distress.
That day of her going there had been no time to
light a candle before the Madonna del Lago. It
had often happened so before, but never before had
she forgotten the omission. She remembered it at
Brescia where they baited the horses. The stab

was momentary. And at Milan I must leave her with this remark, that among the many things she learned there which a girl needed or needed not to know, the lighting of a votive taper to keep memory green was not one. It had, indeed, been nearer her desire more than once to propitiate the shrouded altars of the Gods of Silence and Oblivion.

But as for Simone della Prova, he had forgotten nothing. He was not of the kind that forgets. The constant lover, it may be, is the man that most loves himself, and cannot bear that the least speck should mar the adorable surface. Simone would have died a hundred deaths sooner than face the thought that he could forget or be forgotten— but Emilia would have died first. Clinging to his faith in her, which was really part of his faith in himself, he performed what was required of him by his nature—sweated, bled, fought, drilled, and killed men. There was a league against Venice in those days: Sforza of Milan, Bentivoglio of Bologna, Gonzaga of Mantua, joining forces, worked to stem back the Republic within her marshy lagoons. On the side of Venice was young Simone, with his Cittadella as an outpost to the North. The war went, as Italian wars always did, with varying fortunes, and more attention to the moves of the game than its objects; but there was enough blood-shedding to show young Della Prova as a master. With two hundred horsemen behind him—young men raised and dragooned by himself—he scoured the Southern

country, killing, burning, pillaging. He excelled
in avoiding dangers and countering upon the dangerous. On one occasion, notably, he escaped, by
hard riding, a large body of Milanese horse sent from
Vicenza to cut him off, crossed the Euganeans by
night, and swept down upon the Mantuan camp at
Legnago in the plain before sunrise. In that encounter, though he spared no one in his path, he
had his horse killed under him. Wounded in the
shoulder, half a dozen of his men bore him off the
field under the very eyes of Cardinal Guido Gonzaga, the warrior-priest of Mantua. That great
man, however, forbade any pursuit of a youngster
so heroic. "No, no," he said, "let him live to
wear the spurs he has won from us. Who is the
young man?"

They told him it was Simone della Prova, called
the Black Dog of Cittadella, and that the Devil
was his friend.

"A useful ally," said the Cardinal. "Where did
he learn arms?"

"His father, my lord, old Malipiero, was a great
leader; but this fellow was for two years with Messer
Spinello Fiordispina of Garda, who was a greater."

"Certainly he was," said the Cardinal; "nobody
knows it better than I do. I remember him in
Calabria. It is a noble blend that should come
out of those two old tigers. I must keep an eye
upon Master Simone—truly, a promising youth."

When Simone's father died, and he reigned instead of him as Lord of Cittadella, the Cardinal fixed two eyes upon him instead of one. He thought he saw a way of ending the weary war.

VII. THE BLACK DOG OF CITTADELLA

About a month after his patronage of Nello, so benevolently bestowed and happily accepted—in September—with a retinue of not more than fifty horse, Cardinal Gonzaga started on a mission; indeed he started upon two. Nello, very trim and very gay—seeming to be the more resplendently in health for his black habit—rode by his side, and received his confidences. Some half-dozen chaplains, cassocked and big-hatted on mules, who were in the next rank, carried with them all the signs of churchmanship which His Eminence chose to display; the Cardinal himself rode out as a warrior, resplendent in arms.

"A man of my rank," he observed, "keeps his mind's eye for Heaven, but with his bodily organs directs the world. God is not to be mocked by the ill-ordering of that; and Mantua with the dominions thereof are my immediate concern. We have a very delicate task to perform, my Nello, with which I regret to say the Church has little to do."

He outlined the case for his young friend's consideration. Mantua was at war with Venice—Mantua and Milan in league. Milan was extremely necessary to Mantua, the big to the little; but it was by no means so clear that the converse could be maintained. Sforza, in fact, was languid; he did not prosecute the war as he had promised; he was half minded to make peace. If he did that Venice might swallow up Mantua. The Cardinal's business, therefore, was to make friends elsewhere in case of need, but by no means to give up hopes of Sforza. He intended for Milan to arrange a marriage between his niece Dorotea and Sforza's heir, Galeazzo Maria; but first of all he was going to Cittadella. Did Nello know why? Nello did not.

"Did you ever hear," asked the Cardinal, "of the Captain of Cittadella?" Nello nodded.

"Of Simone della Prova—the Black Dog, as they call him? Eminence, yes. I heard of him when I was in Padua. He was a fighting youth—a very demon of the blood and dust. But he is for Venice —it is an old alliance. Men used to say that he learned warfare of Milan, to use it against them. He was the idol of Padua in my day, much trusted by the Republic. All women were in love with him, if for no better reason than that he would never look at one of them. Hippolytus, the son of Theseus, was not more chaste than he."

"We shall see, we shall see," said the Cardinal. "I am going to pay him a visit: so much has been arranged. He and I have met once before—in the field. It was at Legnago, where he made a dawn attack upon our camp and gave us a couple of hours' exquisite anxiety. We rallied, however, and beat

him off. The fellow was wounded; I might have
had him, and he knew it. But I admired him, and
let them carry him off—and he knew that also. I
believe he hated me for it; but I cannot think him
without a bottom of generosity. It is for you and
me to tempt that out of him, my Nello. Tell me
something more of his habits. Women, you say,
made no appeal to him?"

"I think—none at all. He seemed to be proof.
Preoccupation may account for that."

"In what way, my friend?"

"A man of that sort, Eminence—an unreason-
ing, furious man—is generally chaste because he is
a lover. It may be of a woman, it may be of himself, it may be of warfare or statesmanship, or of
the Blessed Virgin. It may even be of virtue;
but this is rare in a captain of horse. As a rule, I
should say that the love of women is a solace to
every man of action who does not happen to be
the lover of one woman in particular—or of himself."

"I think you may be right. Indeed, that is how
I have found it. But now—was our man quarrelsome?"

"He was, Eminence."

"Ruthless?"

"I understood it."

"Revengeful?"

"Bitterly."

"Gluttonous?"

The Love Chase

"A hearty eater, I think."

"A wine-bibber?"

"I never heard it."

"Then you consider—?"

"I consider that this man scorns all women born for the sake of one. Her, I think, he does not love for the sake of her beauty or virtue so much as because she is his. I conceive him perfectly. He is like a great beast of the desert who sets his paw upon some prey, not to adjust it for his meal, but to mark it for his property. His possession of the thing thereafter becomes essential to his comfort, because to lose it would be to lessen his value in his own eyes."

"All this is very acute," said the Cardinal, "but I do not see—"

"Eminence," replied Nello, "this Simone was trained in the castle of Spinello Fiordispina, an old Milanese soldier. I think it very possible that he is tied body and soul to the slim waist of some Lombard girl." Nello's prescience, no doubt, was a thing of calculation. He knew very well, by report, that Simone considered himself betrothed. But the Cardinal evidently had *not* known it. Our young friend took his profit where he found it.

So talking, they went their way through the burnt gardens and by the dusty roads of the Venetian March. They reached Vicenza, at a push, by night — or as near it as was prudent to go. Next morning the Cardinal was up and stamping

245

in the court-yard while Nello was rubbing his eyes.

"We must go carefully to-day," said master to man. "I don't anticipate any treachery from our friend, but it is quite as well to be on the safe side. We will place an ambush at Sampietro and keep in touch with them. You and I, with twenty spears, will push on to Cittadella."

The Cardinal was right—there was no treachery. The gates of Cittadella, a grim little fortress town, spiked and towered, were wide open; the Mantuans were received with elaborate respect. The Prefect of the city, the Bishop and his Chapter, stood before the citadel; the keys were presented on a dish, taken by the Cardinal, and punctiliously returned to their former keeping. The visitors rode into the piazza, dismounted there, entered the Cathedral church, and heard a solemn mass. The Lord of Cittadella, the Lord Simone della Prova, was expected momently from a raid; meantime the citizens hoped that His Eminence would break his fast in the Vescovado hard by. The retinue would be entertained at the public charge in the court-yard of the Palazzo del Governo. The Cardinal, very urbane, very much the great bow unstrung, rubbed his gross hands and smiled his thanks.

At the stroke of noon hoarse cheering by the gates announced the coming of Simone. The Cardinal went out to the balcony of the Vescovado to watch him in.

The Love Chase

"Now, now, if I am not mistaken, I shall have something to show you," he said, eagerly, flicking his fingers together, whetting his lips like a child at a play. Nello, to whom a man-at-arms was but a clothes-peg, or perhaps a stand for ironmongery, was amused. But the Cardinal, more than half a soldier, had an unaffected delight in the display; his eye caught the first glimmer of spears above the massed heads in the piazza.

"Here is the young wolf of the Veneto," said he aloud, "homing to his lair — and with booty between his paws, by the Cross!" It is true, there were prisoners—allies of the Cardinal's, no doubt. But he was here incognito.

The cavalry came jingling by at a quick walking pace, three hundred of them, young men all. As they reached the piazza they opened out and took the sides of the square, so as to hold back the people with a hedge of arms. The enclosed space was bare, save for three or four officials, a sinister figure in red, and the huge gallows, which (it was understood) was never taken down, and very seldom out of exercise in these days.

If Nello noticed this gloomy apparatus the Cardinal did not. His thoughts were centred upon the troops. Their body-clothes were red and yellow, their armor blue steel; upon the pensels of their spears they showed within a bordure the badge of Simone della Prova of Cittadella—a black dog on a white field. All rode black horses, of which they

seemed to be parts; it was truly as if a herd of cen-
taurs had been drilled to obedience. Behind them
came, on foot, a sorry crew of chained prisoners,
the scouring of some burned village—men, women,
children, all white with dust, all limping footsore,
bound neck to neck. Mothers some, and some to
be so soon; bearded men, and young boys with
eyes not yet too tired to be incurious—they had
no special guard set on them but their chains.
Last of all, riding alone, driving this rout of wild
creatures and their prey, armed completely in
black steel, bareheaded and scowling, came the
Black Dog of Cittadella himself—Simone, a sullen
young God of War. He took not the smallest
notice of the people's acclamation—they cried him
"Cane! Cane! Evviva Simone!" — nor of the
grouped grandees on the Bishop's balcony; the
Cardinal of Mantua was nothing to him at this
moment of still triumph; Nello was aghast at such
pride. He sat his horse as if man and beast were
carved out of one block; his face was nearly as
black as his look, burned deep by the sun; he held
his head high, but had lowered eyelids—scorn,
not modesty, bent them. The only hint of attention to living thing which he gave was to his horse.
Once he leaned over the crest and seemed to speak
in the beast's ear. The Cardinal noticed that the
flanks had been fiercely spurred; but he had not
seen the sudden prick of the ears with which the
fine animal heard his master's whisper. This Nello

did see, and it gave him food for thought. The
day was before him when he was to know Simone
and his horse to fatal purpose. When the Cardinal,
therefore, slapped his thigh, and said aloud, "By
the eyes of God, this is a great captain!" his secretary was bound to agree with him, though unwillingly. "I pity from my soul the man or woman
who is in the power of this Dog," thought he. "This
is a wild beast, dowered by Heaven, for some in-
scrutable reason, with the superior rapacity of a
man." The little humanist was faced like a cherub,
but he could criticise with the Assessing Angel.

What followed justified his reason, while it drove
him back to unreason. It made a child of Nello
again—frightened him, appalled him, made him
furious, as children are when they have been frightened. In a breathless silence—a silence from vic-
tims and witnesses alike—the Black Dog hanged
every one of his prisoners. Nello's breast began to
heave at this terrible sight; he could hardly stand,
yet could not keep his eyes from seeing. And while
his heart wailed, his mind must needs admire the
awful elements of the tragedy; the young Condottiere
out there in the empty space, motionless on his
black horse, the figure of a dream; the silent haste
of the executioner, the despairing silence of the
butchered (when scarcely a boy cried above a
whimper); the hush over all the people. Nello clenched his teeth, clenched his hands, gripped the ground
with his toes. "Ah, fiend of hell! Ah, blockish

devil! Ah, smear upon the day's face!'' Tears of impotent rage scalded his young eyes.

The Cardinal was puzzled, yet profoundly interested. "I set no limits to the scope of this fine young man," he said to Nello. "For aught that I can see he may be Doge of Venice or Patriarch of Christendom, if he have a mind for such trifles! He may be imperial Cæsar—what is to stay him? Not I, you may say. Wait, wait. I am a man also."

"But—but—oh, Eminence! he has hanged the women and boys!" Nello was sobbing.

"Curious, curious, curious!" said the Cardinal.

VIII. NELLO AS RECORDER

When the meeting took place the Cardinal's curiosity was gratified. The Black Dog received his august visitor in the Palazzo del Governo, bowed stiffly, kissed with perfunctory stiffness the ringed hand, then invited His Eminence into the Council Chamber. The Cardinal entered, followed by Nello and his letter-bag; Simone walked in after them, alone, and deliberately shut and locked the door. No doubt the Cardinal took a quicker breath; but the other, without lifting his eyes, handed the key to Nello.

"Keep it," he said shortly. "We use no treachery in Cittadella; but you need not know that."

Nello took it in silence and dropped it on the table. He had such a loathing of the man at this time that he could hardly hold a thing polluted by his touch. Was it not drenched in blood—the blood of the poor?

The Cardinal, bursting with wonder, began with a question, which he begged his young friend to answer with a soldier's frankness. Why had it been necessary to hang the prisoners? Simone looked him fully in the face.

"That question can be easily answered," he said. "Your Eminence is here to deal with a man of whom you know little. I thought it proper that Your Eminence should know more." The Cardinal was delighted, rose, held out his hand.

"I suspected it! A rare stroke! Young sir, we will shake hands, if you please. I am face to face with a plain bargainer. Trust me now, as you deal with me, so I with you." Nello felt himself blush to the roots of his hair. O Shades of Academe! O fading, classic Porch! O greensward, where the Muses dance enlaced! Where were ye, O clean-breathed groves? To such men as these two traffickers of souls poor tarnished Pernetta were a wholesome lass.

They settled to business, the Cardinal very large and suave—Simone keen, quiet, and stiff as a rod—Nello behind them, covering his eyes with his hand. The Cardinal praised the enthusiasm of the populace, who knew their master and the beneficent severity of his rod; the other shrugged ever so slightly, to show his contempt of the populace. The appearance and discipline of the troops came next in review—"as clean a company of horse as I have seen since I served with Fortebraccio in Calabria," said the Cardinal with conviction. Simone never blinked an eyelid. He was waiting. But so was his opponent.

"You will remember," the Cardinal went on, steadfastly urbane, "that I have reason to know something of their valor. We have met in the field, Simone."

"I remember it very well," replied the young man. "I drove you out of Legnago."

The Cardinal, who had deliberately provoked this, and had been waiting for it, suddenly changed his manner and his voice with it. His eyes grew narrow and hard; his smile remained, but had stiffened.

"I think you should remember it indeed. You were wounded in the groin, your shoulder was broken under your horse, I think?"

Simone nodded. "It is true."

"You were surrounded by men—by the enemy —by men in red and white."

Simone's eyes flashed, but he said nothing.

"But you were not made prisoner," said the Cardinal.

The youth started up, red in the face. "No, by the splendor of God, I was not."

The Cardinal rose in his turn, and towered above the other. Nello was struck by the stern strength latent in his bulk.

"I will tell you, Simone," he said, "why you

252

were not taken in chains to Mantua, why you were
not treated, it may be, as you treated those dazed
wretches this day. It was because I called my
men off. It was because I saw stuff in your hot
head too good for a short rope and seven-foot post.
You owe your life, your generalship, your gallows,
and your brave displays to my clemency. Now,
sir, are you disposed to treat a Prince of the Church
and a Gonzaga with civility?"

The whole thing had been finely done, and Nello
saw that it was to be successful. Simone tried
bluster, and looked as if he might try worse. He
looked, for that matter, murderous, and for some
two minutes or more the issue may have been in
doubt. But Nello had no need to snatch at the
key. The Cardinal was superb, plainly the greater
man; Simone, with all the rage which burned in
his deep-set eyes, could not hold out beyond that
brace of minutes. He mumbled some kind of
apology—a soldier's life, distance from courts, etc.
—and pointed to the chairs, not yet cold. The Cardinal, quite easy after his little triumph, sat down
at once, crossed his leg, and took up the discourse
as if nothing had disturbed it.

"I have heard," he said, "of the death of Malipiero, your father, and regret the fact, though not
the manner of the fact. To die of a sword, with a
sword in his hand, was to die as he had lived, as
you doubtless hope to die. It was a brave end to
a brave chain of events."

The storm had not yet cleared; but the young man showed some consciousness of the honor done to his father.

"With such an example before us," continued Gonzaga, "I could not hesitate for a moment to make the suggestion I make now, this—namely, that you should throw the weight of Cittadella and your array into the scale against the Republic. You know Mantua, Simone, and whether it can be a generous foe. Judge from that what sort of a friend it may prove. You know Milan, too—"

Simone said fiercely, as if, Nello thought, he felt himself being pushed against the wall, "You should have asked my father whether his house loved Milan."

"On the contrary," said the Cardinal, "I prefer to ask his son. You, at least, know something of Milan. You studied arms under Spinello Fiordispina, an old ally of that duchy." He watched his man, and Nello, watching too, saw the telltale flame kindle in eyes and dusky cheeks. He knew the meaning of that. Simone, it seemed, could not trust himself to speak. His lips moved, fashioned a word—one word; but neither of his companions could read it. Certainly, however, a shot had gone home.

"If then," said the Cardinal, "you can think kindly of Fiordispina, you can hardly refuse merit in Fiordispina's allies, patrons, friends—the Duke of Milan, the Marquess of Mantua. Believe me,

they are solid men, with solid benefits to confer on
those who love them, however late in the day. I
am not inviting you to turn your coat at a venture. I am inviting you to fight with Spinello
Fiordispina, your old friend—and mine." After a
pause he added, "I am now going to Milan."

It was deeply interesting to Nello now to see
Simone struggling against unexpected odds. At the
name of Fiordispina he had watched him fire, at
that of Milan he saw him blench, as though in the
one he exulted, but feared the other. What was
the connection? What was the missed clue?
Here was the blood-botched despot morally on his
knees at the mere name of Milan.

"Milan," Simone stammered—he had lost his
breath—"you go to Milan! You will be in Milan
in a day—two days?"

"That is my intention," said the Cardinal, blandly. "Can I do you a service there?"

Simone was tearing at himself, to get his breast-
plate away. He broke the straps of the gorget,
wrenched the mail apart, threw it with a clatter on
the flags. He fumbled in his leather doublet, his
eyes all alight, his breath most short. Flushing
like any boy, he produced a something from his
bosom, a something which he kept smothered in
his fist, and stood with it before the Cardinal. He
stared—his words came in jerks. "All I have is in
Milan—at this hour—four years it has been there
—without a word—without a sign. What I have

suffered — perdition!" He stopped suddenly as if he had betrayed himself—then, "No, no, I must speak—now, at last," he grumbled to himself.

He addressed the Cardinal. "If you go to Milan, Eminence, you may serve me if you will. Nay, I will say this much, that without such service I shall have nothing to say to these proposals of yours."

"Be sure of me, Simone, my friend. In what can I serve you?"

"There is at Milan—in the service of Bianca the Duchess—entrusting her honor and extreme youth —there is, I say—Pest!" he cried, striking his forehead, "I am no speaker of such things."

"There is at Milan—?" said the Cardinal.

"There is a lady there, Eminence, a lady very young, Madonna Emilia Fiordispina—maid of honor to the Duchess Bianca. She is betrothed to me. If Your Eminence think fit to reward me service for service—"

"It shall be my particular care, Simone," said the Cardinal, by no means exhibiting the amusement he felt. "Having sought and found her, my friend —assume both in my favor—what am I to do with her?"

Simone held out in the palm of his hand a thin gold ring—an affair of a twisted wire, having a blue jewel in a loop.

"You will say, my lord, that you are from the Veneto, bearing this token—but name no names.

Much hangs on this. She will take it, smiling a
little, a little lifting her eyebrows, coloring ever so
faintly, for she is by nature pale." He closed his
eyes here, and seemed as if dreaming. "She will
ask Your Eminence from whom is this token, and
to what intent. You will say, 'It is thus con-
signed: To La Colombina, from him who only knows
that name.' That is all—my name need not be
mentioned; she will not have forgotten it.' That
title, which is hers by right, for she certainly par-
takes of the nature of the dove, will be sufficient
reminder. None knows it but she and I; none has
used it, I am certain of it. There is the utmost
prayer I have to make of Your Highness. I shall
consider your attention to it a friendly act. The
rest may be a matter of arrangement. If terms
are proposed, I will consider them—as is open to
me: I am by no means bound. Should they approve
themselves, in consideration of your service performed, I shall be prepared to become the friend
of Mantua."

The Cardinal bestowed the ring in his bosom.
"You will be friend of both Milan and Mantua,"
he corrected.

"Of Mantua, Lord Cardinal," said Simone, steadily, and Nello marked that. Gonzaga shrugged.

"As you will. I cannot refuse the courtesy you
do my house. Now, shall we get some of this into
writing?"

"All of it, as you choose," said Simone, holding up his head. Nello was beckoned into action.

The youth advanced with his portfolio to the table, and sat mending the head of a pen, ready with a cool head, though his heart was on fire. Boyish, or even girlish, as he looked beside these two, with his face like a flower and his head in a cloud of gold, the slim and buoyant creature was as tense as a bowstring, and could have strangled Simone by the mere strength of his hatred. Hatred! The word is thin, and what it implies was worn thin. He had hated him once for what he had done—his detestable, cold murdering; now he loathed him for what he was and stood to be, as one abhors a dusty snake. A snake he thought him, rather than a dog—flat-headed, slit-eyed, adust, staring into stupor a girl with the neck and breast of a dove. La Colombina—poor dove, indeed, under this freezing spell! If Nello could have killed anything born, he could have killed Simone, and gone singing to Hell for it. Beside him, in his Cardinal, he saw an amateur of policy, who could admire the intricate interworkings of brain and brain, and delight in the force of villain as well as hero. This was, he would argue, a lawful state of the soul. And indeed the greater strength and longer calculation of this fine Gonzaga had been admirably displayed. But he was too righteously shocked with the Condottiere to be obsequious. While he was waiting for the word—his pen adjusted—he looked at him with

grave, undisguised rebuke. Simone's scornful eyelids were intolerable; Nello's not once blinked before them. In fact he looked too shrewdly and too
long to please the other.

"You should know me by now, Master Scribe,"
said Simone with a scowl.

"Not yet, not yet," Nello replied.

"You shall know this much of me at once, that
this is not a cabinet of curiosities, nor I here to be
valued."

Nello looked to his paper. "So much," he said,
"you have demonstrated." No more was said between them.

Many and diverse were the comments of Cardinal
Gonzaga as, with Nello by his side, he pursued the
road to Milan. He congratulated his secretary
highly upon his remarkable prescience. "To have
touched the soft spot in that steel-trap before you
set eyes on him!" he crowed. "Confess now, my
Nello, that I know something of men. That was
a happy day for me when you went into the Gabbia.
Mehercle! but you read your Simone like a church-
book. Now we must see what you can do with
women. My notion is that Monna Colombina will
receive her token with mixed feelings. It is not
every young woman who would wish to be fuel to
such a roaring fire as our friend there."

"Our knowledge of women," said Nello, senten-
tiously, "is apt to be prejudiced by our desire to
know them. The fancy imposes a portrait before-

hand, from which it does not willingly depart. I feel very sure what sort of a lady we shall find La Colombina to be, and for that reason beg you not to prove me."

He had indeed made a picture for himself. "Very young—rather pale—partaking the nature of a dove." A fair thought—a fair soul in a delicate body—and, O God, under the paw of the Black Dog! "Here," he considered, "are the elements of a tragic scene, which I pray Heaven may not move across my vision. Love might ruin me." And with all his horror and hatred of Simone, he was forced to allow a sense of reality in the fierce youth. The man knew what he wanted and how to get it.

Busy as he was, forecasting and reflecting, he found time to answer a letter which he received at Treviglio from La Pernetta. The penitent fair also, it seemed, knew what she wanted; she wrote in an ecstasy of renunciation:

"Excellent Messer Nello, my unique tutor," she said, "I let you have this news of me because I desire you to praise me. I have wrung the necks of my parrots, and sold my black slave-boy Toffolo. I go to Mass every day and fast three days in the week. I have begun the study of Latin, and find it most severe. These things I do that I may attain to some power over myself, hoping that I may find approval in your eyes. I am well in health, and keep no company. I drink only water. It was truly said by you that the pleasures of denial are more curiously sweet than those of gratification. I am often hungry, but get happy dreams thereby. I kiss your hands.

"La Pernetta."

The Love Chase

To this he replied very shortly:

"Madonna, I rejoice in your account of yourself. Socrates sacrificed a cock to Æsculapius, you parrots—to the same end. Yet I would warn you against enthusiasm. It is better to feast upon dainties than to grow lean on visions. It is not well to neglect the care of the body, for that is a temple made by the hands of God, and always fair whether it enshrine a saint or a demon. Beware of exaltation. As to water-drinking, Epictetus says it is not matter for self-flattery. Do it, saith he, unto yourself, and not unto the world. 'And do not,' he adds, 'embrace the statues; but some time, when you are exceedingly thirsty, take a mouthful of cold water, and spit it out, and say nothing about it.'

"Madonna, keep your health and the remembrance of my desire to serve you.

"ANGELUS DE ANGELIS, Secretarius."

IX. THE PASSIONATE QUEST

True to his conceptions of himself as a statesman, it was no emblazoned captain of armed men who entered the Porta Venezia of Milan that hour before noon, but a vested Cardinal-Legate in cope and mitre, borne in a great swaying chair, with cross-bearer and singing men, with hat-bearer and ring-bearer, with torches and silver trumpets— with all the sanction of the Vatican on his surroundings, and all the rune of the Gospel graven on his abstracted face. Cardinal Guido, indeed, as he fully intended, looked superb; strong as a saint and impassive as an image of Cæsar. Sforza on horseback with his suite, in gilded armor, the ducal sword erect before him, found a stiffer than himself in this vacant-eyed effigy, who blessed the

261

people as he swayed above them, and passing the
Duke without a sign, and the balconied ladies
without a hint of knowledge, was carried forward
to the steps of the Cathedral, and received there,
still sitting enthroned, the homage of the Archbishop and the Chapter. It was most impressive,
and most politic, but it had been learned on the
journey. Just as in little Cittadella the tyrant of
the town had kept the Prince of Mantua waiting,
so now Cardinal Gonzaga, in towered Milan, taught
Duke Francesco Sforza his place. Nello smiled to
know it.

"Policy, policy!" he said to himself, chuckling;
"but my master is a greater man than I thought
him, since he is not above learning a lesson from
the very man whom he has recently taught one.
Now which of these flowering bosoms, I wonder,
holds the Colombine heart?" If the Cardinal saw
no ladies, Nello saw many. They were all beautiful—so much so that he swore them all virtuous.
From one glancing head to another his eye roved
for what he had pictured La Colombina to be. In
front, upon a draped tribune, were the princesses
of the house of Sforza with their mother, or her
who stood for such—fine, bold-eyed ladies, Ippolita,
Polissena, Maddalena, Anna: behind were the maids
of honor, ranked like angels in a fresco of Paradise.
"Very young, rather pale, partaking the nature of
a dove"—he sought among these beauties to fulfil
his words. Whose was that dividing curtain of

dark hair? Whose the moonlit brow it draped? He may just have had a glimpse of Emilia Fiordispina, but nothing to what she had of him. "There rides a beautiful person," said one of her mates, with a nudge; "look, look, Nina. One pace behind the litter—all black with a golden head."

"He is lovely—but not all black. See his scarlet garter. Who should he be? A nephew?"

"No, no—not he. If he were nephew he would be before the chair. 'Tis a secretary—that is his livery. He is a servant of the household."

"May be, Isotta. But I am sure he is wise."

"It will be for you to be wise, child," said Isotta, "for it is certain he looked only at you." For answer Emilia pinched her friend's finger.

After high mass was done, sitting on a throne in the Chapter House, the Cardinal received the Duke of Milan. Sforza, grinning fearfully, came limping in between two of his gentlemen, the whole force of his brocaded court, chamberlains, chancellors, secretaries, poets, esquires, historiographers, soothsayers, Latin orators, behind him. Nello had never seen his patron so monumental as when Sforza, old, sanguine, hacked by battle, crept painfully up the degrees of the throne, and, looking as if he could mangle it, kissed the sacred ring. Gonzaga spared him nothing, pitied nothing in him. Neither his gout, at its worst that day, nor his rank, nor the villanies he had done, nor those he had power to do, saved him one wriggle up the

steps, one inch of reverence. So with the others;
all proud heads must stoop, all stiff knees be bent.
Galeazzo Maria, the heir, a splendid youth, black
and white, slim, straight, carven—down he must go;
Lodovico, the blond prince, Ascanio; the bastards
—Don Hermes, Don Tristan, Don Dioneo: all Milan
must abase itself, for the Cardinal played out the
game. "Zeus the Olympian, the lightnings bun-
dled in his hand," thought Nello, admiring.

After the men, and after a banquet at the Castle,
it was the ladies' turn. The household of the
Duchess received all the benevolence and more
than the scrutiny which they looked for. The
Duchess Bianca was a stately and handsome woman,
in a fierce snow-and-fire sort; her excellence was
known, and her Visconti lineage. The Cardinal,
after her obeisance, raised her up and saluted her
forehead in a brotherly fashion. He patted Donna
Ippolita's head; Donna Maddalena he touched on
the chin; Donna Polissena on the cheek. Last came
the ladies of the household—half a dozen in a row
—to kneel for his blessing. La Colombina must be
here, the pledged bride of the Black Dog of Cittadella, the dove cowering before the snake's cold
eye.

The Cardinal's heavy gaze lurched over their
ranked, obsequious heads, wandered to their young
bosoms, their folded hands. Nello's bright glances
were untiringly there, casting far and wide. "Very
young, rather pale, partaking the nature of a dove."

264

The elements pleased him; the picture he had made from them pleased him more. Now he would see if he was not right.

At the extreme left knelt Isotta de' Nervi, black-haired, small-headed, very pale, in a straight robe of black with gold threads, and underdress of red. She knelt stiffly and looked straight before her. "Young enough, too pale, more hawk than dove," said Nello. Alessandra Ciappelletti, a Veronese lady, was next—color of Venice, opal-pink, golden and white, sumptuous and confident. "An impossible victim of Simone." Francesca del Vescovo, like a clinging silver reed, thin and swaying, what of her? "I reserve her," said Nello, "though against my better judgment. Whom have we here?" A maid, with a bent-down head, and hands folded at her neck, came next. Her lips were pale, but a smile just touched and seemed to tinge them, as the sun warms with color a wintry landscape. "A little nun? A nun in Carnival, pleased and scared, wary and hardy at once? A nun in green, with rose-tipped daisies strewn about her! She smiles askance. Why? Timidity? Partly. Mischief, malice? Partly these; for her danger may teach her to be dangerous. She is pale, smooth, her neck astonishingly white; she hath deep gray eyes! Demure, secret, meek, kind as the earth. Why do you look so wistfully at me, little lady? Do you know that I have conversed with you already—in dreams? Do you carry your fate in your face?

Are you dedicated, set apart, afraid? Very young, rather pale—and, by Heaven, she wears a columbine in her breast! You are she! you are she!" He had no thought, no eyes left, but for her.

The Cardinal, after his benediction, gave his more worldly salutation. He held the hand of Isotta, kissed the cheek of Alessandra, took Emilia by the chin, and because she looked down, held her head up that she might be seen. "To one of you fair maids," he said, as he held her, "I have a message. Which of you is called Madonna Emilia?" The tremor of what he held in his hand warned him. "Oho!" said he, "I have you, Mistress Emilia, eh?"

"Yes, Your Eminence, indeed," says La Colombina. The others looked sideways at this play.

"There is time enough for message and messenger, my child," said the great man. "All I hear of you is good." He stooped his great head and kissed her on each cheek. "One for myself and one for a friend of ours," he added, to her extreme confusion. Nello watched him as a cat a mouse. "The bird in the net of the fowler. Here is a more redoubtable hunter than Simone." He felt that he might grow to hate his master. Was he jealous then? Detestable fact.

Soon after this the reception was over. The Cardinal went away to his lodging and his correspondence; but he trifled with it, against his custom—looked out of window, had out his jewellery-boxes, turned over cameos and gems—by-and-by produced Simone's token. "Here is a reminder of an absurd errand of ours, less poignant than that which we have had already," he said. "Simone's little mistress has a haunting face—it nauseates me to think of him with her. What mystery in those judging eyes! For his brute-staring to explore! What touch of demure mockery in those frail lips! As if she could smile at the gross follies of men while she bled for them. Such things lift her out of the category of silken flesh and rounded limbs, my Nello. Women have few charms for me in these days; but that sleek and furtive beauty moved me strangely. I must see her again—certainly I must see her again." He fell into a fit of musing, as he sat there by his window, the huge, appetent man, fingering the thin gold ring. Here, thought Nello with a wry face, was a monstrous big dog in full cry. What disconcerted him precisely was that the very thoughts of the Cardinal were his own. Pity for the flying prey swallowed up his disgust, and made his growing love—like any carnal dealing with such a filamental thing—seem profane. To pursue in any manner, even the gentlest, a creature so recluse seemed to him a brutality. What was he then, but another dog in running—a third hound in the Love Chase?

> Vitas hinnuleo me similis, Chloe—

Alas, alas!

He viewed his own state, too, with profound dismay. It disturbed all his plans, upset his theories, made his stoicism ridiculous. But he could not help it. He now loved this exquisite, elfin, hunted creature—claimed by Simone, pondered by the thick Gonzaga: yes, yes, he too desired her. Not Epictetus himself, had he been raised from the dead, could keep him from haunting Emilia Fiordispina. And yet, and yet—there were a hundred women more beautiful than she—and not one of them fit to kneel before her. The rose and gold, the black and silver, the reedy, the voluptuous, the sprightly, the pensive—not one of them availed beside La Colombina, who went so secretly, smiling to herself, who said so little and judged men out of her gray eyes, and was under the paw of the Black Dog, and now overshadowed by the huge Molossian hound. Love, pity, intense curiosity ached in his bones. He groaned to know it, but could not move.

But it may be guessed what a fine tumult raged in the maids' bosoms that day, and not in theirs alone; it stirred the ladies of the house of Sforza. The Duchess spoke of it, spoke to the girl herself. "It seems," she said, "that you have attracted the Cardinal's attention, child. Let me advise you not to count upon it. These great gentlemen, after dining, feel benevolent, and are easily induced to acts of generosity which the morning's reflection dispels. I have noticed, my child, that you have the power of attraction—you meek women can do that. I shall be the first to congratulate you upon

any real mark of favor, depend upon it. Now, go
to bed, my dear, and don't forget your prayers."

Emilia curtsyed, kissed hands, and withdrew.
Isotta de' Nervi looked wisely at Sigismunda.
Francesca del Vescovo whispered in Alessandra's
ear. They grew very respectful to their mate—
the observed of an Eminence! But Emilia took
the episode with great humility. She had not
lived at the Court of Milan four years without
learning something.

X. ANGELIC SALUTATION

The usher at the door of the Duchess's side told
Nello that Donna Emilia was not on duty at that
hour. It was time of siesta. "That young and
pretty lady, sir, loves to sleep out-of-doors," said
the usher, "and I understand the passion. Very
well I remember that when I came up from the
country—myself am from Battaglia among the
hills—I was always for running out of house to
snuff the air. I used to weep at the sight of the
mountains in those young days, sir: a trickle of
tears, indeed! Milan seemed to me a prison, a
great maze of brick. Now I'm a fireside cat—
you'd never guess me a mouser. Well, well, the
city drains the country blood out of us soon or
late. In the garden, sir, you'll find her. Try the
long walk where the naked ladies, whom they call
the Graces, are. Graces enough, and no fear of
displaying them, in their ladyships. My old mother
would have had smocks on them the first night—

but a week of Milan changes all that. Hey! what's
a little nudity hereabouts? A thousand thanks,
sir, your servant, I salute you."

Nello had come, on his own initiative, to deliver
to Emilia the badge of her servitude; but he had
not come ingenuously, but, rather, under the spur
of his own desire. That could not be justified, he
knew in his heart, though with his head he juggled
himself into some sort of assurance that it could.
The Cardinal, engrossed in affairs of State—which
were not going too well—had forgotten the ring,
the ringer, and the ringed, and had given over the
business to his secretary with a "Va via! Get it
done with, and come back to me." Nello had gone
out to find her, treading on air.

He had seen her, on some pretext or another,
every day, and had fallen irrevocably in love with
the Betrothed of the Black Dog. He fortified himself with sophisms; he was not a humanist for nothing. He told himself that from that moment of
horror when the wretch, new from his shambles,
had revealed her, he, Nello, had been her slave. A
passion of pity, a passionate foresight of the bound
victim—this white Iphigenia, "very young, rather
pale"; a passionate certainty, when he saw her in
the kneeling row of maids; add her mystery, her
nunlike charm, and he was at her feet. He adored
her mutely for a week, feeding upon chance glimpses
of her here and there. He bathed in her light,
drank thirstily of the air about her. He knelt in

270

the same church, or chapel of a church, went to the
Porta Giovia, on one shift or another, a dozen times
a day; and when he was blessed, he went again—
and when he was not blessed, he went again.   He
passed her in the crowded streets, and stood bareheaded till she was by, he jostled in the pack about
the litters when the Duchess and her ladies were
to take the air.   He did his business in a dream.
Emilia bent her head over his pillow as he closed
his eyes; between sleep and waking in the morn-
ings he saw her shy and smiling there.   He was
Endymion, she the white Goddess of the Moon;
once he dreamed that she stooped and kissed him.
Awaking with a cry, he saw the young moon clear
beyond the window.   An omen!   He had been on
Latmos.

Here is enough to account for his errand; for
mortal man cannot feed forever on dreams, nor is
sight enough for him.   A craving to be nearer, to
make her look at him, to make her conscious of
his love, to make her speak; the knowledge that
he could, that the power was his; the temptation,
crawling and deadly, to make his power felt—why,
by one word of Simone he could make her catch
her breath, tremble, go white; and by another,
spoken from his knees, he could comfort her!   He
fought, but could not resist.   Here was something
stronger than himself, under which a man the most
humane may be turned into a wolf.   He pondered,
he prayed, he longed, he trembled—and he fell.

271

The Cardinal gave over to him ring and message.
Emilia, poor bird, was under his net.

The gardens of the Palazzo Porta Giovia were
very extensive. Terrace spread beyond terrace;
vista opened upon vista of white statues, balus-
trades, trees trimmed, garlanded pillars—a wonderful order. By broad steps you descended through
all this ranked pomp of marble and leafage to the
green grass alleys hedged with cypress; half a dozen
of these, like rays of a semicircle, drew the eye to
a distant point—a focus of all the garden's wonder,
the pride of all Milan, a group of the Three Graces
intertwined, supposed by Praxiteles. There was
deep shade at that place, a little grove of pines,
a fountain, tall grass. There Nello found Emilia,
pillowing her cheek upon her arm, coiled and asleep.

He stood, tiptoe and breathless, to look at her.
He was not as yet so much in love with the image
he had fashioned out of her and her pitifulness that
he could not admire her for what she was. In sleep
the simple thing you are or may be, the child, the
savage, or the beast, comes out and sits upon your
quiet brows, and looks about him. The cage door
is open, the keepers are away; out he comes; you
may see him if you watch. The child within Emilia
sat now full-faced, without fear, for Nello to wonder at. All her defences were down, all the little
makeshifts of her daily life, which he found so
pathetic, and loved because he pitied—the anxious
lift of the eyelids at some strange advance, the

quick response of the brows, the fixed smile on the lips, which commits you to nothing—smoothed away now by sleep's soft palms. If she dreamed it was of comfortable things; full and even came her breath; still her hands lay; her brows were not written, her lips were unlocked. Nello sighed as he looked. "Cruel fate that makes me a messenger to this lovely thing! Cruel fate that denies me the right to guard this opening rose!"

He felt so wicked—here on so vile an errand—that by comparison the proffer of his own love as a protection 'against Simone's seemed to him the act of a hero. A traitor? Yes, but to Simone, who himself was a traitor broadcast. How many hearths were staring under that dastard's stroke, how many souls adrift, how many fiends abroad? Was such a wretch then to mar and mangle at his will? His scythe was dripping with the blood of boys, women, children at the breast. Insatiable—like the Minotaur—he fed upon the flesh of virgins. Well, here was Nello ready to be Theseus. He told himself that he had done ill, but that now he was to be redeemed. His eyes, on their lift to heaven with this boast, caught sight of the Graces, the three white women enlaced, pure as the marble in which they lived. In his fancy he saw in them the threefold soul of Emilia escaped from her sleeping body. He could speak to them freely.

He stood before them with stretched-out arms, like a young *Adorante* at his service, and began his prayer.

273

"Pious ladies," said he, softly, "made in the image of the tender thought of God, Thaleia, Aglaia, Euphrosyne, hear me when I cry. In secret come ye forth from your fair, discarded house, and in this marble dwell; but I come praying while she sleeps, that not for long ye shall depart from her, but rather abide to be at once her justification and her shield. For ye are her soul, O women; and without you, what is she? A shell for music, a soft casket whence the jewel has been ravished. Nay, since I do indeed believe that the soul is true Form, without you she is less than this. Alas! she is but the pretty matrix, the gem for the graver. It is ye, it is ye that are the true seal; it is ye that are the young, the holy, the dawn-hued, pious Emilia. To whom, O soul of Emilia, I devote all I know, can learn, hope, or believe, to protect, to comfort, cherish, and defend against the fret and clamor of the world." He thrust forth his arms in an ecstasy; his voice took ardor, thrilled, pierced, and awoke Emilia. When he turned, glowing with devotion, he saw her wondering gaze. Still flushed with sleep, the child not yet dethroned, she lay prone, her face between her hands, and looked at him.

"Are you an angel?" she asked him, as if she dreamed still. The sunny golden cloud of his hair, his rosy face, and slim lines may have deceived her. But Nello dared not play the god. An angel! A messenger! Alas, what a message was his!

"Madonna, I am Nello Nelli, a young man of

Venice. No angels do my work—I serve the Cardinal of Mantua."

"The Venetians are beautiful persons," Emilia pursued her thoughts: the gloss of sleep was still upon her eyes, and her voice was languid with sleep. "They say that gold hair means the sun at birth."

"It is the Moon that shines upon me now," replied Nello, "and turns me to holy desires. That is the holy season, when the moon rides lonely in the sky, frosty, pure, calm as the spaces she inhabits, and sheds a chaste benediction on all burning foreheads upon earth."

Emilia shut her eyes, and sighed. "The thought is good. But such an estate is not for us."

"It is for me—it strengthens me and makes me wise."

Emilia sat up and laughed softly. Acquaintance with an angel seemed easy on these terms. She leaned back on her hand, and smoothed her hair with the other. "I have had those thoughts myself," she said, "but not here. Long ago—in my home—I had them. That place lies by Garda, and at night the moon rises from behind the mountains and sails slowly above the lake. It is impossible to be wicked on such nights; there is no such thing as wickedness. But here in Milan—the moon is yellow and hot." She sighed, and looked older. "The nights are more wicked than the days."

Nello took two steps and cleared the distance

275

between them. He now stood over her. "Wickedness is rife in the world," he said, his voice trembling, "but not for you! Thou shalt tread upon the
lion and adder; the young lion and the dragon shalt
thou tread under thy feet. Because He has set
his love—"

She did not look up; he was too near. "I try
to be good," she said, "but in Milan—"

"There is no goodness under the sky if you are
not good"; his voice shook.

Sleek, she crouched under the caress of his
words.

"Why do you say that? You know me not."

"Yes, yes, I know you. I have known you
since—ah, a long time!"

She was puzzled. "You know me! But how—"

"By heart," said Nello, "in the heart, and
through the heart. You are very young." She
nodded her head.

"Rather pale"—she smiled; but at that moment
she was not at her palest.

"And you partake of the nature of a dove."
She looked quickly up. Their eyes rested long
together.

Gradually she grew frightened. He saw her
pupils dilate; he saw her call up her reserves.

"Since you have learned so much of me—how
I know not—and voice me so high, I must certainly
tell you the truth. You think me very good; perhaps I was so once. But I have been here two

years. Do you know Milan? There is no time to
think in Milan. There is no time to pray. Ah!"
she broke off suddenly, with a strange look of concern, as if she had betrayed a secret—"ah, I am
not good now to be telling you this."

Nello was quick at all points—quick to understand, to feel, and to resolve. As her poor tongue
had hovered over the secret sins of Milan he had
changed the direction of all his desire. Compared
to this hotbed of a city—its staring suns and yellow
moons—wedlock with Simone, the love and the
arms of that ruffian seemed to him a haven for La
Colombina. For what was he—poor hireling—to
save her from storm and wreck? Alas! a swirling
straw. But he could lead her to a rock. And what
was he, poor hireling, but a puff of idle wind? So
be it, but he could bring her to a steady stream.
Yes, yes, Milan was a worse fate for the white dove
than Simone at Cittadella.

He said, then, deliberately: "You are more
good, Madonna, than you can believe, since you
are able, of your mere motion, to turn men's thoughts
towards the good. One such man is known to me
—another such am I. When I came upon you
sleeping, and saw that only then were you at peace,
I learned all that I dreaded, and knew what I must
do. Other hopes, other resolves had I—but now
have only one. Many and splendid dreams were
mine, but I have put them all away. You are in
danger here—you have said it, but I knew it long

before. Well, I have the means to safeguard you, here with me. Listen."

She rose to her feet and stood before him, searching his face, waiting upon his words.

"My master, the Cardinal, and I were at Cittadella before we turned our faces to Milan. Do you know anything of Cittadella?" She shook her head. "Nothing."

"When there we received in charge a certain token—for you."

"A token—for me?"

He held out betwixt finger and thumb the little ring. The lace ruffles at his wrist almost covered his hand.

"This is the token." He waited for the warm flood of color, the telltale blood, rapturous recognition. He was prepared to hold her as she fell. No such thing. Emilia stared vacantly at the jewel.

"I know nothing of this," she said in a dry voice. "Who gave it? Who sent it?"

"I shall repeat you the words which destined it for you. 'It is,' said the giver, 'for La Colombina —for remembrance.'"

Now she put her hand to her side, she gave back a little, she put her hands behind her. "Ah," she said, "now I know. What shall I do?"

"To La Colombina," repeated Nello, looking fixedly at the gray of her cheek—"for remembrance— from him who only knows that name"; and Emilia began to wring her little hands.

"Oh, oh!" she said, "he has never forgotten—
he could never forget! He requires so much—he
will kill me!" She strained her head back—he
thought now that she would fall, and was shocked
at what he had done. · His wits had betrayed
him, and again his passion veered like a weather-
cock.

"Let it never be given," he said, "let the fault
be mine—let the vengeance fall on me." He looked
round for a bog or bottomless morass: the garden
did not supply one; but then Emilia turned about.

"Shall I be serpent instead of dove—and you
make me so? Give me the ring. It is mine, and
I must wear it."

She held out her left hand, the third finger separate and stiff. "Put the ring on, if you please."
But as Nello obeyed her, her large tears collected,
brimmed over, and trickled down her cheeks. This
silent witness of self-pity moved Nello oddly, not
to pity her in his turn, but to harden him against
so dangerous a generosity, to hector her rather.
The prig in man is, after all, the quickliest moved.
There she stood, melting before him; and he, wise
fool, could do no better than work ardently for the
man whom, of all men, he loathed.

"It is not for me to say that you are wise or
unwise; but I may praise your nobility, I hope.
I know not what right Messer Simone had to claim
your loyalty—"

Here she looked very wistful as she considered

her case, and his putting of it, and Nello felt proud of himself. He had given great measure to his enemy—that butcher Simone—and he had made this lovely creature think. To make a maid of honor think in Milan appeared to him to be something. But he was not prepared for the setback which she was to give him. She had the knack, among others, of extremely simple utterance, and by the very directness of her attack could disarm you.

"It is easy to answer you. He was my lover long ago. I was twelve years old."

He was staggered. "Twelve, Madonna! Twelve years old!" She affirmed with the eyes.

"O Heaven! And he—?" She shrugged—she looked very desolate.

"He was older, of course, and very big. My head was here." She touched her bosom with her finger, and let her hand drop again, a dead weight. The stormy picture which Nello instantly made shocked him to the soul. He shivered—round backed his desire to full, warm south. Emilia, who had been watching him without his knowledge, continued her dreary confession.

XI. Emilia's Way

She said, with eagerness strangely in leash, "You will not misjudge me, I hope. I was very young—but a promise is a sacred thing. I loved him—or thought that I did. But do not misjudge Simone either. No, no!" She put her finger up to check

Nello's budding eloquence. "It is easy to misjudge Simone, but I cannot allow it. He is good." Nello was crimson.

"He is not good, by the King of kings! He is vile and horrible—cruel as death. I have seen him—ah! I cannot say what I have seen. He will kill you."

"He will kill me," said Emilia, "if I am not faithful."

Nello went mad. · He took the girl's two hands— She would not look at him, but made no resistance. He held them, and drew her nearer.

"Madonna," he said, "I am nothing to you; but to me you are everything which a woman should be—" She framed "Oh no!" with her shocked lips, but neither looked nor drew away. "Everything," he repeated, "which a woman should be. You are holy, you are sublime, you are the soul of honor. As a mercy to me, wear not this ring of Simone's until such time as he shall prove his right to ask it by better title than the terrors of a child. Will you do this? You will? Ah, but you will!" He drew the ring off her finger and put it in his bosom. He kissed the freed hand, then the other. He was trembling, love was his master; he knew not what he did—

"Madonna Nina," cried a boyish voice behind the girl.

"Death and the Devil!" said Nello.

They were broken in upon by an eager-faced

page, who, pelting down the garden, had pulled up short when he was upon his quarry.

"Forgive me, Madonna Nina; forgive me, Signore? Madonna, you are summoned, the Duchess has called for you twice." He had barely time to bow his little person away before Emilia had composed her own. A very altered, wise, and circumspect young lady turned to face her flushed adorer.

"Signor Nello," she said sedately, "I have been talking foolishly, but I was startled for the moment. I hope that you will understand that. You have been most kind to me, but I must not trouble you any more. I think that you have my ring. Will you give it to me?"

"I will give it to you, Madonna," said Nello, "on condition that you do not wear it. I have a reason for asking what you may think an extraordinary request."

"What is your reason, sir?"

"I will tell you when we have more leisure. It will approve itself to your judgment and clemency at once. It is highly reasonable."

They were ascending a broad flight of steps; at the top they paused. "We should not go any further together," said she.

He protested, but could not move her. He plunged into nonsense, and made her smile, but she did not advance. "We are children with a bogey between us," says he, "which we dare not so much as name. Let us be bolder—come. Tell

282

me what bogey prevents my walking with you, and
I will tell you who it is that drives me to insist."
She started and turned pale. "Look, look!" she
said. He followed her direction, and there was a
bogey indeed. Cardinal Gonzaga stood smiling,
vast and benevolent, peering upon them out of narrowed eyes.

Nello, sober in a moment, dropped upon his
knee; Emilia took to both of hers. The Cardinal
advanced.

"Charming little lady," he said, "happily met!
If my young friend lingers in his farewells it is no
wonder. I should have been tempted myself. Rise,
rise, and come to me." Faltering she came and
kissed his ring. He patted her cheek and put his
hand on her shoulder, which drooped to receive it.

"I sent Master Nello out to you upon a little
errand, which I have no doubt is performed. Is
it so, Madonna Emilia?"

She met his blinking gaze with a faint color, a
curtsey, a bent head. He almost embraced her
with his arm. "Strange, indeed," he said, "that
so young and gentle a lady should be a counter in
the rough games of states—yet so it is. There is
a price upon that pretty head—a great price. Do
you know what it is? It is Mantua, it is Milan, it
is the glory of Venice. Are you prepared for this
fine marketing?" She murmured some inaudible
words, while Nello bit his lips.

"Our friend out yonder," said the Cardinal, and

waved his hand greatly to the east, "is vehement
in many things, as swift as a dry wind. By the
splendor of God, but he is! I have not emulated
him there, my child; I have not been so eager to
do his errand as he is showing himself in the doing
of mine. You shall forgive a vexed statesman,
who is, nevertheless, sincerely your friend. But
now listen to this of our keen Simone. He has lost
no time. He has surprised the Venetians in a
wood near Padua; cut van from rear. The former
he killed to a man, and the latter pursued with such
incredible swiftness that he was upon them—his
butchery done—before they could reach the gates.
He did some steel work under the very walls, and
mocked them rarely—with his *palio* for horsemen.
his foot-race for camp-women, and what not—and
drew off his men in good order, with half a dozen
gonfalons and a lion of Saint Mark for booty. They
tell me that he has burnt up the maize fields for
three leagues about Abano, and turned the contado
into a smoking desert. I say nothing of prisoners,
since he says nothing; but I have little doubt of how
he has served them. And now the Republic has
called in Piccinnino against him, and we shall have
news before long. A fighter—ha! what a lover for
a pretty lady—ha!"

The Cardinal beamed about him, shining and
exalted. Nello sickened, but not so much at Simone
as at this gross priest. He now believed the worst
of the Cardinal, that his eyes had been caught, and

that he had turned his craft towards the entrapping of Emilia for his own house. Watching her by stealth, he saw that her eyes were troubled, and that her lips framed unsounded words. She prayed; she was in deadly fear.

The Cardinal turned about to continue his walk, so Emilia fell to Nello without further demur. Each felt the nearness of the other; there was an urgency to speak, yet neither spoke. That which the Cardinal stood for, that which underlay every word he had said, was dreadfully present to Nello; but his tongue was tied. As for the little lady, he was to learn before long that she by no means told all that she thought. So it was that they returned, charged, but silently, together.

Nello counted the minutes which remained to him. They narrowed fearfully. He dared delay no longer; speak he must.

"Oh, I pity you! oh, I pity you!"

She shook her head, bit her lip, but said nothing. He leaned to her again. "Courage, courage! there must be a way. Ah, let me live to find it!"

She hurried on blindly. At the foot of the last flight of steps she stopped, and spoke in a quick whisper. "To-night—after vespers—remain. I shall come back. I need you." She went from him swiftly. Nello walked with God.

True to her word, she did come back into the chapel glooms, where Nello waited for her with his beating heart, and all his philosophy in rags. What she had to do with him was got by heart, and done swiftly. She was muffled in a cloak, came directly to him, and began to speak in a low and measured voice. The church was empty but for those two, and a white nun at a distant altar adoring the sacrament.

"Long ago," thus she said, "when I was a child, and plighted to a lover, I tried to be most faithful to Simone. Every night after vespers, after he had left us, I lighted a candle before the Madonna del Lago. I promised him that I would, and so I did. Then, afterwards, for some reason, I omitted it. It was long ago. I came to Milan; there were many things to do, much to take care of. I forgot it. I see now that I did wickedly; you have taught me that. I am going to begin again. I will light my candle and pray that I may be kept for Simone. I wish you to pray with me. You must do it. I ask it of you. You know my secret; you have guessed my—my—danger. I trust in you—in no one else—come!"

Nello was bewitched by the strange, secret girl, who spoke as out of a lesson-book, but had a thrill of tears within her voice. She had his hand in her own, which was hot and dry; she led him away to a hidden altar, where a dim picture glowed, half revealed by a lamp and some dying lights. She lit her taper by another, offered it, spiked it, and knelt—Nello by her. Her head was bowed—it may be questioned whether she prayed, or for what.

The Love Chase

Nello had no words, but his agitation was piercing.
He longed for this girl's soul as he had never longed
for anything; he felt that she lifted him up, gave
him wings which he had never dreamed to have.
The piety, the resignation which he saw in this act
of hers, made him faint with rapture; her breath,
so near, all about him, the soft fretting of her robe
where it touched him, the mystery, the silence, his
beating heart, moved him so much that he could
not keep still. In fact, he trembled, as they say,
like a leaf. But whatever fire had nerved her—
whether love of Simone or love of God—the same
burned steadily to the end. She was perfectly still,
perfectly calm, her own mistress—and his. The
devotion done, she rose and held out her hand to
Nello. He could just see the outline of her pale
face, her serious eyes, and moving lips.

"You have made me better than I ever hoped
to be. Your words, your countenance, your prayers have given me great courage. Watch over
me, help me all you can. I mean to do well—but
I go in peril. Pray for me—good-night."

He kissed a little hand, crying to himself that
it was as cold as a stone. That is as it may be.
Quickly she glided out and left him.

He remained motionless for a long while. "She
has forgotten to take her ring. I am done for—
Love is my master—she shall never have it. She
is adorable; there is no woman left in the world.
All are in her; she is the first and the last. Now

may the Gods who gave me love teach me how to
win her. I have never loved before." Dust lay
on the Arabic grammar that night; and had Pernetta any more parrots for strangulation, she would
have strangled them unpraised.

XII. DEVOTIONS OF A VICAR

It was not without some misgivings that our
Nello, when his fever had had time to cool, saw
himself embarked upon the waters of love in a
skiff none too stout in the timbers; nor did it add
to his contentment that his shallop, such as it was,
was not his own. He loved Emilia Fiordispina;
but what of her? She, if he must believe her,
loved duty; and Simone stood for duty. The more
she clung to Nello, therefore, the better seemed
Simone's case; the more Nello followed her, the
less his chance of outwitting this distant menace,
only present in himself. The false position hurt his
sense of dignity, and yet he could not escape it.
The truth may well be, also, that he sighed more
than once as he confessed the reproaches of his
books. Dust upon the fair edges of his Virgil—
the gift of Vittorino da Feltre; dust, alas, upon the
Arabic grammar; and dim with dust looked his
learned future. He shook his head. "What a
scholiast is lost here! What a chair of Rhetoric
is gaping for me in Mantua—gaping in vain." But
the thought of that head so sweetly bent over a
task—the thought of dire Simone, black-avised,
bloody and sudden, spurred him to the fray. He

pushed aside his books, huddled his notes together. The day was fair; the golden trees outside, the lazy air, the humming of the bees called him. In the garden he might find Emilia, or from some gallery window might see her at play with her mates. The spring called him, and Emilia's urgent cry of the heart, "I need you, Nello, I need you. I am forgetting Simone. Come!" And he went. Strange destiny for poet and lover—to be vicar to one who was butcher and tyrant. "I am humiliated to the earth. My soul is glued to the pavement. I am wretched, I despise myself—she needs me: I go." He always went.

Again, there was another thing. As we know, he was nothing if not critical; not even the romantic uplifting of his heart could numb this faculty of his head. But observe the curious result—that his heart was now able to turn his head to its service. He could not avoid criticising his Colombina; he could not but see that she was dangerously attractive, nor withhold from his private mind the opinion that she was not insensible to the power she had; but he was able, by some intricate juggling of his parts, to assure himself that he adored her more than ever. Her "kindness" was charity, her secretiveness was "mystery," her candor (for she was both secret and open, as she chose) was innocence.

Her lovers, declared and undeclared, were innumerable. There was not a maid at Court who

had half so many. Behind the Duchess's chair—
who whispered in her ear as he passed? to whom
did she listen with vague and wandering eyes? for
whom did those sober lips part and gleam? for
what, at what, did that shy smile hover for a moment, and flicker and fade out? Alas, it was not
for one only! Now it was the magnificent, black-
and-white young lord, heir of Milan, Galeazzo-
Maria; now it was Don Tristano; now Don Hermes
—Sforzas all three, who fought with knives for her;
now it was Messer Filelfo, most unphilosophic philosopher, greasy with sin and over-eating; now it
was a Pallavicini; now a Bentivoglio. There were
rumors about her; it was she who made Don Galeazzo cold upon the Mantuan marriage; it was she—
but enough of that! La Nina and the Cardinal—
Heavens, what a lover's tale! And then the evi-
dence of the eyes — what of that? Billets were
passed up below the table where the maids sat dining;
Nello could see them go. From lap to lap they
went—from Gismonda to Isotta, from her to Bianca,
to Susanna, to Violante-Maria—but on La Nina's
lap they rested—that was always the ark of their
pilgrimage; and Nello, if he happened to be present, watched that she should open and declare the
contents by her face. But she never opened, and
he swore to himself that she was wise; and his
heart instructed his head to say that it was for her
wisdom he loved her. That obsequious head of a
sophist that he had!

The Love Chase

Sometimes he surprised her at intimate quarters with some splendid youth—in the gardens—on the terraces—in the great, coffered chambers. She would be biting the stalk of a flower, he leaning over her, pouring out a fiery stream of rhetoric. She would say little, she would scarcely smile; she looked down always—listened, judged, considered. So the game went on. So wise a head on so young and tender a body! So wary a heart to throb with blood so new! "Is she a miracle? Do I love a witch? A Siren? Calypso, Queen of Faery? Morgan le Fay herself?" he asked, but could not answer himself. Wonder of wonders—he never reproached her; he was entirely her slave—her right hand, her conscience, she used to say, when she made him help her, as she did every day. On the contrary, he accepted everything that she did, and was perfectly loyal to the fiction which held him to her side. His books had no chance with his infatuation. He could not bear to see them lest, regretting their dusty sides, he should seem untrue to Emilia.

Yet, anomalous as they were, he had to own that the privileges which she gave him were signal. So far as he could tell no other lover of hers was so highly favored as he, or Simone in him. Not a day passed but he met her, and more than once; not a day but she confided some secret to him or accorded him some begged gratuity. They swam, he told himself, the strong flood of Milan together, he breasting it gallantly in her quarrel, she, on her side, taking her line from him. She grew to be dangerously frank, did not always disguise what he had darkly feared, and with her confidences stabbed and anointed him in one breath.

This, however, was after he had had ocular testimony of what she chose to confide more than once. He had seen Don Galeazzo with her in the lemon-garden; he had seen Don Tristano in the orchard—and then she told him about it. "Oh, Nello, last night Don Galeazzo ——," or "Dearest friend, in the orchard Don Tristano took me by both my hands. Alas, I did wickedly by my poor Simone!" Again it was, with breathlessness and with tears, "Nello, Nello, I must speak with you for a moment—indeed it is urgent, my Nello. This afternoon the horrible Messer Filelfo followed me into the rose-garden, and made proposals—" The proposals could only be hinted—nor was more needed. She fairly broke down over that business. Nello pulled the philosopher's nose, to the great scandal of his young wife—a staring Greek girl. "Heyday, do you batter a learned man in his own house?" cried she. "Madam," says Nello, "you may well ask. Permit me to explain." But as he very well knew, that was exactly what he would not be allowed to do. Filelfo, with a fearful grin, protested that the assault was a joke between him and his "dear young friend," and there were no more complaints of him from Emilia. These things were of frequent occurrence, and Nello, between his Car-

dinal and his mistress, was stretched as far as his
nerves would go. The odd part about his love-
affair is that the more she confided him of her escapades the more madly he loved her. It would
seem that all that could be necessary to his perfect
happiness would be that some fine gentleman of
Milan should ruin her in earnest. But she was not
of the sort to be ruined.

By these means and others, by the possession of
a common secret, by common understanding, and
by strong predilections, Nello and his Emilia were
bound up together. It could not be long, you
would have said, before some surging of one or the
other of them in the bonds should turn them breast
to breast. That was the expectation of their acquaintance in Milan—that such warm lips as theirs,
throbbing in concert at every pulse of the hour,
could not long be held apart. After their first
meeting in the chapel at dusk Nello had taken
leave to wait there for her every night. Together
they went through the mystical ceremony of the
taper, together bowed their heads, and prayed, or
seemed to pray, in Simone's interest. If ever the
Madonna winked (as the Protestants fable) she
might be excused for it here. The taper was kindled
for Simone, but it kindled a more secret flame. Not
only was Nello there every night; every night
Emilia counted on his being there. The first turn
of her quick eyes was to that pillar against which
he always leaned; she almost ran to meet him; her

hand sought his; without knowing the why or the
why not, she nestled to his side as she spoke. The
witch! how they whispered together: there was always something to say—some ruse whereby the
Duchess should not miss her, some wise forethought
which provided the Cardinal with employment. Her
face came close to his; he stooped his head that it
should be closer. She grew more earnestly con-
fidential, there seemed no bounds to their inter-
course—and then a sigh escaped him, a word of
rapture, an "anima mia," or a "dearest," and that
broke the spell. Emilia became serious at once.
"Come, Nello, we forget poor Simone's candle."
Then he lit it for her, because he was the taller, and
she offered it; they knelt before the veiled picture;
and if their hands did not meet half-way through
the droll performance, and so stay until the rite was
done, Nello thought that he had wasted a day.
They rose up. "Good-night, dear Nello." "Good-
night; happy dreams to my Nina." Or else it
was, "Shall you be at the masquerade this evening?" or "The Cardinal will be at the Duchess's
circle. I shall see my Ninetta again"—and so it
went on.

As well as this, by hook or crook, he contrived
to cross her path half a dozen times in the week.
Sometimes, as you know, the moment was ill-
chosen. He saw her with this one or that—saw
her sometimes when she was unaware, biting a
flower, or twiddling her fingers, listening, smiling,

while some curled and anointed golden youth whispered in her ear. At such times it is to his credit
to say that he tore himself from the place, and that,
though he suffered the torments of the damned,
she never knew it. He might have guessed from
such unwholesome sights that all was not well.
There were whole sections of the days and nights
when he could not see her. But, God help the
boy, he was a loyal soul, and thought her a minister of Heaven.

On her account—mysterious, slow-smiling little
creature—there was no telling. What lay behind
those locked lips, which seemed forever on the
point of a confidence and forever refusing it at the
last, there was nobody in Milan could say. There
were at least a dozen who believed that they could,
but Nello was not one of them. He was perfectly
honest with himself; he had no notion whether she
loved him or not. He knew that she trusted him,
and that in spite of his very obvious passion. Sometimes he believed, and sometimes could not bring
himself to believe that she was using him only as
Simone's proxy—detestable, inglorious office! What
he did not know—one of many things—was that
his name had got into her letters to old Father
Pandolfo, her confessor of old when she was a slip
of a girl by Garda. That white-haired, peaceful
man had more of the truth from her than anybody.

Reverend my father, last night the Cardinal of Mantua
paid me great attention at the Duchess's assembly. Her

Grace asked me upon going to bed what it meant. I could not tell her. He said that I had dove's eyes, and that La Colombina was my rightful name. Did you ever hear me called by that? . . . Messer Nello Nelli was not present. He is the most clever of all the young gentlemen in Milan, and excessively learned. I read Seneca with him sometimes, and sometimes the Songs of Catullus. He calls me Lesbia, and has tamed a sparrow for me, but we call the bird Simone. Do you remember Messer Simone della Prova, who was squire to my father long ago? He is winning great battles in the Veneto for our party. His name is on all lips—that is why we have given it to our sparrow. Messer Nello Nelli thinks him very strong, but the Cardinal of Mantua yesterday advised me to have nothing to say to him should I ever meet him again—which is improbable.

It was true about the sparrow—that she had named it. "Passer, deliciae meae puellae," Nello had said; and she, soberly, "Ah, in that case we will call him Simone." Nello, ruefully, had to see this Simone sip his full of sugar from the most tormenting, beautiful, changeable mouth in the world.

Father Pandolfo, rather perturbed, wrote in reply:

Have a care, my daughter. Your Messer Nello is evidently a talented youth, and has caught the knack of appearing good. Before you bestow upon him your treasure, however, I advise you to inquire of his bankers.

Emilia answered at once:

We have lost each other, dearest father in Jesus Christ. What is this of treasure and a bank? Last evening the magnificent Don Galeazzo, etc., etc.

"It's a bad case," quoth Father Pandolfo to the cat on his knee.

It was a worse case than the good man supposed. The Cardinal had sent a messenger to Mantua with orders to put in complete furniture the Palazza Senzanoja which had not been occupied since the demise of Donna Vittoria Pico, of the princely house of Mirandola. La Pernetta heard of it, among others; in fact all Mantua was interested.

XIII. THE RIVEN HEART

It may seem incredible, and yet is perfectly true, that Nello, sharp-eyed lover as he was, had no notion of that affair of Senzanoja; and while he suspected every gallant in Milan of meditating the murder of his bliss, did not include in the host the one man of them all who meant it most. One reason is that he could not, poor youth, look every way at once, and another that his Nina's confidences were not so generous as he believed them. Nothing had been said of the Cardinal's dealings with her. And yet those dealings had never ceased since the day when he held her chin at the audience of his entry. She had been forced upon his attention then by Simone della Prova's charge; she had remained in it by her own powers. It was certain that she could attract men without seeming so to do: the Duchess knew it, Nello knew it, everybody knew it. The Cardinal, it has been said, was not at all scandalous in his life and conversation; far from that, he had been very little worse than Saint

Paul's supposed bishop. He had been as much the
husband of Donna Vittoria Pico as the law allowed
him; and when she died he had mourned her in
deed as well as at heart. However, he was forty
years old and a fine man, and could not be expected to mourn her forever.

He had not, perhaps, been able to see so much
of Emilia as his secretary had; but he had been
able, either from absence of tact or a disregard of
it, to go nearly as far. And this without Nello's
knowledge, for the simple reason that he had not
chosen that Nello should know. Tact is one thing,
discretion another. He was very well aware that
he had a rival in that bright-faced young man; he
did not fear him, but saw no occasion to provoke
him. "All's fair in the game we play here," he
would have said. "If I mean to give Della Prova
the go-by, my Master Nello has the same intentions
with regard to the pair of us. He has his talents
and ingenuity, his beauty, his wit, his singing-voice
and his blessed, blessed youth on his side. Let
him thrive, in God's name. I wish him every good
but one."

It was discretion in the Cardinal, not forgetfulness, which gave over the ring and the message to
Nello; it was discretion which enlarged upon Simone's fury of fighting in the hearing of the lady.
These were statesman's methods, and show that
he had something on his side.

He certainly had: he was a prince. It is not

every maid of honor that can hold a Cardinal captive to her petticoat. Emilia was made aware of
that at all hours of the day. The Sforza princesses
petted and teased her on account of it; her mates
were jealous or envious, it matters not which, for
one symptom was as flattering as the other. It
was not, and could not be, without a flutter of the
heart that she met this great lover, almost so declared; it hardly occurred to her to resist. What
were her poor little weapons of defence—her poor
little walls of silence, her poor little screens of
secrecy—against such artillery as his? She heard
him speak—and he spoke well; she received his
presents, and he was splendid at giving as at all
else; she read his notes—and kept them to herself.
But Nello was perhaps the only person at Court who
was ignorant of all this.

The Cardinal had sent her some half-dozen little
notes, each with a ring, or a jewel, or a painted
book bound in silver. These notes were not signed,
but bore upon the wax the impression of a Greek
gem—Hercules at the distaff and Omphale leaning
over his shoulder—a beautiful piece of work. It
was a famous gem: two Popes had begged it of
Gonzaga. He used it rarely, it was a valuable
thing; but he thought it well employed for this particular service, and told himself with a smile that it
exactly represented his case. He told Emilia so too
—the hero's neck, the hero's bulk prone beneath her
little foot! How could she avoid a leap of the heart?

There was, for the rest, no harm in any one of his notes. Some were rather pretty. That which covered a jewel bearing a Pelican in Piety (in white and red enamel) said, "So, lady, would I bleed if you might thereby be served. But, alas! what is pious duty in the bird, in the man may be presumption." No harm in that, I hope: at most a foolishness in Cardinals. Another said, "Take my Little Hours, Madonnetta mia; for even as your pure prayers rise up to the great Goddess of the Christians, so mine (poor pagan!) wander round your feet." The prayers of Cardinals should be otherwise directed—but let it pass. The man was strenuously in love; and in any case, enough of his notes.

Now, when August came and Milan lay blistering in dust and red heat, the Ducal Court moved to Pavia, where there was a castle, a green park, hunting for the men, and grass to cool the feet of ladies. Thither went the Duchess and her household; thither went Emilia the demure; but thither the Cardinal, detained by business from Rome and a state-marriage which hung fire, could not go. Love, when it cannot feed on words, makes shift with letters; and if, during these weeks of aching, Nello was living on the letter-bag, so was the Cardinal his master. Whence, suddenly, there blazed a thunderbolt, which fell between them and rove the solid earth. Into the yawning gulf so made must tumble Nello, Emilia, Mantua, Milan, and all.

It was Nello's duty to open the great man's let-

ter-bag while he himself was at his prayers. With
what a shock it came upon him to discover a folded
square within it, in Emilia's fine hand, I leave you
to judge who have learned the youth by this time,
and know what he had and had not of Emilia's
little affairs. The blood swirled in his head; his
heart gave a wild surge upwards into his throat;
then sank like a leaden ball, and he knew that all
the color, all the rhythm, all the music had shud-
dered out of life. "Riverendissimo in Xpo patri
ac domino, Domino Guidoni Principi Cardinali de
Sancta Maria in Cosmedin," etc. There was no
doubt: the flourish, the thin penmanship, the spell-
ing, the seal—Hercules and Omphale, the priceless
Smyrniote gem, sought by two Popes—Emilia's
letter, the Cardinal's gift! O God, the wreck, the
wreck!

The Cardinal, glowing from his prayer, found
his secretary peering at this hideous fact; saw the
little square fact itself shaking in his hand. He
was instantly aware, and made up his mind in an
instant. Now was the time for a sudden stroke.

"Aha, my Nello. What is this pretty thing?
Let me see the seal. It seems familiar. Ha, the
little Colombina!" He did not keep the letter, but
having turned it over and looked at the seal, put
it back into Nello's hand. He sat down comfortably in his deep leathern chair, crossed his leg,
clasped his knee.

"Well, well," he said, "we have known each

other quite a season, my Nello. By a bold stroke
you claimed my protection, deserved, and won it.
It is time that you should learn more of your master, what manner of man he is, by my head, when
the priest is taking a walk and the prince a siesta;
when the soldier is at his ease, unarmed, and the
statesman can smooth out the creases in his brow.
Hey, my little humanist! You whose study is
mankind—let me show you Guido Gonzaga, the
naked man—ha!"

"Foul flesh—a mountain of it!" Nello shivered
all through himself. The Cardinal sat well back,
and put his hands behind his head.

"Come," he said, "let me hear what the lady of
Garda has to tell me. She is a sleek little witch,
by the Blood—and has charmed away my seal
from me. And has used it, by Hercules himself!"
Nello did not move.

"She has pricked me—Nello, I will own it. I
am a man, not insensible to pricks.

> Ne sit ancillae tibi amor pudori—

Ha! So say I, so say I. We have had some talk
together—she has approved herself to me—modest,
sensible, frugal of favors, of sufficient nobility—in
fine, I contemplate a pleasant bondage. But read,
Nello, read, what my shy Omphale pleads."

Atrocious pain for Nello, but not to be refused.

It was a humble letter enough, creditable to the
writer at least. The Cardinal thought it remark-

able. Did not Nello think it so? That so young a lady should be so guarded—extraordinary! Here it is:

"Sacred and most eminent Prince, father and lord," wrote Emilia, "I return on my knees my humble thanks for his princely thought of me, esteeming it miraculous that so perexcellent a lord should stoop to the grass in his path—"

"Ah, she outvies modesty itself!" the Cardinal protested with shut eyes. "But proceed, proceed."

"—in his path. As to what Your Eminence is so gracious as to say of myself, I am thankful to have pleased him. All my life I shall strive to win and to deserve that pleasure; for to what other end do I, do all bondmaidens, live, but to give pleasure to those whom we serve? So far as my duties about the serene person of Madonna the Duchess may comport, I beg Your Eminence to believe me studious to obey him in all things commanded.
I prostrate myself at the Eminent feet,
Praying that they will believe me
Of Your Eminence
The most humble, devout, grateful, pious
servant, EMILIA FIORDISPINA."

Of Nello it may be truly said that the prevailing sense he had was of pity so unutterable that he was able to detach Emilia from his heart, and contemplate her for what she seemed—a white ghost of a girl, shivering and doomed, in some infernal Sabbath of devils. Tonguing thieves, lust and clamor personified, came leaping about her; ruin, horror, nameless life and death, were hers. He saw her end—bloodless, a shredded rag—who had been lovely once; he saw her ghost—she gibbered at him, a mocking sepulchre, the spurned husk of a fair woman, trodden like an orange-skin after all the sweet joy had been sucked out. Beside such a fate as this, a bondage to Simone della Prova seemed perfect freedom. All his love wailing in him cried upon the evil; and yet he was dumb before it. He knew himself a coward, and sickened to know it. He dared not gainsay the Cardinal. Vacant and frozen as he sat, the letter in his hand, he was suddenly shaken into life by the sound of his name.

"Come hither, Nello," said the Cardinal.

The machinery obeyed. He knelt before his master, who put a hand upon his shoulder, and kissed him. "My dear," said Gonzaga, "I have loved you from the first moment of our meeting, and I believe that you love me also. You have so served me at any rate—and now you shall serve me again. My senses are all alight, but I am not acting without judgment. I need that little person extremely, more, perhaps, than you might have thought reasonable in me. But think again. There is nothing so wayward as the fancy of a strong man. What says your Horace?

> Arsit Atrides medio in triumpho
> Virgine rapta—

It is so, indeed. You put wine before him, some great vintage that has lain deep in the earth for two decades, browned ruby, smooth, silky as balm, holding fire, as it were, in essence. He will have none of it: his fancy for the hour is—milk! So with women. A hot Venetian, all burning kisses and straining arms; a slim white Tuscan; a strapping Veronese—basta! basta! He passes them all without a quiver, and lights upon a staid mouse of a girl, like this Fiordispina; her will he have—no other. Strange that it should be so. But I assure you, my friend, she has set me afire. Well, I might talk forever; let me give you directions. This accursed business of my niece Dorotea's marriage will tie me here for another fortnight; meantime my shy captive flutters in the springes of Pavia. You shall leave me, Nello, take her a letter, and plead my cause. What I cannot well write, you shall say. You know me very well—for an honest man, a prince not without wisdom to temper his power. Tell her I am coming on wings. Ah, my boy, I may be a happy man yet. What! Am I a lover? By my soul, I am. Does this entertain you? To see the puller of imperial strings, the genius of battle— which I have been called by good judges—with a white hand under his chin? Anima mia—ha! Leave me, child, to write my letter. Prepare you for your journey—and away."

Nello, in a white garment of rage, took the road for Pavia.

XIV. The Power of the Dog

Riding up through the dappled glades of the park—the towered castle of Pavia in the level sun

of afternoon—he saw a herd more absorbing to his
eyes than the twinkling, antlered deer: a party of
silken ladies and lords—in yellow, in green, in
white—who walked slowly over the grass. He saw
the sun strike on Polissena Sforza's hair, on Donna
Anna's white arm, on Don Tristano's sword. And
then he saw two ladies who strolled apart. Their
heads were near together, one's arm was round the
other's waist. Even at that distance his deadly
fear told him that it was Emilia who was held, and
Ippolita Sforza who held her.

His heart jumped with fear, but with rage also—
for he was a man. He stopped, white and staring.
"She shall have it now—before her friends and lovers
—the Judas-price, the unholy thing. Yes, while
the rage is on me, and my tongue can tell. A little
more sight of her and I should love her again—a
disgrace to my manhood." He signed to his servant to lead on his horse, dismounted, and strode
over the grass.

Presently he saw that he was seen. Ippolita Sforza
observed him first and spoke to Emilia, a laughing
whisper in her neck. He saw Emilia falter, look
quickly up, but guardedly, but never cease looking
towards him. "She feels her shame: it beats down
her head: yet she must have it." The rest of the
party were at some distance—by a great oak. The
cavaliers were spreading their cloaks that the ladies
might sit. Ippolita Sforza drew Emilia to meet
Nello; shyly she came, and dared to wave her hand.

Nello bared his head and came on to execute judgment. As he neared he might have seen the blush of welcome, the bright light in Emilia's eyes—if his rage had let him. But to him, as then he was, she appeared all scarlet, cloaked in that monstrous love; she leered, as it were, out of the Cardinal's cassock. He could not have spared her then had she worn an angel's stole. When he came up he was trembling all over and like to die.

But he knelt to kiss Donna Ippolita's friendly hand.

"Where is his great Eminence?" she asked him, while Emilia hung behind. "Here we have everything to delight him—but he comes not."

Nello fired at this bitter truth.

"I am His Eminence's legate, princess. I have a message from him to your companion. It is no secret, I believe, from your Grace. Have I your leave to deliver it?"

"Oh, of course, of course." Seeing Emilia through red mist, he held out to her the abhorred letter.

"Madonna Emilia"—she did not know his voice —"His Eminence, my master, bids me thank you for your letter—which it was my privilege to read to him. He would have answered it in person but that business holds him still in Milan. Here he has written all that your ladyship can desire to know. He is yours, lady. The bargain is struck —your wishes—the honor that pertains. I take my leave—O God, have I told you all of it?"

He strained his face away that she might not
see it, but his voice broke, and she heard that.

"Now, what in the world—" began Ippolita
Sforza in a ringing voice. Emilia broke away and
plucked at his sleeve.

"Nello, Nello, dear friend, what is this? Never
abandon me, Nello! Speak to me for pity."

Nello turned upon her a bloodless face, quivering and furious.

"Ah, how could you stoop down there in the
mire! Fie, a man-mountain, a hill of flesh! Will
you be buried in the ruins of a church? After your
prayers, your weeping to the cross, your— Why,
if all the tapers you have lighted to show love pure
were turned upon you now, they would show you
speckled, Emilia, spotted like a snake. Ah, come
now, come now, see yourself: let me show you your
similitude in a glass. One, two, four, six, ten,
twenty—jewels, girdles, chains, verses—hey! the
great Cardinal gives like a prince. Of whom else
have you had so much and so many times?" He
pointed to her neck, the Smyrna gem was there,
burning his eyes. "Hercules and Omphale, done
by a Greek in chalcedony! Now, is not this a
curious sin, when so small a woman tames a
bulk—"

"Stop, or I kill you," flashed Ippolita Sforza.
"The girl is down."

Down she was, struggling with dry sobs which
nearly cut her in half. Nello stood mute above

her, surveying his fine piece of work. Ippolita scorned him.

"You are at liberty to take what pride you can in this successful performance, young sir. For my part, I consider you more coward than fool, if that is possible."

"She is the lure of the Cardinal—"

"Dolt, she loves you only."

"She wrote meekly to him—"

"Are you a flint?"

"I can recite you her letter—"

"Have you read his? I am ashamed of you. Go."

"Pity me, princess. I adore her."

"Adore? Do you call this love? Pooh, you love yourself, as all men do. They use women as ointment, to smear themselves; and when they have coated themselves sick—angry, they break the pot. Foh! who would love a man?"

"Ah, Nello, Nello!" Emilia moaned where she lay—and down went he beside her.

"My soul, my soul—look upon me—pity me—I am in hell."

"You deserve to be, my friend," said Ippolita Sforza.

Donna Polissena, her sister, came lightly up. The others followed her, curious.

"What is this comedy you are at, sister? And why are we not to behold it? Who are your prostrate comedians?"

Nello, on his knees, faced about. He had some honesty left in him, and some of his old quality at command. He stretched out his arms, as if asking for punishment.

"Strike down, Madonna," he said, "strike down without ruth a graceless villain—a suicide who would slay his best self—an atheist who denies his revelation of Heaven. Have no mercy—do a piety to God!"

"The matter is this, sister," said Donna Ippolita, "that little fool on her face has given her heart to this little fool on his knees. This little fool whips her for a spendthrift. He has eaten up what she gave him, I suppose, and now reviles her because there is no more in her cupboard."

The haggard misery of the youth would have struck any eye which had not first seen the girl's despair. It struck Polissena Sforza.

"This is too bad, sister," said she. "These poor children are aching for each other. Let us leave them in peace to sob the truth out between them. Come, sister, come, Isotta, come, Manfredo. Tristano, come you especially. We do harm if we stop. Let them kiss, you let them cry; let them cry, you loosen their poor tongues. Once they talk all is well. Come, ladies—come, sirs."

And now Ippolita chose to be generous. She put up her hand.

"Stay, sister—you are always an hour before the clock. Let us bind them—let there be a treaty.

They ought to be plighted with a ring: never were there two lovers more disposed to each other. Give them a sanction, they will never stray again. For they are pious children, after all. Let us have a betrothal—here are witnesses enough. Signori, do you stand by Nello. Donzelle, lead the Betrothed. Come, come."

Polissena fired. "Pretty finale! Under the green tree."

They plighted Emilia and Nello in the approved Lombard fashion. Ippolita Sforza said the words: it was more than half a play and quite a pretty scene. Polissena and Isotta led forward the shrinking Fidanzata: the princess held out the hand for the ring of troth. Nello, squired by Tristano Sforza, by Manfredo Bentivoglio, and a swarthy young Orsini from Rome, was brought to the tryst. Fated to be a vicar, he betrothed her with Simone's thin gold ring, put it on her finger whence he had drawn it once already, held the cold little hand, and so remained until the words were done. Bidden then to kiss the bride, he touched her cheek. "Now leave we them," said Polissena, and so it was done. The long velvet shadows sank them deeper into the dark, the deer fed round about them; so handfasted stood those two, serious at the end of a game.

"You have me now, Nello. Are you pleased with me?"

"Give me back the letter." She handed it to him unopened, without a word of protest.

"It is yours with the rest of me, Nello." He looked up and saw her tears falling fast.

"O God, what a devil gnaws me!" he cried out. Then he tore the letter across and across. "Thus I scatter all dark clouds between me and thee. No more protestation, no backward looks, no doubting, no faint hearts. No, but trust in each other—courage, hope, love—wings for Heaven! with thee, my saint, with thee!" He took her in his arms and kissed her. She lay all silken and still.

With Nello, as with poets in general, words stood for things. To say that he loved and to love were one and the same act; to cry out his hopes was to have them; to pray was to have prayer answered. Not so with her; but she needed the sanction of a thing done before she could express her acquiescence. The thing was done now; she gave him kiss for kiss, returned him love for love. Deep in her shining eyes he saw himself enthroned, and swore her the most perfect, the pattern of women. The joy of which he supped filled him full. He thought he could never hunger again.

There was no time for more than rapture that night; their last clinging, their last kisses robbed speech. Emilia fled away to her duty; Nello testified to the new moon, and walked home to his lodging nursing his new heart. Next day, when their full joy might have begun—perversity of fate! they could get nothing but alarms. Each had a sharp dread, each a vain comfort for the other. Emilia pointed awfully to the ring on her finger. "Simone's pledge, Nello," she said; and when he kissed away her fright, "Thus Simone might have kissed." In the act to take her he saw Hercules plying the distaff on her bosom. "Gonzaga's mark, O God!" he groaned, and she fell crying in his arms, "Save me from Gonzaga!"

The two panics beat their courses above these young heads. They were like children, crouching under the trees, while above, in the black air, storm met storm and pealed ruin on the world. It was a feverish time, without stay, or peace, or assurance, a time of straining together, of kisses, of hot tears, and cold shivers, of doubt and misgiving. He could not trust her, nor she him. She paled and burned, till she crept about like a Reproach made flesh; Nello bit his nails to the quick, and started at every touch on the shoulder. Such hours as they had, not spent in the glades of the park, they passed, tearless and speechless, in one church or another. From altar to altar they dragged one another, from saint to saint, from Mary of the Seven Dolours to Mary of the Seven Wounds. What courage he had to spare her, he lent. It was all to Gonzaga's advantage; for she could think only of Simone—that he would come and kill her. "Ah, Simone, my soul! I have seen the Cardinal beat Simone. He handled him as if he had been a raw colt; he left him trembling all over, broken to the

voice." She smiled wofully and shook her head.
"We have to face Simone's master," says Nello.
"Yes—but Simone!" says she. It is a poor way
of gaining courage in the dark to learn that the
day is still more dreadful. Emilia took fright of
Gonzaga, but she lost none of Simone. His scowling black shadow was forever looming, turned all
her sweets to sours, and drove her at last to desperate measures.

Nello found her on a day at their place of meeting, and went to embrace her. She clapped her
arms across her bosom and shrank from him. "No,
no; leave me," she muttered, frowning and white.
"I am a snake—unclean." He took her in spite
of herself, and swore her his holy one. He kissed
her clay-cold lips, but could not move or warm her.
"Perjured, most false!" she cried. "O Nello, my
soul is dead. Pity me, Nello, and forgive."

He gave her what comfort he had; she lay trembling, uninspired, inert. "I think the plague is
upon me, Nello. I feel one taint. I am deep in
perjury. Simone betrayed, the Cardinal betrayed,
and now you, my love—O Lord Christ!"

She held up fearfully the left hand. "The traitor hand! Burn it, burn it, Nello, before Simone
come. Be sure he will come, be sure of it. Kiss
me once, my Nello, but never again. We have done
sinfully who meant to do well. O love, good-by."

All he could win of her was the grace to see her
as chance might afford. She agreed that he need

not return to Milan until he was sent for; but there must be no more secret meetings, "assignations," she called them now. "All's to do again," he groaned. "She loves me—but wretchedly. I can only pray." His courage was gone, his resource, his philosophy, such as it was, even his wit. One thing only stayed him from entering religion, the necessity of seeing her. Much good might that do him; he became her miserable shadow. He haunted her footsteps, but never spoke to her, and she never looked his way. He slunk out of sight of the Court, dared not be seen, yet had to see. More unhappy young man than Nello Nelli the history of Pavia has not yet revealed.

The Cardinal wrote daily with messages and enclosures. Nello sent them on to Emilia by a trusty hand. What was done, doing, or to be done upon them he could not learn; but the Cardinal announced his speedy arrival. And meanwhile Emilia passed and repassed before him where he lurked, walking staidly behind the Duchess, riding with the princesses, with the young lords and esquires of the household. Marvel! he saw her laugh, talk, ask questions, give light replies. It was as if she saw him not, as if she had never known him—never put her lips to his, never felt his arms about her, nor clung to him with hers. "She laughs, O Heaven! Are women devils, then? Was a woman the Mother of God? Harlot-hearted—O Saviour, save my Emilia!" Nello was in hell, it seems.

But Emilia, paler than she ought to be perhaps, yet shapely and adorned, sleek in silk, with a jewel in the midst of her forehead, and a very fine-cut gem on her breast, went about her daily work as if all were well—sang to her Duchess, laughed when her princesses were merry, was gentle in reply to Sforza or Borromeo, Manfredi or Belgiojoso; said her prayers, made her confessions, took the Cardinal's gifts, read his letters, and answered them dutifully; was never seen to cry or heard to moan. Women are your real stoics. One of the maids told Nello that in her sleep she tossed about and muttered, too fast for them to catch the sense. She was not thought to be happy: let that comfort him in his own misery. Was she miserable then? Who knows? A maid of honor has no business with misery. She is there to be courteous. Emilia's courtesy could never be called in question, for she was of great family, a Fiordispina of Garda, of a house famous for loyalty to the Dynasty of Milan and to all princely stocks in alliance with that. Ah, there need be no fear but that Emilia would do her duty.

She did her duty indeed! She did it when the Cardinal wrote naming the day of his arrival; but she said not a word of it to any living soul.

XV. The Incredible Stoop

At this time, it is to be related, Simone della Prova, now tyrant of seven citadels on the Venetian frontier, received a letter. He was sitting in the

hall at Castelfranco—one of his added towns—
when it came, in conference with two square-faced
men in red robes. He took his letter, and held it
tossing in his hand while he continued his talk.

"What do you say to us, Simone? Is it a bargain?"

"I will consider what you report."

"We answer for Sforza, remember."

"So I understand you. I have your master's
letter. And the money—"

"The money is here. Now, as to the Cardinal—"

"Leave the Cardinal to me," said Simone.

When the Venetians had taken their leave he
opened his letter and read it slowly, twice through.
He sat staring at it, chewing his tongue for maybe
half an hour; at the end of that paroxysm he
laughed, or barked rather—like a wolf at night in
the snow. "Trick for trick, hey?" he said, and
called for his secretary in a voice which made the
fellow tremble as he ran.

"Write, Tebbaldo," said he.

The secretary sat on the floor. "Ready, sir."

"Write thus: 'Traitress, I come in judgment.'
That is all. Seal."

"The direction, my lord?"

"Madonna Emilia Fiordispina, at the Castle of
Milan. Now send me Fabrizio—go."

Fabrizio, a blunt Venetian of the inland, came
blinking to his master. Simone put a heavy hand
on his shoulder.

"Saddle two horses, and gallop. You are to be at Milan by noon to-morrow, though you break the hearts of both good beasts. If she whom you seek with this letter be not in the city, you are to find her. Here is your safe-conduct. I start six hours after you, and take the same road, with what speed you who know me and Renegado will guess. If I am nearer to you by thirty minutes at any stage of the journey, I shall kill you, Fabrizio. You are riding for your life. Now be off."

Those six hours of his in his subject burgh were memorable. Never was known such a case of dreadful deliberation and performance. He was as vibrant as a stretched cord, his very voice cut the air. He did judgment in the court-yard and saw it executed, with a square full of hushed people waiting on his commands. There were nine-foot walls, grass ramparts, and a moat between him and them; yet had he been in their midst, a whip in his hand, he could not have kept them in silence more absolute. When the bodies had been huddled into the death-cart he called up his captains, chose a viceregent from among them, and gave him minute orders for the six days following. At the stroke of noon on the sixth day he would be back, he told them, and was believed. To Cittadella, to Campodarsego, to Montebelluna, to San Martino, to Camposampiero, and to San Giorgio delle Pertiche, all his towns, he sent governors with plenary powers. He ate hardly anything, and drank nothing at all. At the end of his time he gave order to saddle Renegado, his black barb; and at the prick of the hour appointed, cantered smoothly out of his town gates, and heard them clang behind him.

Passing Cittadella at a steady pace, but not drawing rein, he had the satisfaction to be challenged by his own outposts, to give them the word of the day, and to see afar off, at the end of the avenue of dusty acacias, his own well-barred gates. In an hour from that Renegado was swimming the Brenta. He had no need to whisper in those tender ears, laid flat for a sign; his was a great horse, full of heart, who knew that much was to be required of him before nightfall. Simone let him go his own pace, a swinging gallop, let the reins hang free; he was, as always, from the knees upwards a part of the lunging beast: so much so that he seemed not to be human. He breathed wholly through his nose, and looked dead before him, in a stare.

He skirted Vicenza in the brown dusk, crossed two little racing streams which merge just there—the turbid and the green water—to form the Bachiglione; then coming to some common land, where the sunburnt sods afforded certain softness to the feet, he checked his shining Renegado, and walked him for an hour. At Arzignano, a little village just outside the debatable country, where a long spur of the Alps lies like a rugged finger over the fields, he baited for the first time since leaving Castelfranco. Fabrizio had come in and gone just six hours before. He had changed horses there, and dosed one with meal and water. Both were in a lather, and one pretty well gored in the flanks. Simone saw to Renegado with great care, cooled him, washed and rubbed him down, fed and watered him. He took his own food standing, and at the end of two hours and a half was ambling through chestnut woods, watched by a shy young moon.

He reached the swirling green Adige by seven in the morning, and refreshed both man and beast by the swim; pushed on desperately to Bussolengo, whence lemon trees and trellised vines stretch to the shores of Garda. There he stayed. Fabrizio had passed through five hours and three-quarters earlier, but—"He'll never reach Milan with the led horse," said the landlord of the inn. "He had better," was Simone's short comment.

Two hours later yet, he rode through Peschiera under a burning sun. Garda itself looked white hot; the tower of the Fiordispina was trembling, the ilex woods all about it were motionless and pale with dust. He had not been there since that night when he had held Emilia to his heart and sworn her his forever; but he took no sort of notice. If any memory touched him he opened not his mouth, if his rage goaded him he did not grind his teeth. He rode through the place, under the very shadow of the tower, unwinking, unregarding, undeterred. Like a carved man's his eyes were blank; the hand

that held the reins to the pommel might have been
blocked out of stone.

Flagging crest and drooping quarters: Renegado
cried to him. At Bagnolo he stayed three hours.
He washed the good horse's legs, his face, and chest
with *aqua vitae*, fed him stoutly, and went to get
news of Fabrizio. "Five and a half hours away,
sir," they tell him. "He has left a dead horse a
mile down the Garda road. Cracked his heart by
order, as I understood him to say."

"I saw nothing of it," says Simone. "Hey, that
may very well be, my lord," says the man with a
grin. "Perhaps he knew what he was about."
"May be so, but he has lost his law."

He spent the rest of his time walking up and
down the inn yard, his hands behind his back, his
face rigid and expressionless. He ate nothing.
"There's a maggot groping in that signore's head,"
said one groom to another, "which numbs his
brains. Wait a bit, wait a bit, till your worm works
another inch—and then pity the fine beast he rides."
There was no fear for Renegado; but Simone be-
strode more beasts than one.

Folk upon the road, the stir of the day's affairs;
heavy ox-carts, little companies of dusty soldiers,
priests by twos and threes, friars silent, cowled, in
file, loitering girls, warned him where he was. Then
afar off, in the misty gray of the heat, marble pin-
nacles, towers, the bulk of some huge fortress, walls,
battlements, a dome. He reached Milan before

nightfall and made such a clamor at the gate, you would have thought the Venetians there in force. "La Fiordispina, sir!" cried a guard. "Dio mio, how many more urgencies upon this lady's account? Is she Queen of Sheba then? Is she Empress of the East? Five hours gone there came a man all panic on a horse all blood with the same cry. I told him what I tell your lordship—she is not here, she is away. She is with the Court of Madama at Pavia—taking the air—bathing her eyes in green. Seek her on the grass, and don't leave me a dead horse on my hands."

"Ha! so he left a dead horse?"

"I can show you the skin, or what remains of it —peppered with spurs like a sieve. Our man flew away on foot as if the devil was behind him— And I think that the devil was," he added, as Simone pounded back to find the Pavia road.

All night he pushed on; and Renegado, whose noble heart was nourished by a purer flame, never denied him. But Renegado was nearly spent. Simone's mouth was at his ear continually, and at every fierce whisper of his voice it was pretty to see the sensitive twitch, the gallant attack, and pitiful to see the flagging come so soon. The end was near—none too soon for the horse. The tower of San Michele uncertain in the foggy dawn, the convent roof, deep in green, far off to the left; the massed clouds, which were the trees of the park; last of all the castle turrets, the lodges, the tents about the walls; the banner of Sforza lazy in the still air—"Courage, my soul! Courage, my good beast!" breathed Simone to his horse. "We are here; thy work is done, and mine is at hand. God comfort thee, my Renegado, that deniest only fear." Whatever else he hated, he loved his horse.

In the yard of an inn of Pavia, Fabrizio was heavily asleep, but awoke at the clatter of Renegado's hoofs, saw his master, and began to pray vehemently. Simone ignored him until he had seen to his horse. But when all was done which could be done; in a few strides he was upon him.

"You have delivered the letter?"

"Sissignoria."

"When?"

"Eh, Dio mio! So many hours ago—six, seven, eight! Who can tell?"

"You are lying. It was less than three. It is now ten. You delivered it at the coming out from mass at seven."

"Sir, sir, have a little mercy! My horses failed me—you cannot flog dead flesh. I came from Milan to Pavia afoot—and ah, saints in heaven, how I ran! I am nearly dead, Signore, nearly a dead man. Look, master, look!" He held up his boot —with half the sole away. Simone was unmoved.

"You have killed my horses—you, that had two to my one. I have killed nothing—as yet—and have gained three hours upon you. A messenger

who cannot ride—humor his beasts—who disobeys
my orders, is useless. I will see you presently."

Fabrizio clung to his knees. "My lord, my lord,
pity me!"

"Speak of that later," said Simone, and spurned
and left him.

XVI. Resumption

Lurking under the beech boughs, loathing himself
for the slave he was become, on watch (as always)
for Emilia, Nello saw her come in company over the
park that early forenoon. It so happened that he
was expecting the Cardinal from hour to hour. He
wondered, with a sickening of the heart, whether
that was her expectation also. He dreaded it so
much that he could almost have prayed at any
time now that the end should come: the end,
and the worst, that so he might despair in
peace. He little knew what the poor girl's expect-
ance was, what tryst she was out there to keep,
what turned her faint between the flashes of the
talk.

She was walking with her mates Isotta and
Sigismunda, a black-haired Manfredi, and two or
three chattering pages, who chased each other in
and out of the trees. This company passing very
near where Nello was hidden, she with one sidelong
cast of the eye saw his shadow there. Just at the
moment Manfredi had paid her a daring compliment; between her blush and dextrous parry she
had seen Nello and he her. But she was in com-

324

pany and he was not, and if the sight of him hurt her heart, no one must know it.

He heard the general laugh at Manfredi's bold attack, saw Emilia turn her head to meet it full. "Heartless—harlot-hearted, O God!" groaned the miserable boy; but stayed where he was, peering. Impossible to help it! He followed all their progress over the grass—from shade to sun, to shade again.

A page struck a chord of music, and began to sing in saucy, boyish tones—a song of light love. He walked backwards before the rest, improvised audaciously, and more so, and more: he was resolved to make La Nina laugh. So they went on by degrees and degrees, Nello keeping at his distance, until presently he saw Emilia stop short, stagger for a minute, lean her head as if she was faint, press upon Sigismunda's arm. Sigismunda's questioning look downwards, a quick survey by Isotta, Manfredi's chin in the air, the scared boys —what was this?

Then he saw what they had seen. A tall figure of a man on horseback came pacing up the grass ride—a bareheaded, close-polled, young man in gleaming body-armor, booted to the thighs. Square shoulders, thick neck, small head—"O God, Simone!"

He saw Emilia held between the two girls; Manfredi go to meet the new-comer. The little page dropped his viol. All his bright temerity was gone;

he shrank to a nursery size. All eyes were on
Simone save Emilia's. Hers were cast down, and
intently down. She swayed her bent head about
as if in the troubles of a dream. Nello could see
that she was chalk-white, and had a crying fear.
He broke away from his hiding-place and went
towards her. But Simone reached her first, and
Nello stopped.

When he had dismounted and thrown the reins
to one of the lads; when he was so near that she
could hear his short breath, Emilia looked up. She
said nothing; her eyes were fixed on what he held
in his hand—a letter.

"Is this yours?" He spoke as to a thief caught
in the act.

"Yes, Simone." Nello guessed at the whispered
words. Sigismunda, very red, put her arm round
Emilia's body.

"And you have my answer to it?"

"Yes, Simone."

The savagery smouldering in him broke out in
flame. "Ah, untirable duplicity of women! Ah,
traitress born, hardy merchant that sells to one the
cheek, to another the hand, to another the longing
eye, the word in secret. How long will you be
out on your traffic? Is this tolerable? By life
and death, not so tolerable. Are you an encoun-
terer? do you angle? You, who swore yourself
mine utterly by Garda; you, to whom I vowed all
my faith, from whom I have never once wavered

in my thought, for whose sake all women have been dross in my treasury, laughed out, counted for nought; you, for whom I have fought, bled, killed, conquered, achieved—look now at the end of all my toils and the answer to all my strong prayers, that when I seek for you on high, on the throne where I saw you for a queen, you are not there— the throne is bare, the crown tumbles. No, but you come crawling, trailing through the dust, like a little snake, to fasten on my feet. What are you doing down there in the dust? You were quiring with angels when I left you; you were bathed in the blue. Now you sing *ballate* with pages, go to market with minions, are offered here, shrugged away there, appraised, taken as a makeshift. O Heaven, what bargain is this? But you know me too well, it appears. You falter, you repent. By the soul of God, I will never let you go. However you are, I take what I have won. Hold out your left hand. Whose ring is that?"

"It is yours, Simone."

"I know it; but I never put it there. Is it with that you played me false?"

"Yes." She motioned it with her head.

"Give it me, then."

She held out her hand. Simone pulled off the little blue ring, bit it in half with his teeth, threw down the pieces, and trod them under his heel. "Now," said he, "give me that jewel." Spoil of Smyrna, desired of Popes, the *Hercules and Omphale* was delivered up and ground to powder. Simone took an iron ring from his breast.

"In the presence of these persons I, Simone della Prova, lord of Cittadella and other subjugate cities, betroth you, Emilia Fiordispina, in the name of the holy and immeasurable Trinity." He thrust the iron ring up to the stem of her finger, turned, and left her. Gismonda saved her from a fall; and Nello, running forward too late, was brushed out of the way. He felt deadly cold; he shivered. His course was run.

Not quite, however. His was one of those natures which success makes bold, which without approval is palsied. A glance from Emilia would have heartened him into flying at Simone's throat; but she had had no eyes for him; her acquiescence had chilled him to the bone—no human force could have nerved him then.

That figure of bronze, that Simone was a man. He knew his mind, he chose what he wanted, marked it for his own, and in his time took it. To him and the like of him must all created things fall down. The Fates were his servants, for he despised the spindle and mocked at the shears; he had no ruth, nor concern either. "If I take you, you die? Well, die now, sooner than that I should be robbed." The lamb's shoulder, do you see, bore the imprint of the wolf. Horrible, sublime arrogation! But the other was as fine. "If I have you not, I die? Well, let me die, if I may not have my own." In no way can such men as these be moved. They are above the world, masters of the spindle and the shears.

Nello in his misery, outcast and acold, knew that Simone was a lord of the earth, and that he himself, poor vicar, must lay down his cure. He acquiesced; it was reasonable; what had a Nello to do in a world trampled by heroes, except be trampled with the rest? And Emilia, the branded dove? Lonely victim, meek she bowed her head to the sanction of a thing done! She took up her yoke, would go almost gladly into bondage; for the strength of her chain would be a strength to her, and her flower the more exquisite for her garden enclosed in steel. True it was, true it was; no furious domination of a man could rob sacrifice of its virtue. And that virtue, at least, was not denied to the vilest. Vile he was, poor Nello—but he could die.

Naked as he saw himself now, he shivered at his plight, but did not reject it. It was just, he deserved it; his butterfly hour was over. He had spread his gauze wings and glanced in the sun for a day; the storm had come crashing overhead, the rain had fallen; he was draggled, defenceless; he must die. But how? . . . Presently he saw the way. They had taken Emilia from him, and Simone, afar off over the park, was out of his reach. But whose was that cavalcade that came winding by the dusty road? Simone had become aware of it, had reined up his horse to watch, and now was moving warily forward, like some beast of the desert that sees danger in the distance, and prepares to meet it.

It was the Cardinal of Mantua coming to find Emilia. Nello gave a little cry, and ran with all his might towards his fate.

XVII. The Last Bout

Cardinal Gonzaga sniffed mischief in the wind when he saw who the oncomer was, and rose to meet it. His face was a broad sheet, blank and bland. He greeted his enemy with heartiness.

"Bravo, Simone!" cried he, reining up. "Be you the happily met, my champion; and may I be the first of the allies to take your hand. The lion-breaker—ha! The dictator of ·Venice—ha! By the Saint of Padua, my son, but your scamper over Abano will need a new Titus Livy. I have the very man for it. Or will you, like Cæsar, be your own chronicler?"

"I must have a short word with Your Eminence —in private," said Simone.

"Now, my hero, now!" cried the Cardinal. "Upon my soul, I can refuse you nothing." He signed to his retinue to advance, turned his horse over the grass, saw Nello coming, and hailed him. "Here comes my little secretary, Simone," he said. "We three were once before in conference. I have no secrets from him—nor need you have." Simone took no notice. Nello came up and stopped short.

He had forgotten his manners; he did not salute his master.

"Three days ago, Your Eminence, I received this letter. Be pleased to read it." Simone handed over a folded paper. If the Cardinal's breathing troubled him when he saw the famous seal, the hand which took it was unshaken, and he could look steadily at the writing.

"Ha! a lady's letter, if one may judge. My dear Simone, what do you ask me to do?"

"I ask you to read."

The Cardinal handed it over to Nello. "I have secretaries, my good young sir. Nello, read me this letter." Nello read it without a falter.

To her most Excellent Friend and good Lord, Messer
Simone della Prova—

Excellent and dear friend, for many days I have been seeking the force to write you a letter, but have not been able to find it until now. It is perhaps a weakness in women, though it may be (as I hope it is) a law of their nature, which forbids them to intrude themselves, unless required, into the bolder counsels of men; nor (believe me) should I have ventured now if my necessities had not been great.

Excellent lord and friend, I should assuredly have answered your letter if you had ever written any to me or sent me any token of your mind towards me until now of late, when I was shown a ring and learned that you still had me in remembrance. Four years is a long time in which to have no message from a friend—and if I was surprised to receive your ring you will not blame me, I hope. I wear it on my finger, as in duty I ought; but I must tell you the truth, which is that my mind is not altogether as it was when we were together by Garda; nor is that to be wondered at, seeing that I was a child in those days and since then have had experience of many things.

It is not easy in Milan to do well; it is not easy to discover where duty becomes inclination, and inclination is a sin. I have been troubled lately about my soul, seeking by all means safety for it, if that be a possible thing in Milan. And now of late, dear friend, there has been proposed to me a discreet alliance—

The Cardinal caught and stifled an exclamation. Nello read dryly on.

—a discreet alliance which would give me assurance against disaster, comfort to my parents (whose necessities are known to you), and a certain influence in the world. I thought it right and honorable, however, to let you know so much, so that, if you should desire your ring back again, you should send a messenger; or that, at any rate, you should not suppose that I ignored your right to be informed. Alas! we cannot pledge what we have not, and the promises of children, like the kisses of their mouths, testify no more than their simplicity.

With kissing of hands I am,
Your Lordship's friend and servant,
EMILIA FIORDISPINA.

Nello ended. The Cardinal found himself more moved than he could have expected. A certain warmth crept into his voice, and a good deal of honest conviction.

"I protest that is a gentle, virtuous lady, Simone," he said. Simone's face twitched.

"Your Eminence remembers the terms of our alliance?"

"Perfectly, perfectly."

"There has been treachery somewhere. That is clear."

"Ah, by God, I should not say that! No, no. In promising to deliver your token to the lady I did not engage to become her keeper."

"Your Eminence, then, delivered the token?"

The Cardinal squared his shoulders. "I did not. My secretary here delivered it." Simone looked at Nello, who did not flinch. He remembered him now. He had returned him the same steady scrutiny at Cittadella.

"Personally," continued the Cardinal, "I delivered your message—and in doing that much I considered that you could hardly, all things taken into account, call upon me for more. Is it not so?" The eyes of the two men met, and once more Simone had to lower his flag before his adversary. He shifted his ground.

"This matter is very dear to me—it is life and death. I have come at once and taken action. I have destroyed the token which I gave by other hands—unwisely, as it seems—and have substituted one of my own delivery. I am not to be trifled with, let thieves beware. What is mine I keep. And I am no orator, to dispense vain wind. I am for deeds—those who know me say that I have a knack—it is not for me to say. Now I claim Donna Emilia as mine by vows not to be broken. I hold to what I had before—I shall always hold to it. If it is Milan which tampers with treachery against me, let Milan choose. If it is Mantua, Lord Cardinal, let Mantua. Venice was my father's country

formerly, and has been mine. Do you think I
have no letter from Mocenigo? None from Piccinnino their captain? Do you think I have no
price—no market? You are mistaken then. Let
Milan beware—if Milan it be."

The Cardinal put up his hand. "Stop there,"
he said, "resolve your doubts as you will. I will
have none on my account. Do you trust me or
not?"

Simone stared at him for a while, then shrugged.
"Who knows? Whom am I to trust?"

"That is my question. Do you trust me?"

"How am I to say? What do I know—save
this, that there has been treachery?"

"I will tell you what I am ready to do for you,"
said the Cardinal coldly. "I will secure the young
lady's establishment at Mantua, in the household
of my sister the Marchioness. She will be much
under my eyes there—perhaps I shall be able to
serve you—"

It was a time to admire the intense black of the
Cardinal's eyes, if admiration had been in Simone's
way. Nello could never withhold a tribute—even
to villany, if it were bold enough. He could not
withhold it now. And yet he had made up his
mind what he was going to do, and ought to have
been thinking of his end.

Simone had no thanks for this handsome offer,
nor any distrust of it either. His belief at present
was that some Sforza had betrayed his honor. "If

I could be sure—" he began, muttering half to himself; but the Cardinal would have none of that.

"You can be sure of nothing, Simone," he said curtly, "least of all when women are in question."

"It is true, it is true! They will give her no peace—desperate, breathless work!"

"As breathless as you please," said the Cardinal, and believed that he had him. For a second time in his short life Nello saw death cheek by jowl; and now in an uglier guise than when it had worn the executioner's red livery. That had seemed a Carnival death. Here was death by violence; for ugly passion would lend it terror. So must it be; he dared not quail.

"If I could learn whose was the villany—" Simone was grumbling to himself.

"I will tell you, Simone," said Nello, speaking with a croak in his voice. "The time has come. Two traitors are before you. I am one."

Simone stared—then laughed grossly. "You! with your milk teeth! Pooh, you white face."

"Little hound!" cried the Cardinal, and would have ridden him down; but his rein was caught.

"Stop, my lord," Simone said. "We will hear this fellow out."

"Simone," said Nello, "I have loved Donna Emilia and done my utmost against you. I have been no traitor, for I never gave you a pledge—nor has she, for she would take none but yours. But I have kept off a worse than myself. Now,

I tell you that if you let her go to Mantua with this Lord Cardinal it will be her ruin."

The Cardinal gave a short cry. His face was curious to see. He wrung his head round and stared at the sky, as if to get an explanation thence. "Have I nourished a viper—this little snake!" He gaped, could not believe. "Viper! Viper!" The tragic mask, with its grin awry, was his; but not the tragic calm. He leaned over the saddle and studied this little snake with real surprise; and then with his dagger struck down at the boy as you might strike off a wasp, but stabbed Nello deep between neck and shoulder. The lad sobbed, and for a moment or two stood stiffly in his place, staring, nodding his head. He put out his arms to balance himself, swayed, and did not fall. The blood came in a spurt down his black velvet; he looked at it, pondered it, half dazed, half wondering. Slowly then his eyes grew filmy, lost their sight; his arms jerked, and held him no more; he swayed wider, fell, lay beneath the horse.

Simone, quite unmoved, said, "That tells me the tale. Cardinal, you have tricked me; but we will cry quits, for I have tricked you. I have accorded with Venice, and have in my pocket Sforza's proposals to the Ten. He is tired of the war. I think you will hesitate before you continue it. I certainly think so. I salute Your Eminence."

He turned and went back across the park. The Cardinal rode thoughtfully to his lodging.

The Love Chase

Late at night, Emilia, muffled in a hood, rode pillion behind her strong lover, and clasped him close. Going out of the park, the horse swerved violently and nearly threw her; but Simone spurred him forward.

"Dearest lord, what was that?" she cried, her cheek caressing his shoulder.

"'Twas a dead man, or some such thing," said Simone. "A man was stabbed out here this morning. You need not regret it."

"My soul, I have you—I regret nothing!" whispered Emilia, and kissed his shoulder.

EPILOGUE—PHILOSOPHY IN GRAY

NELLO NELLI TO POLITIAN—" . . . Here at Urbino I have books and leisure once more. Apollo, who does not love to see any other served than himself and his chaste sister, has now been appeased. I have been very near to death, and in a case where death seemed the only gain; but martyrdom was denied me—I am not without hope that I can give longer testimony than my blood could have provided. In short, after labors as great as those of Alcides, torments as long as those of Sisyphus, and no more fruitful (you may think), I emerge sane and whole. With my hot blood I poured out my fatal passion, and return to my studies with what appetite you may guess. The Duke is most urbane—as a soldier I have never seen his equal but once; as a philosopher he has none since Pericles fought in Samos. . . .

"But because it is not reasonable that one, who has known the sweets of a woman's mouth—ah, and more—should be without such refreshment, and that, nevertheless, without hindrance to his serious affairs, I now contemplate wedlock. For love, as lovers understand it, is an aching fever, and precludes the study of the ancients; but it is otherwise with marriage. A wise man, desiring to be wiser—and for that purpose desiring above all things leisure—does not choose his wife as he would his mistress, for her fragrance, or mere perfection of parts, nor because she is much sought by others, nor because she greatly seeks himself. Of such dangerous lures I have had more than enough. No, but he asks of his wife comeliness indeed, but also modesty; he asks her to be bountiful to himself, to the world very thrifty; and (as in my own case) requires also experience in the affairs of men and women, and temperance in the pursuit of them. For to pant is a sign of weakness in a horse or of bad *manège* in the rider; and so it is in a household.

". . . The lady is selected, not without mature reflection, after a two years' acquaintance violently begun, violently disrupted, happily resumed. But I have watched her carefully and corresponded with her much; more sparingly I have of late allowed myself to converse with her, but never alone. Like myself, she has drunk of the sweet waters of our life, so thirstily that I cannot but

338

believe her sated. Indeed, I have proved her so, for all her appetite now is for moderation, decorum, and womanly excellence. Like myself also, she has had troubles and shames, self-inflicted, therefore self-paid. Her repentance began where my excesses took hold of me. Her diligence was to learn frugality, mine to taste luxury. Now we are come to a point where we can touch. I know now the heady delights of love, she the calmer pleasures of continence. We esteem each other no less for our frailties overcome than for our virtues fortified.

"She is called Pernetta, and is a daughter of the Adriatic. Rimini saw her birth twenty-one years ago. Of her history I shall report to you by a more discreet conveyance; I have had some share in it which I do not at all regret. She is grateful to me, and is prepared to teach me gratitude. In other words, she desires to get out of my debt in the most pleasant way open to her. Indeed, I believe that she loves me overmuch—a fault in women to which we are apt to be tender. She is a very beautiful person, most modest, most submissive, most willing to do my will. I have had her instructed in the rudiments of Latin, and as soon as I possess her I propose to continue her instruction. We shall read Ovid together: the poet is easy and the task should be congenial. *Amant alterna Camenae!* At the head of my table she will be an ornament, in the chamber a solace, into the study she will never come but by invitation.

339

For she knows just how far a woman can be companion to a man, and is not jealous of my books. In short, my Politian, you may felicitate me upon my nearing bliss.

". . . I meditate an exposition of the *Cantica Canticorum*, mystical and exegetical, in seven books. Your advice will be much.

". . . Messer Vittorino da Feltre, that shepherd of young minds, salutes you. I have spoken twice to the Duchess of Urbino in your regard. She loves you well. The Cardinal of Mantua, I am told, is lately dead. What is this that I hear of a Ferrarese friar—a Dominican—who inveighs against good learning? What says your Laurentius of the ignorant rascal? If we had him in Urbino we would cast him from the Rocca to appease the Nymphs. Valete."

THE END

www.ingramcontent.com/pod-product-compliance
Lightning Source LLC
Chambersburg PA
CBHW032235010726
47494CB00002B/502